Robert Barr (16 September 1849 – 21 October 1912) was a Scottish-Canadian short story writer and novelist. Robert Barr was born in Barony, Lanark, Scotland to Robert Barr and Jane Watson. In 1854, he emigrated with his parents to Upper Canada at the age of four years old. His family settled on a farm near the village of Muirkirk. Barr assisted his father with his job as a carpenter, and developed a sound work ethic. Robert Barr then worked as a steel smelter for a number of years before he was educated at Toronto Normal School in 1873 to train as a teacher. After graduating Toronto Normal School, Barr became a teacher, and eventually headmaster/principal of the Central School of Windsor, Ontario in 1874. While Barr worked as head master of the Central School of Windsor, Ontario, he began to contribute short stories—often based on personal experiences, and recorded his work. On August 1876, when he was 27, Robert Barr married Ontario-born Eva Bennett, who was 21. (Source: Wikipedia)

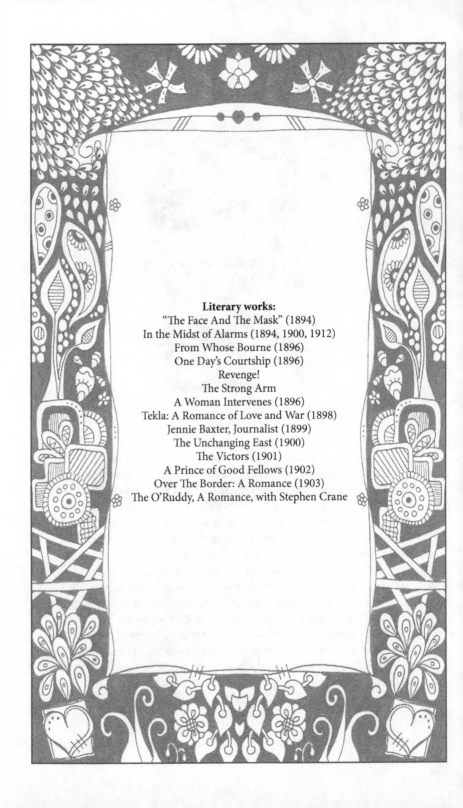

Literary works:
"The Face And The Mask" (1894)
In the Midst of Alarms (1894, 1900, 1912)
From Whose Bourne (1896)
One Day's Courtship (1896)
Revenge!
The Strong Arm
A Woman Intervenes (1896)
Tekla: A Romance of Love and War (1898)
Jennie Baxter, Journalist (1899)
The Unchanging East (1900)
The Victors (1901)
A Prince of Good Fellows (1902)
Over The Border: A Romance (1903)
The O'Ruddy, A Romance, with Stephen Crane

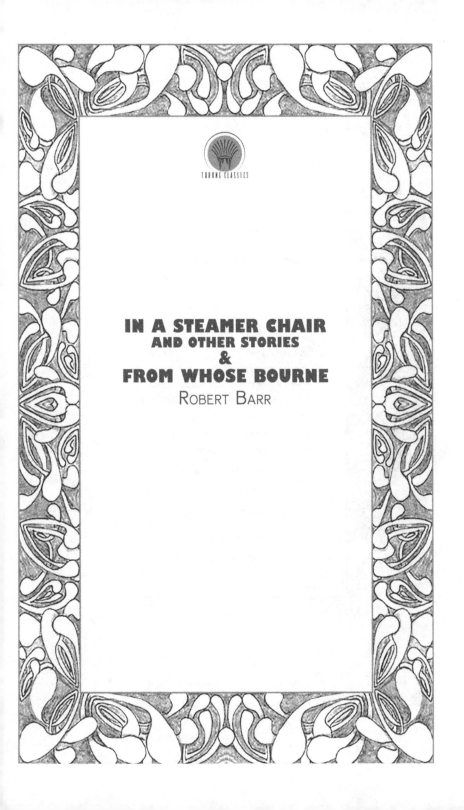

THRONE CLASSICS

IN A STEAMER CHAIR
AND OTHER STORIES
&
FROM WHOSE BOURNE
ROBERT BARR

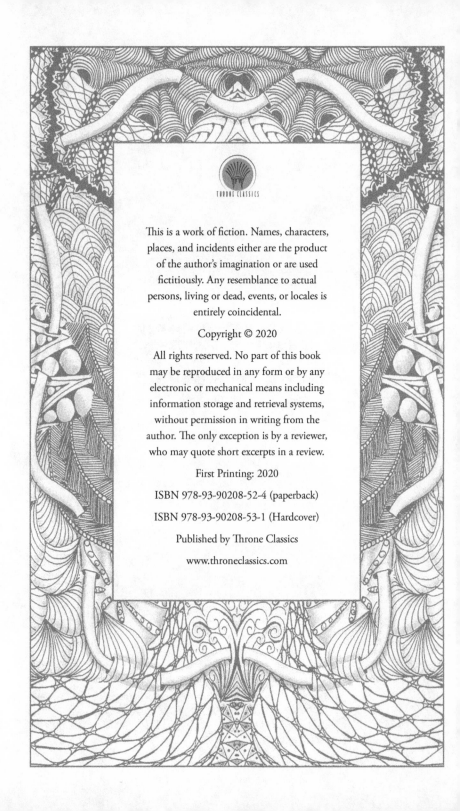

Copyright © 2020

First Printing: 2020

ISBN 978-93-90208-52-4 (paperback)

ISBN 978-93-90208-53-1 (Hardcover)

Published by Throne Classics

www.throneclassics.com

Contents

IN A STEAMER CHAIR, AND OTHER STORIES   9

In a Steamer Chair   13

Mrs. Tremain   99

Share and Share Alike   111

An International Row   116

A Ladies Man   123

A Society For The Reformation Of Poker Players.   136

The Man Who was Not on the Passenger List.   145

The Terrible Experience of Plodkins   152

A Case Of Fever   157

How The Captain Got His Steamer Out   162

My Stowaway   168

The Purser's Story   176

Miss McMillan   183

FROM WHOSE BOURNE   **191**

CHAPTER I.   193

CHAPTER II.   196

CHAPTER III.   202

CHAPTER IV.   209

CHAPTER V.   215

CHAPTER VI.   226

CHAPTER VII.   233

CHAPTER VIII.   244

CHAPTER IX.   251

CHAPTER X.   256

CHAPTER XI.   261

CHAPTER XII.   266

CHAPTER XIII.   270

CHAPTER XIV.   275

CHAPTER XV.   280

CHAPTER XVI.   283

About Author   **287**

NOTABLE WORKS   **290**

IN A STEAMER CHAIR
AND OTHER STORIES
&
FROM WHOSE BOURNE

IN A STEAMER CHAIR, AND
OTHER STORIES

As the incidents related herein took place during voyages between England and America, I dedicate this book to the Vagabond Club of London, and the Witenagemote Club of Detroit, in the hope that, if any one charges me with telling a previously told tale, the fifty members of each club will rise as one man and testify that they were called upon to endure the story in question from my own lips prior to the alleged original appearance of the same.

R. B.

In a Steamer Chair

The First Day

Mr. George Morris stood with his arms folded on the bulwarks of the steamship City of Buffalo, and gazed down into the water. All around him was the bustle and hurry of passengers embarking, with friends bidding good-bye. Among the throng, here and there, the hardworking men of the steamer were getting things in order for the coming voyage. Trunks were piled up in great heaps ready to be lowered into the hold; portmanteaux, satchels, and hand-bags, with tags tied to them, were placed in a row waiting to be claimed by the passengers, or taken down into the state-rooms. To all this bustle and confusion George Morris paid no heed. He was thinking deeply, and his thoughts did not seem to be very pleasant. There was nobody to see him off, and he had evidently very little interest in either those who were going or those who were staying behind. Other passengers who had no friends to bid them farewell appeared to take a lively interest in watching the hurry and scurry, and in picking out the voyagers from those who came merely to say good-bye.

At last the rapid ringing of a bell warned all lingerers that the time for the final parting had come. There were final hand-shakings, many embraces, and not a few tears, while men in uniform with stentorian voices cried, "All ashore." The second clanging of the bell, and the preparations for pulling up the gang-planks hurried the laggards to the pier. After the third ringing the gang-plank was hauled away, the inevitable last man sprang to the wharf, the equally inevitable last passenger, who had just dashed up in a cab, flung his valises to the steward, was helped on board the ship, and then began the low pulsating stroke, like the beating of a heart, that would not cease until the vessel had sighted land on the other side. George Morris's eyes were fixed on the water, yet apparently he was not looking at it, for when it began to spin away from the sides of the ship he took no notice, but still gazed at the mass of seething foam that the steamer threw off from her as she moved through the bay. It was evident that the sights of New York harbour were very familiar to the young man, for he paid no attention to them, and the vessel was beyond Sandy Hook before he changed his position. It is doubtful if he would have changed it then, had not a steward touched him on the elbow, and said— had not a steward touched him on the elbow, and said—

"Any letters, sir?"

"Any what?" cried Morris, suddenly waking up from his reverie.

"Any letters, sir, to go ashore with the pilot?"

"Oh, letters. No, no, I haven't any. You have a regular post-office on

board, have you? Mail leaves every day?"

"No, sir," replied the steward with a smile, "not every day, sir. We

send letters ashore for passengers when the pilot leaves the ship. The next mail, sir, will leave at Queenstown."

The steward seemed uncertain as to whether the passenger was trying to joke with him or was really ignorant of the ways of steamships. However, his tone was very deferential and explanatory, not knowing but that this particular passenger might come to his lot at the table, and stewards take very good care to offend nobody. Future fees must not be jeopardized.

Being aroused, Mr. Morris now took a look around him. It seemed wonderful how soon order had been restored from the chaos of the starting. The trunks had disappeared down the hold; the portmanteaux were nowhere to be seen. Most of the passengers apparently were in their state-rooms exploring their new quarters, getting out their wraps, Tam-o-Shanters, fore-and-aft caps, steamer chairs, rugs, and copies of paper-covered novels. The deck was almost deserted, yet here and there a steamer chair had already been placed, and one or two were occupied. The voyage had commenced. The engine had settled down to its regular low thud, thud; the vessel's head rose gracefully with the long swell of the ocean, and, to make everything complete, several passengers already felt that inward qualm—the accompaniment of so many ocean voyages. George Morris yawned, and seemed the very picture of ennui. He put his hands deeply into his coat pockets, and sauntered across the deck. Then he took a stroll up the one side and down the other. As he lounged along it was very evident that he was tired of the voyage, even before it began. Judging from his listless manner nothing on earth could arouse the interest of the young man. The gong sounded faintly in the inner depths of the ship somewhere announcing dinner. Then, as the steward appeared up the companion way, the sonorous whang, whang became louder, and the hatless official, with the gong in hand, beat that instrument several final strokes, after which he disappeared into the regions below.

"I may as well go down," said Morris to himself, "and see where they have placed me at table. But I haven't much interest in dinner."

As he walked to the companion-way an elderly gentleman and a young lady appeared at the opposite door, ready to descend the stairs. Neither of them saw the young man. But if they had, one of them at least would have doubted the young man's sanity. He stared at the couple for a moment with a look of grotesque horror on his face that was absolutely comical. Then he turned, and ran the length of the deck, with a speed unconscious of all obstacles.

"Say," he cried to the captain, "I want to go ashore. I must go ashore. I want to go ashore with the pilot."

The captain smiled, and said, "I shall be very happy to put you ashore, sir, but it will have to be at Queenstown. The pilot has gone."

"Why, it was only a moment ago that the steward asked me if I had any letters to post. Surely he cannot have gone yet?"

"It is longer than that, I am afraid," said the captain. "The pilot left the ship half an hour ago."

"Is there no way I can get ashore? I don't mind what I pay for it."

"Unless we break a shaft and have to turn back there is no way that I know of. I am afraid you will have to make the best of it until we reach Queenstown."

"Can't you signal a boat and let me get off on her?"

"Well, I suppose we could. It is a very unusual thing to do. But that would delay us for some time, and unless the business is of the utmost necessity, I would not feel justified in delaying the steamer, or in other words delaying several hundred passengers for the convenience of one. If you tell me what the trouble is I shall tell you at once whether I can promise to signal a boat if I get the opportunity of doing so."

Morris thought for a moment. It would sound very absurd to the captain for him to say that there was a passenger on the ship whom he desired very much not to meet, and yet, after all, that was what made the thought of the voyage so distasteful to him.

He merely said, "Thank you," and turned away, muttering to himself something in condemnation of his luck in general. As he walked slowly down the deck up which he had rushed with such headlong speed a few moments before, he noticed a lady trying to set together her steamer chair, which had seemingly given way—a habit of steamer chairs. She looked up appealing at Mr. Morris, but that gentleman was too preoccupied with his own situation to be gallant. As he passed her, the lady said—

"Would you be kind enough to see if you can put my steamer chair together?"

Mr. Morris looked astonished at this very simple request. He had resolved to make this particular voyage without becoming acquainted with anybody, more especially a lady.

"Madam," he said, "I shall be pleased to call to your assistance the deck steward if you wish."

"If I had wished that," replied the lady, with some asperity, "I would have asked you to do so. As it is, I asked you to fix it yourself."

"I do not understand you," said Mr. Morris, with some haughtiness. "I do not see that it matters who mends the steamer chair so long as the steamer chair is mended. I am not a deck steward." Then, thinking he had spoken rather harshly, he added, "I am not a deck steward, and don't understand the construction of steamer chairs as well as they do, you see."

16

The lady rose. There was a certain amount of indignation in her voice as she said—

"Then pray allow me to present you with this steamer chair."

"I—I—really, madam, I do not understand you," stammered the young man, astonished at the turn the unsought conversation had taken.

"I think," replied the lady, "that what I said was plain enough. I beg you to accept this steamer chair as your own. It is of no further use to me."

Saying this, the young woman, with some dignity, turned her back upon him, and disappeared down the companion-way, leaving Morris in a state of utter bewilderment as he looked down at the broken steamer chair, wondering if the lady was insane. All at once he noticed a rent in his trousers, between the knee and the instep.

"Good heavens, how have I done this? My best pair of trousers, too. Gracious!" he cried, as a bewildered look stole over his face, "it isn't possible that in racing up this deck I ran against this steamer chair and knocked it to flinders, and possibly upset the lady at the same time? By George! that's just what the trouble is."

Looking at the back of the flimsy chair he noticed a tag tied to it, and on the tag he saw the name, "Miss Katherine Earle, New York." Passing to the other side he called the deck steward.

"Steward," he said, "there is a chair somewhere among your pile with the name 'Geo. Morris' on it. Will you get it for me?"

"Certainly, sir," answered the steward, and very shortly the other steamer chair, which, by the way, was a much more elegant, expensive, and stable affair than the one that belonged to Miss Katherine Earle, was brought to him. Then he untied the tag from his own chair and tied it to the flimsy structure that had just been offered to him; next he untied the tag from the lady's chair and put it on his own.

"Now, steward," he said, "do you know the lady who sat in this chair?"

"No, sir," said the steward, "I do not. You see, we are only a few hours out, sir."

"Very well, you will have no trouble finding her. When she comes on deck again, please tell her that this chair is hers, with the apologies of the gentleman who broke her own, and see if you can mend this other chair for me."

"Oh yes," said the steward, "there will be no trouble about that. They are rather rickety things at best, sir."

"Very well, if you do this for me nicely you will not be a financial sufferer."

"Thank you, sir. The dinner gong rang some time ago, sir."

"Yes, I heard it," answered Morris.

Placing his hands behind him he walked up and down the deck, keeping an anxious eye now and then on the companion way. Finally, the young lady whom he had seen going down with the elderly gentleman appeared alone on deck. Then Morris acted very strangely. With the stealthy demeanour of an Indian avoiding his deadly enemy, he slunk behind the different structures on the deck until he reached the other door of the companion-way, and then, with a sigh of relief, ran down the steps. There were still quite a number of people in the saloon, and seated at the side of one of the smaller tables he noticed the lady whose name he imagined was Miss Katherine Earle.

"My name is Morris," said that gentleman to the head steward. "Where have you placed me?"

The steward took him down the long table, looking at the cards beside the row of plates.

"Here you are, sir," said the steward. "We are rather crowded this voyage, sir."

Morris did not answer him, for opposite he noticed the old gentleman, who had been the companion of the young lady, lingering over his wine.

"Isn't there any other place vacant? At one of the smaller tables, for instance? I don't like to sit at the long table," said Morris, placing his finger and thumb significantly in his waistcoat pocket.

"I think that can be arranged, sir," answered the steward, with a smile.

"Is there a place vacant at the table where that young lady is sitting alone?" said Morris, nodding in the direction.

"Well, sir, all the places are taken there; but the gentleman who has been placed at the head of the table has not come down, sir, and if you like I will change his card for yours at the long table."

"I wish you would."

So with that he took his place at the head of the small table, and had the indignant young lady at his right hand.

"There ought to be a master of ceremonies," began Morris with some hesitation, "to introduce people to each other on board a steamship. As it is, however, people have to get acquainted as best they may. My name is Morris, and, unless I am mistaken, you are Miss Katherine Earle. Am I right?"

"You are right about my name," answered the young lady, "I presume you ought to be about your own."

"Oh, I can prove that," said Morris, with a smile. "I have letters to show, and cards and things like that."

Then he seemed to catch his breath as he remembered there was also a young woman on board who could vouch that his name was George Morris This took him aback for a moment, and he was silent. Miss Earle made no reply to his offer of identification.

"Miss Earle," he said hesitatingly at last, "I wish you would permit me to apologise to you if I am as culpable as I imagine. Did I run against your chair and break it?"

"Do you mean to say," replied the young lady, looking at him steadily, "that you do not know whether you did or not?"

"Well, it's a pretty hard thing to ask a person to believe, and yet I assure you that is the fact. I have only the dimmest remembrance of the disaster, as of something I might have done in a dream. To tell you the truth, I did not even suspect I had done so until I noticed I had torn a portion of my clothing by the collision. After you left, it just dawned upon me that I was the one who smashed the chair. I therefore desire to apologise very humbly, and hope you will permit me to do so."

"For what do you intend to apologise, Mr. Morris? For breaking the chair, or refusing to mend it when I asked you?"

"For both. I was really in a good deal of trouble just the moment before I ran against your chair, Miss Earle, and I hope you will excuse me on the ground of temporary insanity. Why, you know, they even let off murderers on that plea, so I hope to be forgiven for being careless in the first place, and boorish in the second."

"You are freely forgiven, Mr. Morris. In fact, now that I think more calmly about the incident, it was really a very trivial affair to get angry over, and I must confess I was angry."

"You were perfectly justified."

"In getting angry, perhaps; but in showing my anger, no—as some one says in a play. Meanwhile, we'll forget all about it," and with that the young lady rose, bidding her new acquaintance good night.

George Morris found he had more appetite for dinner than he expected to have.

Second Day

Mr. George Morris did not sleep well his first night on the City of Buffalo. He dreamt that he was being chased around the deck by a couple of young ladies, one a very pronounced blonde, and the other an equally pronounced brunette, and he suffered a great deal because of the uncertainty as to which of the two pursuers he desired the most to avoid. It seemed to him that at last he was cornered, and the fiendish young ladies began literally, as the slang phrase is, to mop the deck with him. He felt himself being slowly pushed back and forward across the deck, and he wondered how long he would last if this treatment were kept up. By and by he found himself lying still in his bunk, and the swish, swish above him of the men scrubbing the deck in the early morning showed him his dream had merged into reality. He remembered then that it was the custom of the smoking-room steward to bring a large silver pot of fragrant coffee early every morning and place it on the table of the smoking-room. Morris also recollected that on former voyages that early morning coffee had always tasted particularly good. It was grateful and comforting, as the advertisement has it. Shortly after, Mr. Morris was on the wet deck, which the men were still scrubbing with the slow, measured swish, swish of the brush he had heard earlier in the morning. No rain was falling, but everything had a rainy look. At first he could see only a short distance from the ship. The clouds appeared to have come down on the water, where they hung, lowering. There was no evidence that such a thing as a sun existed. The waves rolled out of this watery mist with an oily look, and the air was so damp and chilly that it made Morris shiver as he looked out on the dreary prospect. He thrust his hands deep into his coat pockets, which seemed to be an indolent habit of his, and walked along the slippery deck to search for the smoking-room. He was thinking of his curious and troublesome dream, when around the corner came the brunette, wrapped in a long cloak that covered her from head to foot. The cloak had a couple of side pockets set angleways in front, after the manner of the pockets in ulsters. In these pockets Miss Earle's hands were placed, and she walked the deck with a certain independent manner which Mr. Morris remembered that he disliked. She seemed to be about to pass him without recognition, when the young man took off his cap and said pleasantly, "Good morning, Miss Earle. You are a very early riser."

"The habit of years," answered that young lady, "is not broken by merely coming on board ship."

Mr. Morris changed step and walked beside her.

"The habit of years?" he said. "Why, you speak as if you were an old woman."

"I am an old woman," replied the girl, "in everything but one particular."

21

"And that particular," said her companion, "is the very important one, I imagine, of years."

"I don't know why that is so very important."

"Oh, you will think so in after life, I assure you. I speak as a veteran myself."

The young lady gave him a quick side glance with her black eyes from under the hood that almost concealed her face.

"You say you are a veteran," she answered, "but you don't think so. It would offend you very deeply to be called old."

"Oh, I don't know about that. I think such a remark is offensive only when there is truth in it. A young fellow slaps his companion on the shoulder and calls him 'old man.' The grey-haired veteran always addresses his elderly friend as 'my boy.'"

"Under which category do you think you come, then?"

"Well, I don't come under either exactly. I am sort of on the middle ground. I sometimes feel very old. In fact, to confess to you, I never felt older in my life than I did yesterday. Today I am a great deal younger."

"Dear me," replied the young lady, "I am sorry to hear that."

"Sorry!" echoed her companion; "I don't see why you should be sorry. It is said that every one rejoices in the misfortunes of others, but it is rather unusual to hear them admit it."

"It is because of my sympathy for others that I am sorry to hear you are younger today than you were yesterday. If you take to running along the deck today then the results will be disastrous and I think you owe it to your fellow passengers to send the steward with his gong ahead of you so as to give people in steamer chairs warning."

"Miss Earle," said the young man, "I thought you had forgiven me for yesterday. I am sure I apologised very humbly, and am willing to apologise again to-day."

"Did I forgive you? I had forgotten?"

"But you remembered the fault. I am afraid that is misplaced forgetfulness. The truth is, I imagine, you are very unforgiving."

"My friends do not think so."

"Then I suppose you rank me among your enemies?"

"You forget that I have known you for a day only."

"That is true, chronologically speaking. But you must remember a day on shipboard is very much longer than a day on shore. In fact, I look on you now as an old acquaintance, and I should be sorry to think you looked on me as an enemy."

"You are mistaken. I do not. I look on you now as you do on your own age—sort of between the two."

"And which way do you think I shall drift? Towards the enemy line, or towards the line of friendship?"

"I am sure I cannot tell."

"Well, Miss Earle, I am going to use my best endeavours to reach the friendship line, which I shall make unless the current is too strong for me. I hope you are not so prejudiced against me that the pleasant effort will be fruitless."

"Oh, I am strictly neutral," said the young lady. "Besides, it really amounts to nothing. Steamer friendships are the most evanescent things on earth."

"Not on earth, surely, Miss Earle. You must mean on sea."

"Well, the earth includes the sea, you know."

"Have you had experience with steamer friendships? I thought, somehow, this was your first voyage."

"What made you think so?"

"Well, I don't know. I thought it was, that's all."

"I hope there is nothing in my manner that would induce a stranger to think I am a verdant traveller."

"Oh, not at all. You know, a person somehow classifies a person's fellow-passengers. Some appear to have been crossing the ocean all their lives, whereas, in fact, they are probably on shipboard for the first time. Have you crossed the ocean before?"

"Yes."

"Now, tell me whether you think I ever crossed before?"

"Why, of course you have. I should say that you cross probably once a year. Maybe oftener."

"Really? For business or pleasure?"

"Oh, business, entirely. You did not look yesterday as if you ever had any pleasure in your life."

"Oh, yesterday! Don't let us talk about yesterday. It's to-day now, you know. You seem to be a mind-reader. Perhaps you could tell my occupation?"

"Certainly. Your occupation is doubtless that of a junior partner in a prosperous New York house. You go over to Europe every year—perhaps twice a year, to look after the interests of your business."

"You think I am a sort of commercial traveller, then?"

"Well, practically, yes. The older members of the firm, I should imagine, are too comfortably situated, and care too little for the pleasures of foreign travel, to devote much of their time to it. So what foreign travel there is to be done falls on the shoulders of the younger partner. Am I correct?"

"Well, I don't quite class myself as a commercial traveller, you know, but in the main you are—in fact, you are remarkably near right. I think you must be something of a mind-reader, as I said before, Miss Earle, or is it possible that I carry my business so plainly in my demeanour as all that?"

Miss Earle laughed. It was a very bright, pleasant, cheerful laugh.

"Still, I must correct you where you are wrong, for fear you become too conceited altogether about your powers of observation. I have not crossed the ocean as often as you seem to think. In the future I shall perhaps do so frequently. I am the junior partner, as you say, but have not been a partner long. In fact I am now on my first voyage in connection with the new partnership. Now, Miss Earle, let me try a guess at your occupation."

"You are quite at liberty to guess at it."

"But will you tell me if I guess correctly?"

"Yes. I have no desire to conceal it."

"Then, I should say off-hand that you are a teacher, and are now taking a vacation in Europe. Am I right?"

"Tell me first why you think so?"

"I am afraid to tell you. I do not want to drift towards the line of enmity."

"You need have no fear. I have every respect for a man who tells the truth when he has to."

"Well, I think a school teacher is very apt to get into a certain dictatorial habit of speech. School teachers are something like military men. They are accustomed to implicit obedience without question, and this, I think, affects their manner with other people."

"You think I am dictatorial, then?"

"Well, I shouldn't say that you were dictatorial exactly. But there is a certain confidence—I don't know just how to express it, but it seems to me, you know—well, I am going deeper and deeper into trouble by what I am saying, so really I shall not say any more. I do not know just how to express it."

"I think you express it very nicely. Go on, please."

"Oh, you are laughing at me now."

"Not at all, I assure you. You were trying to say that I was very dictatorial."

"No, I was trying to say nothing of the kind. I was merely trying to say that you have a certain confidence in yourself and a certain belief that everything you say is perfectly correct, and is not to be questioned. Now, do as you promised, and tell me how near right I am."

"You are entirely wrong. I never taught school."

"Well, Miss Earle, I confessed to my occupation without citing any mitigating circumstances. So now, would you think me impertinent if I asked you to be equally frank?"

"Oh, not at all! But I may say at once that I wouldn't answer you."

"But you will tell me if I guess?"

"Yes, I promise that."

"Well, I am certainly right in saying that you are crossing the ocean for pleasure."

"No, you are entirely wrong. I am crossing for business."

"Then, perhaps you cross very often, too?"

"No; I crossed only once before, and that was coming the other way."

"Really, this is very mysterious. When are you coming back?"

"I am not coming back."

"Oh, well," said Morris, "I give it up. I think I have scored the unusual triumph of managing to be wrong in everything that I have said. Have I not?"

"I think you have."

"And you refuse to put me right?"

"Certainly."

"I don't think you are quite fair, Miss Earle."

"I don't think I ever claimed to be, Mr. Morris. But I am tired of walking now. You see, I have been walking the deck for considerably longer than you have. I think I shall sit down for a while."

"Let me take you to your chair."

Miss Earle smiled. "It would be very little use," she said.

The deck steward was not to be seen, and Morris, diving into a dark and cluttered-up apartment, in which the chairs were piled, speedily picked out his own, brought it to where the young lady was standing, spread it out in its proper position, and said—

"Now let me get you a rug or two."

"You have made a mistake. That is not my chair."

"Oh yes, it is. I looked at the tag. This is your name, is it not?"

"Yes, that is my name; but this is not my chair."

"Well, I beg that you will use it until the owner calls for it."

"But who is the owner? Is this your chair?"

"It was mine until after I smashed up yours."

"Oh, but I cannot accept your chair, Mr. Morris."

"You surely wouldn't refuse to do what you desired, in fact, commanded, another to do. You know you practically ordered me to take your chair. Well, I have accepted it. It is going to be put right to-day. So, you see, you cannot refuse mine."

Miss Earle looked at him for a moment.

"This is hardly what I would call a fair exchange," she said. "My chair was really a very cheap and flimsy one. This chair is much more expensive. You see, I know the price of them. I think you are trying to arrange your revenge, Mr. Morris. I think you want to bring things about so that I shall have to apologise to you in relation to that chair-breaking incident. However, I see that this chair is very comfortable, so I will take it. Wait a moment till I get my rugs."

"No, no," cried Morris, "tell me where you left them. I will get them for you."

"Thank you. I left them on the seat at the head of the companion-way. One is red, the other is more variegated; I cannot describe it, but they are the only two rugs there, I think."

A moment afterwards the young man appeared with the rugs on his arm, and arranged them around the young lady after the manner of deck stewards and gallant young men who are in the habit of crossing the ocean.

"Would you like to have a cup of coffee?"

"I would, if it can be had."

"Well, I will let you into a shipboard secret. Every morning on this vessel the smoking-room steward brings up a pot of very delicious coffee, which he leaves on the table of the smoking-room. He also brings a few biscuits—not the biscuit of American fame, but the biscuit of English manufacture, the cracker, as we call it—and those who frequent the smoking-room are in the habit sometimes of rising early, and, after a walk on deck, pouring out a cup of coffee for themselves."

"But I do not expert to be a habitué of the smoking-room," said Miss Earle.

"Nevertheless, you have a friend who will be, and so in that way, you see, you will enjoy the advantages of belonging to the smoking club."

A few moments afterwards, Morris appeared with a camp-stool under his arm, and two cups of coffee in his hands. Miss Earle noticed the smile suddenly fade from his face, and a look of annoyance, even of terror, succeed it. His hands trembled, so that the coffee spilled from the cup into the saucer.

"Excuse my awkwardness," he said huskily; then, handing her the cup, he added, "I shall have to go now. I will see you at breakfast-time. Good morning." With the other cup still in his hand, he made his way to the stair.

Miss Earle looked around and saw, coming up the deck, a very handsome young lady with blonde hair.

Third Day

On the morning of the third day, Mr. George Morris woke up after a sound and dreamless sleep. He woke up feeling very dissatisfied with himself, indeed. He said he was a fool, which was probably true enough, but even the calling himself so did not seem to make matters any better. He reviewed in his mind the events of the day before. He remembered his very pleasant walk and talk with Miss Earle. He knew the talk had been rather purposeless, being merely that sort of preliminary conversation which two people who do not yet know each other indulge in, as a forerunner to future friendship. Then, he thought of his awkward leave-taking of Miss Earle when he presented her with the cup of coffee, and for the first time he remembered with a pang that he had under his arm a camp-stool. It must have been evident to Miss Earle that he had intended to sit down and have a cup of coffee with her, and continue the acquaintance begun so auspiciously that morning. He wondered if she had noticed that his precipitate retreat had taken place the moment there appeared on the deck a very handsome and stylishly dressed young lady. He began to fear that Miss Earle must have thought him suddenly taken with insanity, or, worse still, sea-sickness. The more Morris thought about the matter the more dissatisfied he was with himself and his actions. At breakfast—he had arrived very late, almost as Miss Earle was leaving—he felt he had preserved a glum, reticent demeanour, and that he had the general manner of a fugitive anxious to escape justice. He wondered what Miss Earle must have thought of him after his eager conversation of the morning. The rest of the day he had spent gloomily in the smoking-room, and had not seen the young lady again. The more he thought of the day the worse he felt about it. However, he was philosopher enough to know that all the thinking he could do would not change a single item in the sum of the day's doing. So he slipped back the curtain on its brass rod and looked out into his state-room. The valise which he had left carelessly on the floor the night before was now making an excursion backwards and forwards from the bunk to the sofa, and the books that had been piled up on the sofa were scattered all over the room. It was evident that dressing was going to be an acrobatic performance.

The deck, when he reached it, was wet, but not with the moisture of the scrubbing. The outlook was clear enough, but a strong head-wind was blowing that whistled through the cordage of the vessel, and caused the black smoke of the funnels to float back like huge sombre streamers. The prow of the big ship rose now into the sky and then sank down into the bosom of the sea, and every time it descended a white cloud of spray drenched everything forward and sent a drizzly salt rain along the whole length of the steamer.

"There will be no ladies on deck this morning," said Morris to himself, as he held his cap on with both hands and looked around at the threatening sky. At this moment one wave struck the steamer with more than usual force and raised its crest amidship over the decks. Morris had just time to escape into the companion-way when it fell with a crash on the deck, flooding the promenade, and then rushing out through the scuppers into the sea.

"By George!" said Morris. "I guess there won't be many at breakfast either, if this sort of thing keeps up. I think the other side of the ship is the best."

Coming out on the other side of the deck, he was astonished to see, sitting in her steamer chair, snugly wrapped up in her rugs, Miss Katherine Earle, balancing a cup of steaming coffee in her hand. The steamer chair had been tightly tied to the brass stanchion, or hand-rail, that ran along the side of the housed-in portion of the companion-way, and although the steamer swayed to and fro, as well as up and down, the chair was immovable. An awning had been put up over the place where the chair was fastened, and every now and then on that dripping piece of canvas the salt rain fell, the result of the waves that dashed in on the other side of the steamer.

"Good morning, Mr. Morris!" said the young lady, brightly. "I am very glad you have come. I will let you into a shipboard secret. The steward of the smoking-room brings up every morning a pot of very fragrant coffee. Now, if you will speak to him, I am sure he will be very glad to give you a cup."

"You do like to make fun of me, don't you?" answered the young man.

"Oh, dear no," said Miss Earle, "I shouldn't think of making fun of anything so serious. Is it making fun of a person who looks half frozen to offer him a cup of warm coffee? I think there is more philanthropy than fun about that."

"Well, I don't know but you are right. At any rate, I prefer to take it as philanthropy rather than fun. I shall go and get a cup of coffee for myself, if you will permit me to place a chair beside yours?"

"Oh, I beg you not to go for the coffee yourself. You certainly will never reach here with it. You see the remains of that cup down by the side of the vessel. The steward himself slipped and fell with that piece of crockery in his hands. I am sure he hurt himself, although he said he didn't."

"Did you give him an extra fee on that account?" asked Morris, cynically.

"Of course I did. I am like the Government in that respect. I take care of those who are injured in my service."

"Perhaps, that's why he went down. They are a sly set, those stewards. He knew that a man would simply laugh at him, or perhaps utter some maledictions if he were not feeling in very good humour. In all my ocean voyages I have never had the good fortune to see a steward fall. He knew, also, the rascal, that a lady would sympathise with him, and that he wouldn't lose anything by it, except the cup, which is not his loss."

"Oh yes, it is," replied the young lady, "he tells me they charge all breakages against him."

"He didn't tell you what method they had of keeping track of the breakages, did he? Suppose he told the chief steward that you broke the cup, which is likely he did. What then?"

"Oh, you are too cynical this morning, and it would serve you just right if you go and get some coffee for yourself, and meet with the same disaster that overtook the unfortunate steward. Only you are forewarned that you shall have neither sympathy nor fee."

"Well, in that case," said the young man, "I shall not take the risk. I shall sacrifice the steward rather. Oh, here he is. I say, steward, will you bring me a cup of coffee, please?"

"Yes, sir. Any biscuit, sir?"

"No, no biscuit. Just a cup of coffee and a couple of lumps of sugar, please; and if you can first get me a chair, and strap it to this rod in the manner you do so well, I shall be very much obliged."

"Yes, sir. I shall call the deck steward, sir."

"Now, notice that. You see the rascals never interfere with each other. The deck steward wants a fee, and the smoking-room steward wants a fee, and each one attends strictly to his own business, and doesn't interfere with the possible fees of anybody else."

"Well," said Miss Earle, "is not that the correct way? If things are to be well done, that is how they should be done. Now, just notice how much more artistically the deck steward arranged these rugs than you did yesterday morning. I think it is worth a good fee to be wrapped up so comfortably as that."

"I guess I'll take lessons from the deck steward then, and even if I do not get a fee, I may perhaps get some gratitude at least."

"Gratitude? Why, you should think it a privilege."

"Well, Miss Earle, to tell the truth, I do. It is a privilege that—I hope you will not think I am trying to flatter you when I say—any man might be proud of."

"Oh, dear," replied the young lady, laughing, "I did not mean it in that way at all. I meant that it was a privilege to be allowed to practise on those particular rugs. Now, a man should remember that he undertakes a very great responsibility when he volunteers to place the rugs around a lady on a steamer chair. He may make her look very neat and even pretty by a nice disposal of the rugs, or he may make her look like a horrible bundle."

"Well, then, I think I was not such a failure after all yesterday morning, for you certainly looked very neat and pretty."

"Then, if I did, Mr. Morris, do not flatter yourself it was at all on account

32

of your disposal of the rugs, for the moment you had left a very handsome young lady came along, and, looking at me, said, with such a pleasant smile, 'Why, what a pretty rug you have there; but how the steward has bungled it about you! Let me fix it,' and with that she gave it a touch here and a smooth down there, and the result was really so nice that I hated to go down to breakfast. It is a pity you went away so quickly yesterday morning. You might have had an opportunity of becoming acquainted with the lady, who is, I think, the prettiest girl on board this ship."

"Do you?" said Mr. Morris, shortly.

"Yes, I do. Have you noticed her? She sits over there at the long table near the centre. You must have seen her; she is so very, very pretty, that you cannot help noticing her."

"I am not looking after pretty women this voyage," said Morris, savagely.

"Oh, are you not? Well, I must thank you for that. That is evidently a very sincere compliment. No, I can't call it a compliment, but a sincere remark, I think the first sincere one you have made to-day."

"Why, what do you mean?" said Morris, looking at her in a bewildered sort of way.

"You have been looking after me this morning, have you not, and yesterday morning? And taking ever so much pains to be helpful and entertaining, and now, all at once you say—Well, you know what you said just now."

"Oh yes. Well, you see—"

"Oh, you can't get out of it, Mr. Morris. It was said, and with evident sincerity."

"Then you really think you are pretty?" said Mr. Morris, looking at his companion, who flushed under the remark.

"Ah, now," she said, "you imagine you are carrying the war into the enemy's country. But I don't at all appreciate a remark like that. I don't know

33

but I dislike it even more than I do your compliments, which is saying a good deal."

"I assure you," said Morris, stiffly, "that I have not intended to pay any compliments. I am not a man who pays compliments."

"Not even left-handed ones?"

"Not even any kind, that I know of. I try as a general thing to speak the truth."

"Ah, and shame your hearers?"

"Well, I don't care who I shame as long as I succeed in speaking the truth."

"Very well, then; tell me the truth. Have you noticed this handsome young lady I speak of?"

"Yes, I have seen her."

"Don't you think she is very pretty?"

"Yes, I think she is."

"Don't you think she is the prettiest woman on the ship?"

"Yes, I think she is."

"Are you afraid of pretty women?"

"No, I don't think I am."

"Then, tell me why, the moment she appeared on the deck yesterday morning, you were so much agitated that you spilled most of my coffee in the saucer?"

"Did I appear agitated?" asked Morris, with some hesitation.

"Now, I consider that sort of thing worse than a direct prevarication."

"What sort of thing?"

"Why, a disingenuous answer. You know you appeared agitated. You know you were agitated. You know you had a camp-stool, and that you intended to sit down here and drink your coffee. All at once you changed your mind, and that change was coincident with the appearance on deck of the handsome young lady I speak of. I merely ask why?"

"Now, look here, Miss Earle, even the worst malefactor is not expected to incriminate himself. I can refuse to answer, can I not?"

"Certainly you may. You may refuse to answer anything, if you like. It was only because you were boasting about speaking the truth that I thought I should test your truth-telling qualities. I have been expecting every moment that you would say to me I was very impertinent, and that it was no business of mine, which would have been quite true. There, you see, you had a beautiful chance of speaking the truth which you let slip entirely unnoticed. But there is the breakfast gong. Now, I must confess to being very hungry indeed. I think I shall go down into the saloon."

"Please take my arm, Miss Earle," said the young man.

"Oh, not at all," replied that young lady; "I want something infinitely more stable. I shall work my way along this brass rod until I can make a bolt for the door. If you want to make yourself real useful, go and stand on the stairway, or the companion-way I think you call it, and if I come through the door with too great force you'll prevent me from going down the stairs."

"'Who ran to help me when I fell,'" quoted Mr. Morris, as he walked along ahead of her, having some difficulty in maintaining his equilibrium.

"I wouldn't mind the falling," replied the young lady, "if you only would some pretty story tell; but you are very prosaic, Mr. Morris. Do you ever read anything at all?"

"I never read when I have somebody more interesting than a book to talk to."

"Oh, thank you. Now, if you will get into position on the stairway, I shall make my attempts at getting to the door."

"I feel like a base-ball catcher," said Morris, taking up a position somewhat similar to that of the useful man behind the bat.

Miss Earle, however, waited until the ship was on an even keel, then walked to the top of the companion-way, and, deftly catching up the train of her dress with as much composure as if she were in a ballroom, stepped lightly down the stairway. Looking smilingly over her shoulder at the astonished baseball catcher, she said—

"I wish you would not stand in that ridiculous attitude, but come and accompany me to the breakfast table. As I told you, I am very hungry."

The steamer gave a lurch that nearly precipitated Morris down the stairway, and the next moment he was by her side.

"Are you fond of base-ball?" she said to him.

"You should see me in the park when our side makes a home run. Do you like the game?"

"I never saw a game in my life."

"What! you an American girl, and never saw a game of base-ball? Why, I am astonished."

"I did not say that I was an American girl."

"Oh, that's a fact. I took you for one, however."

They were both of them so intent on their conversation in walking up the narrow way between the long table and the short ones, that neither of them noticed the handsome blonde young lady standing beside her chair looking at them. It was only when that young lady said, "Why, Mr. Morris, is this you?" and when that gentleman jumped as if a cannon had been fired beside him, that either of them noticed their fair fellow-traveller.

"Y—es," stammered Morris, "it is!"

The young lady smiled sweetly and held out her hand, which Morris took in an awkward way.

"I was just going to ask you," she said, "when you came aboard. How ridiculous that would have been. Of course, you have been here all the time. Isn't it curious that we have not met each other?—we of all persons in the world."

Morris, who had somewhat recovered his breath, looked steadily at her as she said this, and her eyes, after encountering his gaze for a moment, sank to the floor.

Miss Earle, who had waited for a moment expecting that Morris would introduce her, but seeing that he had for the time being apparently forgotten everything on earth, quietly left them, and took her place at the breakfast table. The blonde young lady looked up again at Mr. Morris, and said—

"I am afraid I am keeping you from breakfast."

"Oh, that doesn't matter."

"I am afraid, then," she continued sweetly, "that I am keeping you from your very interesting table companion."

"Yes, that does matter," said Morris, looking at her. "I wish you good morning, madam." And with that he left her and took his place at the head of the small table.

There was a vindictive look in the blonde young lady's pretty eyes as she sank into her own seat at the breakfast table.

Miss Earle had noticed the depressing effect which even the sight of the blonde lady exercised on Morris the day before, and she looked forward, therefore, to rather an uncompanionable breakfast. She was surprised, however, to see that Morris had an air of jaunty joviality, which she could not help thinking was rather forced.

"Now," he said, as he sat down on the sofa at the head of the table, "I think it's about time for us to begin our chutney fight."

"Our what?" asked the young lady, looking up at him with open eyes.

"Is it possible," he said, "that you have crossed the ocean and never engaged in the chutney fight? I always have it on this line."

37

"I am sorry to appear so ignorant," said Miss Earle, "but I have to confess I do not know what chutney is."

"I am glad of that," returned the young man. "It delights me to find in your nature certain desert spots—certain irreclaimable lands, I might say—of ignorance."

"I do not see why a person should rejoice in the misfortunes of another person," replied the young lady.

"Oh, don't you? Why, it is the most natural thing in the world. There is nothing that we so thoroughly dislike as a person, either lady or gentleman, who is perfect. I suspect you rather have the advantage of me in the reading of books, but I certainly have the advantage of you on chutney, and I intend to make the most of it."

"I am sure I shall be very glad to be enlightened, and to confess my ignorance whenever it is necessary, and that, I fear, will be rather often. So, if our acquaintance continues until the end of the voyage, you will be in a state of perpetual delight."

"Well, that's encouraging. You will be pleased to learn that chutney is a sauce, an Indian sauce, and on this line somehow or other they never have more than one or two bottles. I do not know whether it is very expensive. I presume it is. Perhaps it is because there is very little demand for it, a great number of people not knowing what chutney is."

"Thank you," said the young lady, "I am glad to find that I am in the majority, at least, even in the matter of ignorance."

"Well, as I was saying, chutney is rather a seductive sauce. You may not like it at first, but it grows on you. You acquire, as it were, the chutney habit. An old Indian traveller, whom I had the pleasure of crossing with once, and who sat at the same table with me, demanded chutney. He initiated me into the mysteries of chutney, and he had a chutney fight all the way across."

"I still have to confess that I do not see what there is to fight about in the matter of chutney."

"Don't you? Well, you shall soon have a practical illustration of the terrors of a chutney fight. Steward," called Morris, "just bring me a bottle of chutney, will you?"

"Chutney, air?" asked the steward, as if he had never heard the word before.

"Yes, chutney. Chutney sauce."

"I am afraid, sir," said the steward, "that we haven't any chutney sauce."

"Oh yes, you have. I see a bottle there on the captain's table. I think there is a second bottle at the smaller table. Just two doors up the street. Have the kindness to bring it to me."

The steward left for the chutney, and Morris looking after him, saw that there was some discussion between him and the steward of the other table. Finally, Morris's steward came back and said, "I am very sorry, sir, but they are using the chutney at that table."

"Now look here, steward," said Morris, "you know that you are here to take care of us, and that at the end of the voyage I will take care of you. Don't make any mistake about that. You understand me?"

"Yes, sir, I do," said the steward. "Thank you, sir."

"All right," replied Morris. "Now you understand that I want chutney, and chutney I am going to have."

Steward number one waited until steward number two had disappeared after another order, and then he deftly reached over, took the chutney sauce, and placed it before Mr. Morris.

"Now, Miss Earle, I hope that you will like this chutney sauce. You see there is some difficulty in getting it, and that of itself ought to be a strong recommendation for it."

"It is a little too hot to suit me," answered the young lady, trying the Indian sauce, "still, there is a pleasant flavour about it that I like."

"Oh, you are all right," said Morris, jauntily; "you will be a victim of the chutney habit before two days. People who dislike it at first are its warmest advocates afterwards. I use the word warmest without any allusion to the sauce itself, you know. I shall now try some myself."

As he looked round the table for the large bottle, he saw that it had been whisked away by steward number two, and now stood on the other table. Miss Earle laughed.

"Oh, I shall have it in a moment," said the young man.

"Do you think it is worth while?"

"Worth while? Why, that is the excitement of a chutney fight. It is not that we care for chutney at all, but that we simply are bound to have it. If there were a bottle of chutney at every table, the delights of chutney would be gone. Steward," said Morris, as that functionary appeared, "the chutney, please."

The steward cast a rapid glance at the other table, and waited until steward number two had disappeared. Then Morris had his chutney. Steward number two, seeing his precious bottle gone, tried a second time to stealthily obtain possession of it, but Morris said to him in a pleasant voice, "That's all right, steward, we are through with the chutney. Take it along, please. So that," continued Mr. Morris, as Miss Earle rose from the table, "that is your first experience of a chutney fight—one of the delights of ocean travel."

Fourth Day

Mr. George Morris began to find his "early coffees," as he called them, very delightful. It was charming to meet a pretty and entertaining young lady every morning early when they had the deck practically to themselves. The fourth day was bright and clear, and the sea was reasonably calm. For the first time he was up earlier than Miss Earle, and he paced the deck with great impatience, waiting for her appearance. He wondered who and what she was. He had a dim, hazy idea that some time before in his life, he had met her, and probably had been acquainted with her. What an embarrassing thing it would be, he thought, if he had really known her years before, and had forgotten her, while she knew who he was, and had remembered him.

He thought of how accurately she had guessed his position in life—if it was a guess. He remembered that often, when he looked at her, he felt certain he had known her and spoken to her before. He placed the two steamer chairs in position, so that Miss Earle's chair would be ready for her when she did appear, and then, as he walked up and down the deck waiting for her, he began to wonder at himself. If any one had told him when he left New York that, within three or four days he could feel such an interest in a person who previous to that time had been an utter stranger to him, he would have laughed scornfully and bitterly at the idea. As it was, when he thought of all the peculiar circumstances of the case, he laughed aloud, but neither scornfully nor bitterly.

"You must be having very pleasant thoughts, Mr. Morris," said Miss Earle, as she appeared with a bright shawl thrown over her shoulders, instead of the long cloak that had encased her before, and with a Tam o' Shanter set jauntily on her black, curly hair.

"You are right," said Morris, taking off his cap, "I was thinking of you."

"Oh, indeed," replied the young lady, "that's why you laughed, was it? I may say that I do not relish being laughed at in my absence, or in my presence either, for that matter."

"Oh, I assure you I wasn't laughing at you. I laughed with pleasure to see you come on deck. I have been waiting for you."

"Now, Mr. Morris, that from a man who boasts of his truthfulness is a little too much. You did not see me at all until I spoke; and if, as you say, you were thinking of me, you will have to explain that laugh."

"I will explain it before the voyage is over, Miss Earle. I can't explain it just now."

"Ah, then you admit you were untruthful when you said you laughed because you saw me?"

"I may as well admit it. You seem to know things intuitively. I am not nearly as truthful a person as I thought I was until I met you. You seem the

41

very embodiment of truth. If I had not met you, I imagine I should have gone through life thinking myself one of the most truthful men in New York."

"Perhaps that would not be saying very much for yourself," replied the young lady, as she took her place in the steamer chair.

"I am sorry you have such a poor opinion of us New Yorkers," said the young man. "Why are you so late this morning?"

"I am not late; it is you who are early. This is my usual time. I have been a very punctual person all my life."

"There you go again, speaking as if you were ever so old."

"I am."

"Well, I don't believe it. I wish, however, that you had confidence enough in me to tell me something about yourself. Do you know, I was thinking this morning that I had met you before somewhere? I feel almost certain I have."

"Well, that is quite possible, you know. You are a New Yorker, and I have lived in New York for a great number of years, much as you seem to dislike that phrase."

"New York! Oh, that is like saying you have lived in America and I have lived in America. We might live for hundreds of years in New York and never meet one another!"

"That is very true, except that the time is a little long."

"Then won't you tell me something about yourself?"

"No, I will not."

"Why?"

"Why? Well, if you will tell me why you have the right to ask such a question, I shall answer why."

"Oh, if you talk of rights, I suppose I haven't the right. But I am willing to tell you anything about myself. Now, a fair exchange, you know—"

"But I don't wish to know anything about you."

"Oh, thank you."

George Morris's face clouded, and he sat silent for a few moments.

"I presume," he said again, "that you think me very impertinent?"

"Well, frankly, I do."

Morris gazed out at the sea, and Miss Earle opened the book which she had brought with her, and began to read. After a while her companion said—

"I think that you are a little too harsh with me, Miss Earle."

The young lady placed her finger between the leaves of the book and closed it, looking up at him with a frank, calm expression in her dark eyes, but said nothing.

"You see, it's like this. I said to you a little while since that I seem to have known you before. Now, I'll tell you what I was thinking of when you met me this morning. I was thinking what a curious thing it would be if I had been acquainted with you some time during my past life, and had forgotten you, while you had remembered me."

"That was very flattering to me," said the young lady; "I don't wonder you laughed."

"That is why I did not wish to tell you what I had been thinking of—just for fear that you would put a wrong construction on it—as you have done. But now you can't say anything much harsher to me than you have said, and so I tell you frankly just what I thought, and why I asked you those questions which you seem to think are so impertinent. Besides this, you know, a sea acquaintance is different from any other acquaintance. As I said, the first time I spoke to you—or the second—there is no one here to introduce us. On land, when a person is introduced to another person, he does not say, 'Miss Earle, this is Mr. Morris, who is a younger partner in the house of So-and-so.' He merely says, 'Miss Earle, Mr. Morris,' and there it is. If you want to find anything out about him you can ask your introducer or ask your friends, and you can find out. Now, on shipboard it is entirely different. Suppose, for instance, that I did not tell you who I am, and—if you will pardon me for suggesting such an absurd supposition—-imagine that you wanted to find out, how could you do it?"

Miss Earle looked at him for a moment, and then she answered—

"I would ask that blonde young lady."

This reply was so utterly unexpected by Morris that he looked at her with wide eyes, the picture of a man dumbfounded. At that moment the smoking-room steward came up to them and said—

"Will you have your coffee now, sir?"

"Coffee!" cried Morris, as if he had never heard the word before. "Coffee!"

"Yes," answered Miss Earle, sweetly, "we will have the coffee now, if you please. You will have a cup with me, will you not, Mr. Morris?"

"Yes, I will, if it is not too much trouble."

"Oh, it is no trouble to me," said, the young lady; "some trouble to the steward, but I believe even for him that it is not a trouble that cannot be recompensed."

Morris sipped his coffee in silence. Every now and then Miss Earle stole a quiet look at him, and apparently was waiting for him to again resume the conversation. This he did not seem in a hurry to do. At last she said—

"Mr. Morris, suppose we were on shipboard and that we had become acquainted without the friendly intervention of an introducer, and suppose, if such a supposition is at all within the bounds of probability, that you wanted to find out something about me, how would you go about it?"

"How would I go about it?"

"Yes. How?"

"I would go about it in what would be the worst possible way. I would frankly ask you, and you would as frankly snub me.

"

"Suppose, then, while declining to tell you anything about myself I were to refer you to somebody who would give you the information you desire, would you take the opportunity of learning?"

"I would prefer to hear from yourself anything I desired to learn."

"Now, that is very nicely said, Mr. Morris, and you make me feel almost sorry, for having spoken to you as I did. Still, if you really want to find out something about me, I shall tell you some one whom you can ask, and who will doubtless answer you."

"Who is that? The captain?"

"No. It is the same person to whom I should go if I wished to have information of you—the blonde young lady."

"Do you mean to say you know her?" asked the astonished young man.

"I said nothing of the sort."

"Well, do you know her?"

"No, I do not."

"Do you know her name?"

"No, I do not even know her name."

"Have you ever met her before you came on board this ship?"

"Yes, I have."

"Well, if that isn't the most astonishing thing I ever heard!"

"I don't see why it is. You say you thought you had met me before. As you are a man no doubt you have forgotten it. I say I think I have met that young lady before. As she is a woman I don't think she will have forgotten. If you have any interest in the matter at all you might inquire."

"I shall do nothing of the sort."

"Well, of course, I said I thought you hadn't very much interest. I only supposed the case."

"It is not that I have not the interest, but it is that I prefer to go to the person who can best answer my question if she chooses to do so. If she doesn't choose to answer me, then I don't choose to learn."

"Now, I like that ever so much," said the young lady; "if you will get me another cup of coffee I shall be exceedingly obliged to you. My excuse is that these cups are very small, and the coffee is very good."

"I am sure you don't need any excuse," replied Morris, springing to his feet, "and I am only too happy to be your steward without the hope of the fee at the end of the voyage."

When he returned she said, "I think we had better stop the personal conversation into which we have drifted. It isn't at all pleasant to me, and I don't think it is very agreeable to you. Now, I intended this morning to give you a lesson on American literature. I feel that you need enlightening on the subject, and that you have neglected your opportunities, as most New York men do, and so I thought you would be glad of a lesson or two."

"I shall be very glad of it indeed. I don't know what our opportunities are, but if most New York men are like me I imagine a great many of them are in the same fix. We have very little time for the study of the literature of any country."

"And perhaps very little inclination."

"Well, you know, Miss Earle, there is some excuse for a busy man. Don't you think there is?"

"I don't think there is very much. Who in America is a busier man than Mr. Gladstone? Yet he reads nearly everything, and is familiar with almost any subject you can mention."

"Oh, Gladstone! Well, he is a man of a million. But you take the average

New York man. He is worried in business, and kept on the keen jump all the year round. Then he has a vacation, say for a couple of weeks or a month, in summer, and he goes off into the woods with his fishing kit, or canoeing outfit, or his amateur photographic set, or whatever the tools of his particular fad may be. He goes to a book-store and buys up a lot of paper-covered novels. There is no use of buying an expensive book, because he would spoil it before he gets back, and he would be sure to leave it in some shanty. So he takes those paper-covered abominations, and you will find torn copies of them scattered all through the Adirondacks, and down the St. Lawrence, and everywhere else that tourists congregate. I always tell the book-store man to give me the worst lot of trash he has got, and he does. Now, what is that book you have with you?"

"This is one of Mr. Howells' novels. You will admit, at least, that you have heard of Howells, I suppose?"

"Heard of him? Oh yes; I have read some of Howells' books. I am not as ignorant as you seem to think."

"What have you read of Mr. Howells'?"

"Well, I read The American, I don't remember the others."

"The American! That is by Henry James."

"Is it? Well, I knew that it was by either Howells or James, I forgot which. They didn't write a book together, did they?"

"Well, not that I know of. Why, the depth of your ignorance about American literature is something appalling. You talk of it so jauntily that you evidently have no idea of it yourself."

"I wish you would take me in hand, Miss Earle. Isn't there any sort of condensed version that a person could get hold of? Couldn't you give me a synopsis of what is written, so that I might post myself up in literature without going to the trouble of reading the books?"

"The trouble! Oh, if that is the way you speak, then your case is hopeless! I suspected it for some time, but now I am certain. The trouble! The delight of reading a new novel by Howells is something that you evidently have not the remotest idea of. Why, I don't know what I would give to have with me a novel of Howells' that I had not read."

"Goodness gracious! You don't mean to say that you have read everything he has written?"

"Certainly I have, and I am reading one now that is coming out in the magazine; and I don't know what I shall do if I am not able to get the magazine when I go to Europe."

"Oh, you can get them over there right enough, and cheaper than you can in America. They publish them over there."

"Do they? Well, I am glad to hear it."

"You see, there is something about American literature that you are not acquainted with, the publication of our magazines in England, for instance. Ah, there is the breakfast gong. Well, we will have to postpone our lesson in literature until afterwards. Will you be up here after breakfast?"

"Yes, I think so."

"Well, we will leave our chairs and rugs just where they are. I will take your book down for you. Books have the habit of disappearing if they are left around on shipboard."

After breakfast Mr. Morris went to the smoking-room to enjoy his cigar, and there was challenged to a game of cards. He played one game; but his mind was evidently not on his amusement, so he excused himself from any further dissipation in that line, and walked out on deck. The promise of the morning had been more than fulfilled in the day, and the warm sunlight and mild air had brought on deck many who had not been visible up to that time. There was a long row of muffled up figures on steamer chairs, and the deck steward was kept busy hurrying here and there attending to the wants of the passengers. Nearly every one had a book, but many of the books were turned face downwards on the steamer rugs, while the owners either talked to those next them, or gazed idly out at the blue ocean. In the long and narrow open space between the chairs and the bulwarks of the ship, the energetic pedestrians were walking up and down.

At this stage of the voyage most of the passengers had found congenial companions, and nearly everybody was acquainted with everybody else. Morris walked along in front of the reclining passengers, scanning each one eagerly to find the person he wanted, but she was not there. Remembering then that the chairs had been on the other side of the ship, he continued his walk around the wheel-house, and there he saw Miss Earle, and sitting beside her was the blonde young lady talking vivaciously, while Miss Earle listened.

Morris hesitated for a moment, but before he could turn back the young lady sprang to her feet, and said—"Oh, Mr. Morris, am I sitting in your chair?"

"What makes you think it is my chair?" asked that gentleman, not in the most genial tone of voice.

"I thought so," replied the young lady, with a laugh, "because it was near Miss Earle."

Miss Earle did not look at all pleased at this remark. She coloured slightly, and, taking the open book from her lap, began to read.

"You are quite welcome to the chair," replied Morris, and the moment the words were spoken he felt that somehow it was one of those things he would rather have left unsaid, as far as Miss Earle was concerned. "I beg that you will not disturb yourself," he continued; and, raising his hat to the lady, he continued his walk.

A chance acquaintance joined him, changing his step to suit that of Morris, and talked with him on the prospects of the next year being a good business season in the United States. Morris answered rather absent-mindedly, and it was nearly lunch-time before he had an opportunity of going back to see whether or not Miss Earle's companion had left. When he reached the spot where they had been sitting he found things the very reverse of what he had hoped. Miss Earle's chair was vacant, but her companion sat there, idly turning over the leaves of the book that Miss Earle had been reading. "Won't you sit down, Mr. Morris?" said the young woman, looking up at him with a winning smile. "Miss Earle has gone to dress for lunch. I should do the same thing, but, alas! I am too indolent."

Morris hesitated for a moment, and then sat down beside her.

"Why do you act so perfectly horrid to me?" asked the young lady, closing the book sharply.

"I was not aware that I acted horridly to anybody," answered Morris.

"You know well enough that you have been trying your very best to avoid me."

"I think you are mistaken. I seldom try to avoid any one, and I see no reason why I should try to avoid you. Do you know of any reason?"

The young lady blushed and looked down at her book, whose leaves she again began to turn.

"I thought," she said at last, "that you might have some feeling against me, and I have no doubt you judge me very harshly. You never did make any allowances."

Morris gave a little laugh that was half a sneer.

"Allowances?" he said.

"Yes, allowances. You know you always were harsh with me, George, always." And as she looked up at him her blue eyes were filled with tears, and there was a quiver at the corner of her mouth. "What a splendid actress you would make, Blanche," said the young man, calling her by her name for the first time.

She gave him a quick look as he did so. "Actress!" she cried. "No one was ever less an actress than I am, and you know that."

"Oh, well, what's the use of us talking? It's all right. We made a little mistake, that's all, and people often make mistakes in this life, don't they, Blanche?"

"Yes," sobbed that young lady, putting her dainty silk handkerchief to her eyes.

"Now, for goodness sake," said the young man, "don't do that. People will think I am scolding you, and certainly there is no one in this world who has less right to scold you than I have."

"I thought," murmured the young lady, from behind her handkerchief, "that we might at least be friends. I didn't think you could ever act so harshly towards me as you have done for the past few days."

"Act?" cried the young man. "Bless me, I haven't acted one way or the other. I simply haven't had the pleasure of meeting you till the other evening, or morning, which ever it was. I have said nothing, and done nothing. I don't see how I could be accused of acting, or of anything else."

"I think," sobbed the young lady, "that you might at least have spoken kindly to me."

"Good gracious!" cried Morris, starting up, "here comes Miss Earle. For heaven's sake put up that handkerchief."

But Blanche merely sank her face lower in it, while silent sobs shook her somewhat slender form.

Miss Earle stood for a moment amazed as she looked at Morris's flushed face, and at the bowed head of the young lady beside him; then, without a word, she turned and walked away.

"I wish to goodness," said Morris, harshly, "that if you are going to have a fit of crying you would not have it on deck, and where people can see you."

The young woman at once straightened up and flashed a look at him in which there were no traces of her former emotion.

"People!" she said, scornfully. "Much you care about people. It is because Miss Katherine Earle saw me that you are annoyed. You are afraid that it will interfere with your flirtation with her."

"Flirtation?"

51

"Yes, flirtation. Surely it can't be anything more serious?"

"Why should it not be something more serious?" asked Morris, very coldly. The blue eyes opened wide in apparent astonishment.

"Would you marry her?" she said, with telling emphasis upon the word.

"Why not?" he answered. "Any man might be proud to marry a lady like Miss Earle."

"A lady! Much of a lady she is! Why, she is one of your own shop-girls. You know it."

"Shop-girls?" cried Morris, in astonishment.

"Yes, shop-girls. You don't mean to say that she has concealed that fact from you, or that you didn't know it by seeing her in the store?"

"A shop-girl in my store?" he murmured, bewildered. "I knew I had seen her somewhere."

Blanche laughed a little irritating laugh.

"What a splendid item it would make for the society papers," she said. "The junior partner marries one of his own shop-girls, or, worse still, the junior partner and one of his shop-girls leave New York on the City of Buffalo, and are married in England. I hope that the reporters will not get the particulars of the affair." Then, rising, she left the amazed young man to his thoughts.

George Morris saw nothing more of Miss Katherine Earle that day.

"I wonder what that vixen has said to her," he thought, as he turned in for the night.

Fifth Day

In the early morning of the fifth day out, George Morris paced the deck alone.

"Shop-girl or not," he had said to himself, "Miss Katherine Earle is much more of a lady than the other ever was." But as he paced the deck, and as Miss Earle did not appear, he began to wonder more and more what had been said to her in the long talk of yesterday forenoon. Meanwhile Miss Earle sat in her own state-room thinking over the same subject. Blanche had sweetly asked her for permission to sit down beside her.

"I know no ladies on board," she said, "and I think I have met you before."

"Yes," answered Miss Earle, "I think we have met before."

"How good of you to have remembered me," said Blanche, kindly.

"I think," replied Miss Earle, "that it is more remarkable that you should remember me than that I should remember you. Ladies very rarely notice the shop-girls who wait upon them."

"You seemed so superior to your station," said Blanche, "that I could not help remembering you, and could not help thinking what a pity it was you had to be there."

"I do not think that there is anything either superior or inferior about the station. It is quite as honourable, or dishonourable, which ever it may be, as any other branch of business. I cannot see, for instance, why my station, selling ribbons at retail, should be any more dishonourable than the station of the head of the firm, who merely does on a very large scale what I was trying to do for him on a very limited scale."

"Still," said Blanche, with a yawn, "people do not all look upon it in exactly that light."

"Hardly any two persons look on any one thing in the same light. I hope you have enjoyed your voyage so far?"

"I have not enjoyed it very much," replied the young lady with a sigh.

"I am sorry to hear that. I presume your father has been ill most of the way?"

"My father?" cried the other, looking at her questioner.

"Yes, I did not see him at the table since the first day."

"Oh, he has had to keep his room almost since we left. He is a very poor sailor."

"Then that must make your voyage rather unpleasant?"

The blonde young lady made no reply, but, taking up the book which Miss Earle was reading, said, "You don't find Mr. Morris much of a reader, I presume? He used not to be."

"I know very little about Mr. Morris," said Miss Earle, freezingly.

"Why, you knew him before you came on board, did you not?" questioned the other, raising her eyebrows.

"No, I did not."

"You certainly know he is junior partner in the establishment where you work?"

"I know that, yes, but I had never spoken to him before I met him on board this steamer."

"Is that possible? Might I ask you if there is any probability of your becoming interested in Mr. Morris?"

"Interested! What do you mean?"

"Oh, you know well enough what I mean. We girls do not need to be humbugs with each other, whatever we may be before the men. When a young woman meets a young man in the early morning, and has coffee with him, and when she reads to him, and tries to cultivate his literary tastes, whatever they may be, she certainly shows some interest in the young man, don't you think so?"

Miss Earle looked for a moment indignantly at her questioner. "I do not recognise your right," she said, "to ask me such a question."

"No? Then let me tell you that I have every right to ask it. I assure you that I have thought over the matter deeply before I spoke. It seemed to me there was one chance in a thousand—only one chance in a thousand, remember—that you were acting honestly, and on that one chance I took the liberty of speaking to you. The right I have to ask such a question is this—Mr. George Morris has been engaged to me for several years."

"Engaged to you?"

"Yes. If you don't believe it, ask him."

"It is the very last question in the world I would ask anybody."

"Well, then, you will have to take my word for it. I hope you are not very shocked, Miss Earle, to hear what I have had to tell you."

"Shocked? Oh dear, no. Why should I be? It is really a matter of no interest to me, I assure you."

"Well, I am very glad to hear you say so. I did not know but you might have become more interested in Mr. Morris than you would care to own. I think myself that he is quite a fascinating young gentleman; but I thought it only just to you that you should know exactly how matters stood."

"I am sure I am very much obliged to you."

This much of the conversation Miss Earle had thought over in her own room that morning. "Did it make a difference to her or not?" that was the question she was asking herself. The information had certainly affected her opinion of Mr. Morris, and she smiled to herself rather bitterly as she thought of his claiming to be so exceedingly truthful. Miss Earle did not, however, go up on deck until the breakfast gong had rung.

"Good morning," said Morris, as he took his place at the little table. "I was like the boy on the burning deck this morning, when all but he had fled. I was very much disappointed that you did not come up, and have your usual cup of coffee."

"I am sorry to hear that," said Miss Earle; "if I had known I was disappointing anybody I should have been here."

"Miss Katherine," he said, "you are a humbug. You knew very well that I would be disappointed if you did not come."

The young lady looked up at him, and for a moment she thought of telling him that her name was Miss Earle, but for some reason she did not do so.

"I want you to promise now," he continued, "that to-morrow morning you will be on deck as usual."

"Has it become a usual thing, then?"

"Well, that's what I am trying to make it," he answered. "Will you promise?"

"Yes, I promise."

"Very well, then, I look on that as settled. Now, about to-day. What are you going to do with yourself after breakfast?"

"Oh, the usual thing, I suppose. I shall sit in my steamer chair and read an interesting book."

"And what is the interesting book for to-day?"

"It is a little volume by Henry James, entitled The Siege of London."

"Why, I never knew that London had been besieged. When did that happen?"

"Well, I haven't got very far in the book yet, but it seems to have happened quite recently, within a year or two, I think. It is one of the latest of Mr. James's short stories. I have not read it yet."

"Ah, then the siege is not historical?"

"Not historical further than Mr. James is the historian."

"Now, Miss Earle, are you good at reading out loud?"

"No, I am not."

"Why, how decisively you say that. I couldn't answer like that, because I don't know whether I am or not. I have never tried any of it. But if you will allow me, I will read that book out to you. I should like to have the good points indicated to me, and also the defects."

"There are not likely to be many defects," said the young lady. "Mr. James is a very correct writer. But I do not care either to read aloud or have a book read to me. Besides, we disturb the conversation or the reading of any one else who happens to sit near us. I prefer to enjoy a book by reading it myself."

"Ah, I see you are resolved cruelly to shut me out of all participation in your enjoyment."

"Oh, not at all. I shall be very happy to discuss the book with you afterwards. You should read it for yourself. Then, when you have done so, we might have a talk on its merits or demerits, if you think, after you have read it, that it has any."

"Any what? merits or demerits?"

"Well, any either."

"No; I will tell you a better plan than that. I am not going to waste my time reading it."

"Waste, indeed!"

"Certainly waste. Not when I have a much better plan of finding out what is in the book. I am going to get you to tell me the story after you have read it."

"Oh, indeed, and suppose I refuse?"

"Will you?"

"Well, I don't know. I only said suppose."

"Then I shall spend the rest of the voyage trying to persuade you."

"I am not very easily persuaded, Mr. Morris."

"I believe that," said the young man. "I presume I may sit beside you while you are reading your book?"

"You certainly may, if you wish to. The deck is not mine, only that portion of it, I suppose, which I occupy with the steamer chair. I have no authority over any of the rest."

"Now, is that a refusal or an acceptance?"

"It is which ever you choose to think."

"Well, if it is a refusal, it is probably softening down the No, but if it is an acceptance it is rather an ungracious one, it seems to me."

"Well, then, I shall be frank with you. I am very much interested in this book. I should a great deal rather read it than talk to you."

"Oh, thank you, Miss Earle. There can be no possible doubt about your meaning now."

"Well, I am glad of that, Mr. Morris. I am always pleased to think that I can speak in such a way as not to be misunderstood."

"I don't see any possible way of misunderstanding that. I wish I did."

"And then, after lunch," said the young lady, "I think I shall finish the book before that time;—if you care to sit beside me or to walk the deck with me, I shall be very glad to tell you the story."

"Now, that is perfectly delightful," cried the young man. "You throw a person down into the depths, so that he will appreciate all the more being brought up into the light again."

"Oh, not at all. I have no such dramatic ideas in speaking frankly with you. I merely mean that this forenoon I wish to have to myself, because I am interested in my book. At the end of the forenoon I shall probably be tired of my book and will prefer a talk with you. I don't see why you should think it odd that a person should say exactly what a person means."

"And then I suppose in the evening you will be tired of talking with me, and will want to take up your book again."

"Possibly."

"And if you are, you won't hesitate a moment about saying so?"

"Certainly not."

"Well, you are a decidedly frank young lady, Miss Earle; and, after all, I don't know but what I like that sort of thing best. I think if all the world were honest we would all have a better time of it here."

"Do you really think so?"

"Yes, I do."

"You believe in honesty, then?"

"Why, certainly. Have you seen anything in my conduct or bearing that would induce you to think that I did not believe in honesty?"

"No, I can't say I have. Still, honesty is such a rare quality that a person naturally is surprised when one comes unexpectedly upon it."

George Morris found the forenoon rather tedious and lonesome. He sat in the smoking room, and once or twice he ventured near where Miss Earle sat engrossed in her book, in the hope that the volume might have been put aside for the time, and that he would have some excuse for sitting down and talking with her. Once as he passed she looked up with a bright smile and nodded to him.

"Nearly through?" he asked dolefully.

"Of The Siege of London?" she asked.

"Yes."

"Oh, I am through that long ago, and have begun another story."

"Now, that is not according to contract," claimed Morris. "The contract was that when you got through with The Siege of London you were to let me talk with you, and that you were to tell me the story."

"That was not my interpretation of it. Our bargain, as I understood it, was that I was to have this forenoon to myself, and that I was to use the forenoon for reading. I believe my engagement with you began in the afternoon."

"I wish it did," said the young man, with a wistful look.

"You wish what?" she said, glancing up at him sharply.

He blushed as he bent over towards her and whispered, "That our engagement, Miss Katherine, began in the afternoon."

The colour mounted rapidly into her cheeks, and for a moment George Morris thought he had gone too far. It seemed as if a sharp reply was ready on her lips; but, as on another occasion, she checked it and said nothing. Then she opened her book and began to read. He waited for a moment and said—

"Miss Earle, have I offended you?"

"Did you mean to give offence?" she asked.

"No, certainly, I did not."

"Then why should you think you had offended me?"

"Well, I don't know, I—" he stammered.

Miss Earle looked at him with such clear, innocent, and unwavering eyes that the young man felt that he could neither apologise nor make an explanation.

"I'm afraid," he said, "that I am encroaching on your time."

"Yes, I think you are: that is, if you intend to live up to your contract, and let me live up to mine. You have no idea how much more interesting this book is than you are."

"Why, you are not a bit flattering, Miss Earle, are you?"

"No, I don't think I am. Do you try to be?"

"I'm afraid that in my lifetime I have tried to be, but I assure you, Miss Earle, that I don't try to be flattering, or try to be anything but what I really am when I am in your company. To tell the truth, I am too much afraid of you."

Miss Earle smiled and went on with her reading, while Morris went once more back into the smoking-room.

"Now then," said George Morris, when lunch was over, "which is it to be? The luxurious languor of the steamer chair or the energetic exercise of the deck? Take your choice."

"Well," answered the young lady, "as I have been enjoying the luxurious languor all the forenoon, I prefer the energetic exercise, if it is agreeable to you, for a while, at least."

"It is very agreeable to me. I am all energy this afternoon. In fact, now that you have consented to allow me to talk with you, I feel as if I were imbued with a new life."

"Dear me," said she, "and all because of the privilege of talking to me?"

"All."

"How nice that is. You are sure that it is not the effect of the sea air?"

"Quite certain. I had the sea air this forenoon, you know."

"Oh, yes, I had forgotten that."

"Well, which side of the deck then?"

"Oh, which ever is the least popular side. I dislike a crowd."

"I think, Miss Earle, that we will have this side pretty much to ourselves. The madd'ing crowd seems to have a preference for the sunny part of the ship. Now, then, for the siege of London. Who besieged it?"

"A lady."

"Did she succeed?"

"She did."

"Well, I am very glad to hear it, indeed. What was she besieging it for?"

"For social position, I presume.

"Then, as we say out West, I suppose she had a pretty hard row to hoe?"

"Yes, she had."

"Well, I never can get at the story by cross-questioning. Now, supposing that you tell it to me."

"I think that you had better take the book and read it. I am not a good story-teller."

"Why, I thought we Americans were considered excellent story-tellers.'

"We Americans?"

"Oh, I remember now, you do not lay claim to being an American. You are English, I think you said?"

"I said nothing of the kind. I merely said I lay no claims to being an American."

"Yes, that was it."

"Well, you will be pleased to know that this lady in the siege of London was an American. You seem so anxious to establish a person's nationality that I am glad to be able to tell you at the very first that she was an American, and, what is more, seemed to be a Western American."

"Seemed? Oh, there we get into uncertainties again. If I like to know whether persons are Americans or not, it naturally follows that I am anxious to know whether they were Western or Eastern Americans. Aren't you sure she was a Westerner?"

"The story, unfortunately, leaves that a little vague, so if it displeases you I shall be glad to stop the telling of it."

"Oh no, don't do that. I am quite satisfied to take her as an American citizen; whether she is East or West, or North or South, does not make the slightest difference to me. Please go on with the story."

"Well, the other characters, I am happy to be able to say, are not at all indefinite in the matter of nationality. One is an Englishman; he is even more than that, he is an English nobleman. The other is an American. Then there is the English nobleman's mother, who, of course, is an English woman; and the American's sister, married to an Englishman, and she, of course, is English-American. Does that satisfy you?"

"Perfectly. Go on."

"It seems that the besieger, the heroine of the story if you may call her so, had a past."

"Has not everybody had a past?"

"Oh no. This past is known to the American and is unknown to the English nobleman."

"Ah, I see; and the American is in love with her in spite of her past?"

"Not in Mr. James's story."

"Oh, I beg pardon. Well, go on; I shall not interrupt again."

"It is the English nobleman who is in love with her in spite of his absence of knowledge about her past. The English nobleman's mother is very much against the match. She tries to get the American to tell what the past of this woman is. The American refuses to do so. In fact, in Paris he has half promised the besieger not to say anything about her past. She is besieging London, and she wishes the American to remain neutral. But the nobleman's mother at last gets the American to promise that he will tell her son what he knows of this woman's past. The American informs the woman what he has promised the nobleman's mother to do, and at this moment the nobleman enters the room. The besieger of London, feeling that her game is up, leaves them together. The American says to the nobleman, who stands rather stiffly before him, 'If you wish to ask me any questions regarding the lady who has gone out I shall be happy to tell you.' Those are not the words of the book, but they are in substance what he said. The nobleman looked at him for a moment with that hauteur which, we presume, belongs to noblemen, and said quietly, 'I wish to know nothing.' Now, that strikes me as a very dramatic point in the story."

"But didn't he wish to know anything of the woman whom he was going to marry?"

"I presume that, naturally, he did."

"And yet he did not take the opportunity of finding out when he had the chance?"

"No, he did not."

"Well, what do you think of that?"

"What do I think of it? I think it's a very dramatic point in the story."

"Yes, but what do you think of his wisdom in refusing to find out what sort of a woman he was going to marry? Was he a fool or was he a very noble man?"

"Why, I thought I said at the first that he was a nobleman, an Englishman."

"Miss Katherine, you are dodging the question. I asked your opinion of that man's wisdom. Was he wise, or was he a fool?"

"What do you think about it? Do you think he was a fool, or a wise man?"

"Well, I asked you for your opinion first. However, I have very little hesitation in saying, that a man who marries a woman of whom he knows nothing, is a fool."

"Oh, but he was well acquainted with this woman. It was only her past that he knew nothing about."

"Well, I think you must admit that a woman's past and a man's past are very important parts of their lives. Don't you agree with me?"

"I agree with you so seldom that I should hesitate to say I did on this occasion. But I have told the story very badly. You will have to read it for yourself to thoroughly appreciate the different situations, and then we can discuss the matter intelligently."

"You evidently think the man was very noble in refusing to hear anything about the past of the lady he was interested in."

"I confess I do. He was noble, at least, in refusing to let a third party tell him. If he wished any information he should have asked the lady himself."

"Yes, but supposing she refused to answer him?"

"Then, I think he should either have declined to have anything more to do with her, or, if he kept up his acquaintance, he should have taken her just as she was, without any reference to her past."

"I suppose you are right. Still, it is a very serious thing for two people to marry without knowing something of each other's lives."

"I am tired of walking," said Miss Earle, "I am now going to seek comfort in the luxuriousness, as you call it, of my steamer chair."

"And may I go with you?" asked the young man.

"If you also are tired of walking."

"You know," he said, "you promised the whole afternoon. You took the forenoon with The Siege, and now I don't wish to be cheated out of my half of the day."

"Very well, I am rather interested in another story, and if you will take The Siege of London, and read it, you'll find how much better the book is than my telling of the story."

George Morris had, of course, to content himself with this proposition, and they walked together to the steamer chairs, over which the gaily coloured rugs were spread.

"Shall I get your book for you?" asked the young man, as he picked up the rugs.

"Thank you," answered Miss Earle, with a laugh, "you have already done so," for, as he shook out the rugs, the two books, which were small handy volumes, fell out on the deck.

"I see you won't accept my hint about not leaving the books around. You will lose some precious volume one of these days."

"Oh, I fold them in the rugs, and they are all right. Now, here is your volume. Sit down there and read it." "That means also, 'and keep quiet,' I suppose?"

"I don't imagine you are versatile enough to read and talk at the same time. Are you?"

"I should be very tempted to try it this afternoon."

Miss Earle went on with her reading, and Morris pretended to go on with his. He soon found, however, that he could not concentrate his attention on the little volume in his hand, and so quickly abandoned the attempt, and spent his time in meditation and in casting furtive glances at his fair companion over the top of his book. He thought the steamer chair a perfectly delightful invention. It was an easy, comfortable, and adjustable apparatus, that allowed a person to sit up or to recline at almost any angle. He pushed his chair back a little, so that he could watch the profile of Miss Katherine Earle, and the dark tresses that formed a frame for it, without risking the chance of having his espionage discovered.

"Aren't you comfortable?" asked the young lady, as he shoved back his chair.

"I am very, very comfortable," replied the young man.

"I am glad of that," she said, as she resumed her reading.

George Morris watched her turn leaf after leaf as he reclined lazily in his chair, with half-closed eyes, and said to himself, "Shop-girl or not, past or not, I'm going to propose to that young lady the first good opportunity I get. I wonder what she will say?"

"How do you like it?" cried the young lady he was thinking of, with a suddenness that made Morris jump in his chair.

"Like it?" he cried; "oh, I like it immensely."

"How far have you got?" she continued.

"How far? Oh, a great distance. Very much further than I would have thought it possible when I began this voyage."

Miss Earle turned and looked at him with wide-open eyes, as he made this strange reply.

"What are you speaking of?" she said.

"Oh, of everything—of the book, of the voyage, of the day."'

"I was speaking of the book," she replied quietly. "Are you sure you have not fallen asleep and been dreaming?"

"Fallen asleep? No. Dreaming? Yes."

"Well, I hope your dreams have been pleasant ones."

"They have."

Miss Earle, who seemed to think it best not to follow her investigations any further, turned once more to her own book, and read it until it was time to dress for dinner. When that important meal was over, Morris said to Miss Earle: "Do you know you still owe me part of the day?"

"I thought you said you had a very pleasant afternoon."

"So I had. So pleasant, you see, that I want to have the pleasure prolonged. I want you to come out and have a walk on the deck now in the starlight. It is a lovely night, and, besides, you are now halfway across the ocean, and yet I don't think you have been out once to see the phosphorescence. That is one of the standard sights of an ocean voyage. Will you come?"

Although the words were commonplace enough, there was a tremor in his voice which gave a meaning to them that could not be misunderstood. Miss Earle looked at him with serene composure, and yet with a touch of reproachfulness in her glance. "He talks like this to me," she said to herself, "while he is engaged to another woman."

"Yes," she answered aloud, with more firmness in her voice than might have seemed necessary, "I will be happy to walk on the deck with you to see the phosphorescence."

He helped to hinder her for a moment in adjusting her wraps, and they went out in the starlit night together.

"Now," he said, "if we are fortunate enough to find the place behind the after-wheel house vacant we can have a splendid view of the phosphorescence."

"Is it so much in demand that the place is generally crowded?" she asked.

"I may tell you in confidence," replied Mr. Morris, "that this particular portion of the boat is always very popular. Soon as the evening shades prevail the place is apt to be pre-empted by couples that are very fond of—"

"Phosphorescence," interjected the young lady.

"Yes," he said, with a smile that she could not see in the darkness, "of phosphorescence."

"I should think," said she, as they walked towards the stern of the boat, "that in scientific researches of that sort, the more people who were there, the more interesting the discussion would be, and the more chance a person would have to improve his mind on the subject of phosphorescence, or other matters pertaining to the sea."

"Yes," replied Morris. "A person naturally would think that, and yet, strange as it may appear, if there ever was a time when two is company and three is a crowd, it is when looking at the phosphorescence that follows the wake of an ocean steamer."

"Really?" observed the young lady, archly. "I remember you told me that you had crossed the ocean several times."

The young man laughed joyously at this repartee, and his companion joined him with a laugh that was low and musical.

"He seems very sure of his ground," she said to herself. "Well, we shall see."

As they came to the end of the boat and passed behind the temporary wheel-house erected there, filled with debris of various sorts, blocks and tackle and old steamer chairs, Morris noticed that two others were there before them standing close together with arms upon the bulwarks. They were standing very close together, so close in fact, that in the darkness, it seemed like one person. But as Morris stumbled over some chains, the dark, united shadow dissolved itself quickly into two distinct separate shadows. A flagpole stood at the extreme end of the ship, inclining backwards from the centre of the bulwarks, and leaning over the troubled, luminous sea beneath. The two who had taken their position first were on one side of the flag-pole and Morris and Miss Earle on the other. Their coming had evidently broken the spell for the others. After waiting for a few moments, the lady took the arm of the gentleman and walked forward. "Now," said Morris, with a sigh, "we have the phosphorescence to ourselves."

"It is very, very strange," remarked the lady in a low voice. "It seems as if a person could see weird shapes arising in the air, as if in torment."

The young man said nothing for a few moments. He cleared his throat several times as if to speak, but still remained silent. Miss Earle gazed down at the restless, luminous water. The throb, throb of the great ship made the bulwarks on which their arms rested tremble and quiver.

Finally Morris seemed to muster up courage enough to begin, and he said one word—

"Katherine." As he said this he placed his hand on hers as it lay white before him in the darkness upon the trembling bulwark. It seemed to him that she made a motion to withdraw her hand, and then allowed it to remain where it was.

"Katherine," he continued, in a voice that he hardly recognised as his own, "we have known each other only a very short time comparatively; but, as I think I said to you once before, a day on shipboard may be as long as a month on shore. Katherine, I want to ask you a question, and yet I do not know—I cannot find—I—I don't know what words to use."

The young lady turned her face towards him, and he saw her clear-cut profile sharply outlined against the glowing water as he looked down at her. Although the young man struggled against the emotion, which is usually experienced by any man in his position, yet he felt reasonably sure of the answer to his question. She had come with him out into the night. She had allowed her hand to remain in his. He was, therefore, stricken dumb with amazement when she replied, in a soft and musical voice—

"You do not know what to say? What do you usually say on such an occasion?"

"Usually say?" he gasped in dismay. "I do not understand you. What do you mean?"

"Isn't my meaning plain enough? Am I the first young lady to whom you have not known exactly what to say?"

Mr. Morris straightened up, and folded his arms across his breast; then, ridiculously enough, this struck him as a heroic attitude, and altogether unsuitable for an American, so he thrust his hands deep in his coat pockets.

"Miss Earle," he said, "I knew that you could be cruel, but I did not think it possible that you could be so cruel as this."

"Is the cruelty all on my side, Mr. Morris?" she answered. "Have you been perfectly honest and frank with me? You know you have not. Now, I shall be perfectly honest and frank with you. I like you very much indeed. I have not the slightest hesitation in saying this, because it is true, and I don't care whether you know it, or whether anybody else knows it or not."

As she said this the hope which Morris had felt at first, and which had been dashed so rudely to the ground, now returned, and he attempted to put his arm about her and draw her to him; but the young lady quickly eluded his grasp, stepping to the other side of the flag-pole, and putting her hand upon it.

"Mr. Morris," she said, "there is no use of your saying anything further. There is a barrier between us; you know it as well as I. I would like us to be friends as usual; but, if we are to be, you will have to remember the barrier, and keep to your own side of it."

"I know of no barrier," cried Morris, vehemently, attempting to come over to her side.

"There is the barrier," she said, placing her hand on the flag-pole. "My place is on this side of that barrier; your place is on the other. If you come on this side of that flag-pole, I shall leave you. If you remain on your own side, I shall be very glad to talk with you."

Morris sullenly took his place on the other side of the flag-pole. "Has there been anything in my actions," said the young lady, "during the time we have been acquainted that would lead you to expect a different answer?"

"Yes. You have treated me outrageously at times, and that gave me some hope."

Miss Earle laughed her low, musical laugh at this remark.

"Oh, you may laugh," said Morris, savagely; "but it is no laughing matter to me, I assure you."

"Oh, it will be, Mr. Morris, when you come to think of this episode after you get on shore. It will seem to you very, very funny indeed; and when you speak to the next young lady on the same subject, perhaps you will think of how outrageously I have treated your remarks to-night, and be glad that there are so few young women in the world who would act as I have done."

"Where did you get the notion," inquired George Morris, "that I am in the habit of proposing to young ladies? It is a most ridiculous idea. I have been engaged once, I confess it. I made a mistake, and I am sorry for it. There is surely nothing criminal in that."

"It depends."

"Depends on what?"

71

"It depends on how the other party feels about it. It takes two to make an engagement, and it should take two to break it."

"Well, it didn't in my case," said the young man.

"So I understand," replied Miss Earle. "Mr. Morris, I wish you a very good evening." And before he could say a word she had disappeared in the darkness, leaving him to ponder bitterly over the events of the evening.

Sixth Day

In the vague hope of meeting Miss Earle, Morris rose early, and for a while paced the deck alone; but she did not appear. Neither did he have the pleasure of her company at breakfast. The more the young man thought of their interview of the previous evening, the more puzzled he was.

Miss Earle had frankly confessed that she thought a great deal of him, and yet she had treated him with an unfeelingness which left him sore and bitter. She might have refused him; that was her right, of course. But she need not have done it so sarcastically. He walked the deck after breakfast, but saw nothing of Miss Earle. As he paced up and down, he met the very person of all others whom he did not wish to meet. "Good morning, Mr. Morris," she said lightly, holding out her hand.

"Good morning," he answered, taking it without much warmth.

"You are walking the deck all alone, I see. May I accompany you?"

"Certainly," said the young man, and with that she put her hand on his arm and they walked together the first two rounds without saying anything to each other. Then she looked up at him, with a bright smile, and said, "So she refused you?"

"How do you know?" answered the young man, reddening and turning a quick look at her.

"How do I know?" laughed the other. "How should I know?"

For a moment it flashed across his mind that Miss Katherine Earle had spoken of their interview of last night; but a moment later he dismissed the suspicion as unworthy.

"How do you know?" he repeated.

"Because I was told so on very good authority."

"I don't believe it."

"Ha, ha! now you are very rude. It is very rude to say to a lady that she doesn't speak the truth."

"Well, rude or not, you are not speaking the truth. Nobody told you such a thing."

"My dear George, how impolite you are. What a perfect bear you have grown to be. Do you want to know who told me?"

"I don't care to know anything about it."

"Well, nevertheless, I shall tell you. You told me."

"I did? Nonsense, I never said anything about it."

"Yes, you did. Your walk showed it. The dejected look showed it, and when I spoke to you, your actions, your tone, and your words told it to me plainer than if you had said, 'I proposed to Miss Earle last night and I was rejected.' You poor, dear innocent, if you don't brighten up you will tell it to the whole ship."

"I am sure, Blanche, that I am very much obliged to you for the interest you take in me. Very much obliged, indeed."

"Oh no, you are not; and now, don't try to be sarcastic, it really doesn't suit your manner at all. I was very anxious to know how your little flirtation had turned out. I really was. You know I have an interest in you, George, and always will have, and I wouldn't like that spiteful little black-haired minx to have got you, and I am very glad she refused you, although why she did so I cannot for the life of me imagine."

"It must be hard for you to comprehend why she refused me, now that I am a partner in the firm." Blanche looked down upon the deck, and did not answer.

"I am glad," she said finally, looking up brightly at him with her innocent blue eyes, "that you did not put off your proposal until to-night. We expect to be at Queenstown to-night some time, and we leave there and go on through by the Lakes of Killarney. So, you see, if you hadn't proposed last night I should have known nothing at all about how the matter turned out, and I should have died of curiosity and anxiety to know."

"Oh, I would have written to you," said Morris. "Leave me your address now, and I'll write and let you know how it turns out."

"Oh," she cried quickly, "then it isn't ended yet? I didn't think you were a man who would need to be refused twice or thrice."

"I should be glad to be refused by Miss Earle five hundred times."

"Indeed?"

"Yes, five hundred times, if on the five hundredth and first time she accepted."

"Is it really so serious as that?"

"It is just exactly that serious."

"Then your talk to me after all was only pretence?"

"No, only a mistake."

"What an escape I have had!"

"You have, indeed."

"Ah, here comes Miss Earle. Really, for a lady who has rejected a gentleman, she does not look as supremely happy as she might. I must go and have a talk with her."

"Look here, Blanche," cried the young man, angrily, "if you say a word to her about what we have been speaking of, I'll—"

"What will you do?" said the young lady, sweetly.

Morris stood looking at her. He didn't himself know what he would do; and Blanche, bowing to him, walked along the deck, and sat down in the steamer chair beside Miss Earle, who gave her a very scant recognition.

"Now, you needn't be so cool and dignified," said the lady. "George and I have been talking over the matter, and I told him he wasn't to feel discouraged at a first refusal, if he is resolved to have a shop-girl for his wife."

"What! Mr. Morris and you have been discussing me, have you?"

"Is there anything forbidden in that, Miss Earle? You must remember that George and I are very, very old friends, old and dear friends. Did you refuse him on my account? I know you like him."

"Like him?" said Miss Earle, with a fierce light in her eyes, as she looked at her tormentor. "Yes, I like him, and I'll tell you more than that;" she bent over and added in an intense whisper, "I love him, and if you say another word to me about him, or if you dare to discuss me with him, I shall go up to him where he stands now and accept him. I shall say to him, 'George Morris, I love you.' Now if you doubt I shall do that, just continue in your present style of conversation."

Blanche leaned back in the steamer chair and turned a trifle pale. Then she laughed, that irritating little laugh of hers, and said, "Really I did not think it had gone so far as that. I'll bid you good morning."

The moment the chair was vacated, George Morris strolled up and sat down on it.

"What has that vixen been saying to you?" he asked.

"That vixen," said Miss Earle, quietly, "has been telling me that you and she were discussing me this morning, and discussing the conversation that took place last night."

"It is a lie," said Morris.

"What is? What I say, or what she said, or what she says you said?"

"That we were discussing you, or discussing our conversation, is not true. Forgive me for using the coarser word. This was how it was; she came up to me—"

"My dear Mr. Morris, don't say a word. I know well enough that you would not discuss the matter with anybody. I, perhaps, may go so far as to say, least of all with her. Still, Mr. Morris, you must remember this, that even if you do not like her now—"

"Like her?" cried Morris; "I hate her."

"As I was going to say, and it is very hard for me to say it, Mr. Morris, you have a duty towards her as you—we all have our duties to perform," said Miss Earle, with a broken voice. "You must do yours, and I must do mine. It may be hard, but it is settled. I cannot talk this morning. Excuse me." And she rose and left him sitting there.

"What in the world does the girl mean? I am glad that witch gets off at Queenstown. I believe it is she who has mixed everything up. I wish I knew what she has been saying."

Miss Earle kept very closely to her room that day, and in the evening, as they approached the Fastnet Light, George Morris was not able to find her to tell her of the fact that they had sighted land. He took the liberty, however, of scribbling a little note to her, which the stewardess promised to deliver. He waited around the foot of the companion-way for an answer. The answer came in the person of Miss Katherine herself.

If refusing a man was any satisfaction, it seemed as if Miss Katherine Earle had obtained very little gratification from it. She looked weary and sad as she took the young man's arm, and her smile as she looked up at him had something very pathetic in it, as if a word might bring the tears. They sat in the chairs and watched the Irish coast. Morris pointed out objects here and there, and told her what they were. At last, when they went down to supper together, he said—

"We will be at Queenstown some time to-night. It will be quite a curious sight in the moonlight. Wouldn't you like to stay up and see it?"

"I think I would," she answered. "I take so few ocean voyages that I wish to get all the nautical experiences possible."

The young man looked at her sharply, then he said—

"Well, the stop at Queenstown is one of the experiences. May I send the steward to rap at your door when the engine stops?"

"Oh, I shall stay up in the saloon until that time?"

"It may be a little late. It may be as late as one or two o'clock in the morning. We can't tell. I should think the best thing for you to do would be to take a rest until the time comes. I think, Miss Earle, you need it."

It was a little after twelve o'clock when the engine stopped. The saloon was dimly lighted, and porters were hurrying to and fro, getting up the baggage which belonged to those who were going to get off at Queenstown. The night was very still, and rather cold. The lights of Queenstown could be seen here and there along the semi-circular range of hills on which the town stood. Passengers who were to land stood around the deck well muffled up, and others who had come to bid them good-bye were talking sleepily with them. Morris was about to send the steward to Miss Earle's room, when that young lady herself appeared. There was something spirit-like about her, wrapped in her long cloak, as she walked through the half-darkness to meet George Morris.

"I was just going to send for you," he said.

"I did not sleep any," was the answer, "and the moment the engine stopped I knew we were there. Shall we go on deck?"

"Yes," he said, "but come away from the crowd," and with that he led her towards the stern of the boat. For a moment Miss Earle seemed to hold back, but finally she walked along by his side firmly to where they had stood the night before. With seeming intention Morris tried to take his place beside her, but Miss Earle, quietly folding her cloak around her, stood on the opposite side of the flagpole, and, as if there should be no forgetfulness on his part, she reached up her hand and laid it against the staff.

"She evidently meant what she said," thought Morris to himself, with a sigh, as he watched the low, dim outlines of the hills around Queenstown Harbour, and the twinkling lights here and there.

"That is the tender coming now," he said, pointing to the red and green lights of the approaching boat. "How small it looks beside our monster steamship."

Miss Earle shivered.

"I pity the poor folks who have to get up at this hour of the night and go ashore. I should a great deal rather go back to my state-room."

"Well, there is one passenger I am not sorry for," said Morris, "and that is the young woman who has, I am afraid, been saying something to you which has made you deal more harshly with me than perhaps you might otherwise have done. I wish you would tell me what she said?"

"She has said nothing," murmured Miss Earle, with a sigh, "but what you yourself have confirmed. I do not pay much attention to what she says."

"Well, you don't pay much attention to what I say either," he replied. "However, as I say, there is one person I am not sorry for; I even wish it were raining. I am very revengeful, you see."

"I do not know that I am very sorry for her myself," replied Miss Earle, frankly; "but I am sorry for her poor old father, who hasn't appeared in the saloon a single day except the first. He has been sick the entire voyage."

"Her father?" cried Morris, with a rising inflection in his voice.

"Certainly."

"Why, bless my soul! Her father has been dead for ages and ages."

"Then who is the old man she is with?"

"Old man! It would do me good to have her hear you call him the old man. Why, that is her husband."

"Her husband!" echoed Miss Earle, with wide open eyes, "I thought he was her father."

"Oh, not at all. It is true, as you know, that I was engaged to the young lady, and I presume if I had become a partner in our firm sooner we would have been married. But that was a longer time coming than suited my young lady's convenience, and so she threw me over with as little ceremony as you would toss a penny to a beggar, and she married this old man for his wealth, I presume. I don't see exactly why she should take a fancy to him otherwise. I felt very cut up about it, of course, and I thought if I took this voyage I would at least be rid for a while of the thought of her. They are now on their wedding trip. That is the reason your steamer chair was broken, Miss Earle. Here I came on board an ocean steamer to get rid of the sight or thought of a certain woman, and to find that I was penned up with that woman, even if her aged husband was with her, for eight or nine days, was too much for me. So I raced up the deck and tried to get ashore. I didn't succeed in that, but I did succeed in breaking your chair."

Miss Earle was evidently very much astonished at this revelation, but she said nothing. After waiting in vain for her to speak, Morris gazed off at the dim shore. When he looked around he noticed that Miss Earle was standing on his side of the flagstaff. There was no longer a barrier between them.

Seventh Day

If George Morris were asked to say which day of all his life had been the most thoroughly enjoyable, he would probably have answered that the seventh of his voyage from New York to Liverpool was the red-letter day of his life. The sea was as calm as it was possible for a sea to be. The sun shone bright and warm. Towards the latter part of the day they saw the mountains of Wales, which, from the steamer's deck, seemed but a low range of hills. It did not detract from Morris's enjoyment to know that Mrs. Blanche was now on the troubleless island of Ireland, and that he was sailing over this summer sea with the lady who, the night before, had promised to be his wife.

During the day Morris and Katherine sat together on the sunny side of the ship looking at the Welsh coast. Their books lay unread on the rug, and there were long periods of silences between them.

"I don't believe," said Morris, "that anything could be more perfectly delightful than this. I wish the shaft would break."

"I hope it won't," answered the young lady; "the chances are you would be as cross as a bear before two days had gone past, and would want to go off in a small boat."

"Oh, I should be quite willing to go off in a small boat if you would come with me. I would do that now."

"I am very comfortable where I am," answered Miss Katherine. "I know when to let well enough alone."

"And I don't, I suppose you mean?"

"Well, if you wanted to change this perfectly delightful day for any other day, or this perfectly luxurious and comfortable mode of travel for any other method, I should suspect you of not letting well enough alone."

"I have to admit," said George, "that I am completely and serenely happy. The only thing that bothers me is that to-night we shall be in Liverpool. I wish this hazy and dreamy weather could last for ever, and I am sure I could stand two extra days of it going just as we are now. I think with regret of how much of this voyage we have wasted."

"Oh, you think it was wasted, do you?"

"Well, wasted as compared with this sort of life. This seems to me like a rest after a long chase."

"Up the deck?" asked the young lady, smiling at him.

"Now, see here," said Morris, "we may as well understand this first as last, that unfortunate up-the-deck chase has to be left out of our future life. I am not going to be twitted about that race every time a certain young lady takes a notion to have a sort of joke upon me."

"That was no joke, George. It was the most serious race you ever ran in your life. You were running away from one woman, and, poor blind young man, you ran right in the arms of another. The danger you have run into is ever so much greater than the one you were running away from."

"Oh, I realise that," said the young man, lightly; "that's what makes me so solemn to-day, you know." His hand stole under the steamer rugs and imprisoned her own.

"I am afraid people will notice that," she said quietly.

"Well, let them; I don't care. I don't know anybody on board this ship, anyhow, except you, and if you realised how very little I care for their opinions you would not try to withdraw your hand."

"I am not trying very hard," answered the young woman; and then there was another long silence. Finally she continued—

"I am going to take the steamer chair and do it up in ribbons when I get ashore."

"I am afraid it will not be a very substantial chair, no matter what you do with it. It will be a trap for those who sit in it."

"Are you speaking of your own experience?"

"No, of yours."

"George," she said, after a long pause, "did you like her very much?"

"Her?" exclaimed the young man, surprised. "Who?"

"Why, the young lady you ran away from. You know very well whom I mean."

"Like her? Why, I hate her."

"Yes, perhaps you do now. But I am asking of former years. How long were you engaged to her?"

"Engaged? Let me see, I have been engaged just about—well, not twenty-four hours yet. I was never engaged before. I thought I was, but I wasn't really."

Miss Earle shook her head. "You must have liked her very much," she said, "or you never would have proposed marriage to her. You would never have been engaged to her. You never would have felt so badly when she—"

81

"Oh, say it out," said George, "jilted me, that is the word."

"No, that is not the phrase I wanted to use. She didn't really jilt you, you know. It was because you didn't have, or thought you didn't have, money enough. She would like to be married to you to-day."

George shuddered.

"I wish," he said, "that you wouldn't mar a perfect day by a horrible suggestion."

"The suggestion would not have been so horrible a month ago."

"My dear girl," said Morris, rousing himself up, "it's a subject that I do not care much to talk about, but all young men, or reasonably young men, make mistakes in their lives. That was my mistake. My great luck was that it was discovered in time. As a general thing, affairs in this world are admirably planned, but it does seem to me a great mistake that young people have to choose companions for life at an age when they really haven't the judgment to choose a house and lot. Now, confess yourself, I am not your first lover, am I?"

Miss Earle looked at him for a moment before replying.

"You remember," she said, "that once you spoke of not having to incriminate yourself. You refused to answer a question I asked you on that ground. Now, I think this is a case in which I would be quite justified in refusing to answer. If I told you that you were my first lover, you would perhaps be manlike enough to think that after all you had only taken what nobody else had expressed a desire for. A man does not seem to value anything unless some one else is struggling for it."

"Why, what sage and valuable ideas you have about men, haven't you, my dear?"

"Well, you can't deny but what there is truth in them."

"I not only can, but I do. On behalf of my fellow men, and on behalf of myself, I deny it."

"Then, on the other hand," she continued, "if I confessed to you that

I did have half a score or half a dozen of lovers, you would perhaps think I had been jilting somebody or had been jilted. So you see, taking it all in, and thinking the matter over, I shall refuse to answer your question."

"Then you will not confess?"

"Yes, I shall confess. I have been wanting to confess to you for some little time, and have felt guilty because I did not do so."

"I am prepared to receive the confession," replied the young man, lazily, "and to grant absolution."

"Well, you talk a great deal about America and about Americans, and talk as if you were proud of the country, and of its ways, and of its people."

"Why, I am," answered the young man.

"Very well, then; according to your creed one person is just as good as another."

"Oh, I don't say that, I don't hold that for a moment. I don't think I am as good as you, for instance."

"But what I mean is this, that one's occupation does not necessarily give one a lower station than another. If that is not your belief then you are not a true American, that is all."

"Well, yes, that is my belief. I will admit I believe all that. What of it?"

"What of it? There is this of it. You are the junior partner of a large establishment in New York?"

"Nothing criminal in that, is there?"

"Oh, I don't put it as an accusation, I am merely stating the fact. You admit the fact, of course?"

"Yes. The fact is admitted, and marked Exhibit A, and placed in evidence. Now, what next?"

"In the same establishment there was a young woman who sold ribbons to all comers?"

"Yes, I admit that also, and the young lady's name was Miss Katherine Earle."

"Oh, you knew it, then?"

"Why, certainly I did."

"You knew it before you proposed to me."

"Oh, I seem to have known that fact for years and years."

"She told it to you."

"She? What she?"

"You know very well who I mean, George. She told it to you, didn't she?"

"Why, don't you think I remembered you—remembered seeing you there?"

"I know very well you did not. You may have seen me there, but you did not remember me. The moment I spoke to you on the deck that day in the broken chair, I saw at once you did not remember me, and there is very little use of your trying to pretend you thought of it afterwards. She told it to you, didn't she?"

"Now, look here, Katherine, it isn't I who am making a confession, it is you. It is not customary for a penitent to cross-examine the father confessor in that style."

"It does not make any difference whether you confess or not, George; I shall always know she told you that. After all, I wish she had left it for me to tell. I believe I dislike that woman very much."

"Shake hands, Kate, over that. So do I. Now, my dear, tell me what she told you."

"Then she did tell you that, did she?"

"Why, if you are so sure of it without my admitting it, why do you ask again?"

"I suppose because I wanted to make doubly sure."

"Well, then, assurance is doubly sure. I admit she did."

"And you listened to her, George?" said Katherine, reproachfully.

"Listened? Why, of course I did. I couldn't help myself. She said it before I knew what she was going to say. She didn't give me the chance that your man had in that story you were speaking of. I said something that irritated her and she out with it at once as if it had been a crime on your part. I did not look on it in that light, and don't now. Anyhow, you are not going back to the ribbon counter."

"No," answered the young lady, with a sigh, looking dreamily out into the hazy distance. "No, I am not."

"At least, not that side of the counter," said George.

She looked at him for a moment, as if she did not understand him; then she laughed lightly.

"Now," said Morris, "I have done most of the confession on this confession of yours. Supposing I make a confession, and ask you to tell me what she told you."

"Well, she told me that you were a very fascinating young man," answered Katherine, with a sigh.

"Really. And did after-acquaintance corroborate that statement?"

"I never had occasion to tell her she was mistaken."

"What else did she say? Didn't mention anything about my prospects or financial standing in any way?"

"No; we did not touch on that subject."

"Come, now, you cannot evade the question. What else did she say to you about me?"

"I don't know that it is quite right to tell you, but I suppose I may. She said that you were engaged to her."

"Had been."

"No, were."

"Oh, that's it. She did not tell you she was on her wedding tour?"

"No, she did not."

"And didn't you speak to her about her father being on board?"

Katherine laughed her low, enjoyable laugh.

"Yes," she said, "I did, and I did not think till this moment of how flustered she looked. But she recovered her lost ground with a great deal of dexterity."

"By George, I should like to have heard that! I am avenged!"

"Well, so is she," was the answer.

"How is that?"

"You are engaged to me, are you not?"

Before George could make any suitable reply to this bit of humbug, one of the officers of the ship stopped before them.

"Well," he said, "I am afraid we shall not see Liverpool to-night."

"Really. Why?" asked George.

"This haze is settling down into a fog. It will be as thick as pea-soup before an hour. I expect there will be a good deal of grumbling among the passengers."

As he walked on, George said to Katherine, "There are two passengers who won't grumble any, will they, my dear?"

"I know one who won't," she answered.

The fog grew thicker and thicker; the vessel slowed down, and finally stopped, sounding every now and then its mournful, timber-shaking whistle.

<u>Eighth Day</u>

On the afternoon of the eighth day George Morris and Katherine Earle stood together on the deck of the tender, looking back at the huge steamship which they had just left.

"When we return," he said, "I think we shall choose this ship."

"Return?" she answered, looking at him.

"Why, certainly; we are going back, are we not?"

"Dear me," she replied, "I had not thought of that. You see, when I left America I did not intend to go back."

"Did you not? I thought you were only over here for the trip."

"Oh no. I told you I came on business, not on pleasure."

"And did you intend to stay over here?"

"Certainly."

"Why, that's strange; I never thought of that."

"It is strange, too," said Katherine, "that I never thought of going back."

"And—and," said the young man, "won't you go?"

She pressed his arm, and stood motionless.

"Where thou goest, I will go. Thy people shall be my people."

"That's a quotation, I suppose?" said George.

"It is," answered Katherine.

"Well, you see, as I told you, I am not very well read up on the books of the day."

"I don't know whether you would call that one of the books of the day or not," said Katherine; "it is from the Bible."

"Oh," answered the other. "I believe, Kate, you will spend the rest of your life laughing at me."

"Oh no," said the young lady, "I always thought I was fitted for missionary life. Now, look what a chance I have."

"You have taken a big contract, I admit."

They had very little trouble with their luggage. It is true that the English officials looked rather searchingly in Katherine's trunk for dynamite, but, their fears being allayed in that direction, the trunks were soon chalked and on the back of a stout porter, who transferred them to the top of a cab.

"I tell you what it is," said George, "it takes an American Custom-house official to make the average American feel ashamed of his country."

"Why, I did not think there was anything over there that could make you feel ashamed of your country. You are such a thorough-going American."

"Well, the Customs officials in New York have a knack of making a person feel that he belongs to no place on earth."

They drove to the big Liverpool hotel which is usually frequented by Americans who land in that city, and George spent the afternoon in attending to business in Liverpool, which he said he did not expect to have to look after when he left America, but which he desired very much to get some information about.

Katherine innocently asked if she could be of any assistance to him, and he replied that she might later on, but not at the present state of proceedings.

In the evening they went to a theatre together, and took a long route back to the hotel.

"It isn't a very pretty city," said Miss Earle.

"Oh, I think you are mistaken," replied her lover. "To me it is the most beautiful city in the world."

"Do you really mean that?" she said, looking at him with surprise.

"Yes, I do. It is the first city through which I have walked with the lady who is to be my wife."

"Oh, indeed," remarked the lady who was to be his wife, "and have you never walked with—"

"Now, see here," said Morris, "that subject is barred out. We left all those allusions on the steamer. I say I am walking now with the lady who is to be my wife. I think that statement of the case is perfectly correct, is it not?"

"I believe it is rather more accurate than the average statement of the average American."

"Now, Katherine," he said, "do you know what information I have been looking up since I have been in Liverpool?"

"I haven't the slightest idea," she said. "Property?"

"No, not property."

"Looking after your baggage, probably?"

"Well, I think you have got it this time. I was looking after my baggage. I was trying to find out how and when we could get married."

"Oh!"

"Yes, oh! Does that shock you? I find they have some idiotic arrangement by which a person has to live here three months before he can be married, although I was given some hope that, by paying for it, a person could get a special licence. If that is the case, I am going to have a special licence to-morrow."

"Indeed?"

"Yes, indeed. Then we can be married at the hotel."

"And don't you think, George, that I might have something to say about that?"

"Oh, certainly! I intended to talk with you about it. Of course I am talking with you now on that subject. You admitted the possibility of our getting married. I believe I had better get you to put it down in writing, or have you say it before witnesses, or something of that sort."

"Well, I shouldn't like to be married in a hotel."

"In a church, then? I suppose I can make arrangements that will include a church. A parson will marry us. That parson, if he is the right sort, will have a church. It stands to reason, therefore, that if we give him the contract he will give us the use of his church, quid pro quo, you know."

"Don't talk flippantly, please. I think it better to wait until to-morrow, George, before you do anything rash. I want to see something of the country. I want us to take a little journey together to-morrow, and then, out in the country, not in this grimy, sooty city, we will make arrangements for our marriage."

"All right, my dear. Where do you intend to go?"

"While you have been wasting your time in getting information relating to matrimony, I have been examining time-tables. Where I want to go is two or three hours' ride from here. We can take one of the morning trains, and when we get to the place I will allow you to hire a conveyance, and we will have a real country drive. Will you go with me?"

"Will I? You better believe I will. But you see, Katherine, I want to get married as soon as possible. Then we can take a little trip on the Continent before it is time for us to go back to America. You have never been on the Continent, have you?"

"Never."

"Well, I am very glad of that. I shall be your guide, philosopher, and friend, and, added to that, your husband."

"Very well, we will arrange all that on our little excursion to-morrow."

Ninth Day

Spring in England—and one of those perfect spring days in which all rural England looks like a garden. The landscape was especially beautiful to American eyes, after the more rugged views of Transatlantic scenery. The hedges were closely clipped, the fields of the deepest green, and the hills far away were blue and hazy in the distance.

"There is no getting over the fact," said Morris, "that this is the prettiest country in the whole world."

During most of the journey Katherine Earle sat back in her corner of the first-class compartment, and gazed silently out of the flying windows. She seemed too deeply impressed with the beauty of the scene to care for conversation even with the man she was to marry. At last they stopped at a pretty little rural station, with the name of the place done in flowers of vivid colour that stood out against the brown of the earth around, them and the green turf which formed the sloping bank.

"Now," said George, as they stood on the platform, "whither away? Which direction?"

"I want to see," said she, "a real, genuine, old English country home."

"A castle?"

"No, not a castle."

"Oh, I know what you want. Something like Haddon Hall, or that sort of thing. An old manor house. Well, wait a minute, and I'll talk to the station master, and find out all there is about this part of the country."

And before she could stop him, he had gone to make his inquiry of that official. Shortly after he came back with a list of places that were worth seeing, which he named.

"Holmwood House," she repeated. "Let us see that. How far is it?"

George again made inquiries, and found that it was about eight miles away. The station-master assured him that the road thither was one of the prettiest drives in the whole country.

"Now, what kind of a conveyance will you have? There are four-wheeled cabs, and there is even a hansom to be had. Will you have two horses or one, and will you have a coachman?"

"None of these," she said, "if you can get something you can drive yourself—I suppose you are a driver?"

"Oh, I have driven a buggy."

"Well, get some sort of conveyance that we can both sit in while you drive."

"But don't you think we will get lost?"

"We can inquire the way," she said, "and if we do get lost, it won't matter. I want to have a long talk with you before we reach the place."

They crossed the railway by a bridge over the line, and descended into a valley along which the road wound.

The outfit which George had secured was a neat little cart made of wood in the natural colour and varnished, and a trim little pony, which looked ridiculously small for two grown people, and yet was, as George afterwards said, "as tough as a pine knot."

The pony trotted merrily along, and needed no urging. George doubtless was a good driver, but whatever talents he had in that line were not brought into play. The pony was a treasure that had apparently no bad qualities. For a long time the two in the cart rode along the smooth highway silently, until at last Morris broke out with—

"Oh, see here! This is not according to contract. You said you wanted a long talk, and now you are complacently saying nothing."

"I do not know exactly how to begin."

"Is it so serious as all that?"

"It is not serious exactly—it is merely, as it were, a continuation of the confession."

"I thought we were through with that long ago. Are there any more horrible revelations?"

She looked at him with something like reproach in her eyes.

"If you are going to talk flippantly, I think I will postpone what I have to say until another time."

"My dear Kate, give a man a chance. He can't reform in a moment. I never had my flippancy checked before. Now then, I am serious again. What appalling—I mean—you see how difficult it is, Katherine—I mean, what serious subject shall we discuss?"

"Some other time."

"No—now. I insist on it. Otherwise I will know I am unforgiven."

"There is nothing to forgive. I merely wanted to tell you something more than you know about my own history."

"I know more now than that man in the story."

"He did not object to the knowledge, you know. He objected to receiving it from a third person. Now I am not a third person, am I?"

"Indeed, you are not. You are first person singular—at present—the first person to me at least. There, I am afraid I have dropped into flippancy again."

"That is not flippancy. That is very nice." The interval shall be unreported.

At last Katherine said quietly, "My mother came from this part of England."

"Ah! That is why you wanted to come here."

"That is why I wanted to come here. She was her father's only daughter, and, strange to say, he was very fond of her, and proud of her."

"Why strange?"

"Strange from his action for years after. She married against his will. He never forgave her. My father did not seem to have the knack of getting along in the world, and he moved to America in the hope of bettering his condition. He did not better it. My father died ten years ago, a prematurely broken down man, and my mother and I struggled along as best we could until she died two years ago. My grandfather returned her letter unopened

93

when mother wrote to him ten years ago, although the letter had a black border around it. When I think of her I find it hard to forgive him, so I suppose some of his nature has been transmitted to me."

"Find it hard? Katherine, if you were not an angel you would find it impossible."

"Well, there is nothing more to tell, or at least, not much. I thought you should know this. I intended to tell you that last day on shipboard, but it seemed to me that here was where it should be told—among the hills and valleys that she saw when she was my age."

"Katherine, my dear, do not think about it any more than you can help. It will only uselessly depress you. Here is a man coming. Let us find out now whether we have lost our way or not."

They had.

Even after that they managed to get up some wrong lanes and byways, and took several wrong turnings; but by means of inquiry from every one they met, they succeeded at last in reaching the place they were in search of.

There was an old and grey porter's lodge, and an old and grey gateway, with two tall, moss-grown stone pillars, and an iron gate between them. On the top of the pillars were crumbled stone shields, seemingly held in place by a lion on each pillar.

"Is this Holmwood House?" asked Morris of the old and grey man who came out of the porter's lodge.

"Yes, sir, it be," replied the man.

"Are visitors permitted to see the house and the grounds?"

"No, they be'ant," was the answer. "Visitors were allowed on Saturdays in the old Squire's time, but since he died they tell me the estate is in the courts, and we have orders from the London lawyers to let nobody in."

"I can make it worth your while," said George, feeling in his vest pocket; "this lady would like to see the house."

The old man shook his head, even although George showed him a gold piece between his finger and thumb. Morris was astonished at this, for he had the mistaken belief which all Americans have, that a tip in Europe, if it is only large enough, will accomplish anything.

"I think perhaps I can get permission," said Katherine, "if you will let me talk a while to the old man."

"All right. Go ahead," said George. "I believe you could wheedle anybody into doing what he shouldn't do."

"Now, after saying that, I shall not allow you to listen. I shall step down and talk with him a moment and you can drive on for a little distance, and come back."

"Oh, that's all right," said George, "I know how it is. You don't want to give away the secret of your power. Be careful, now, in stepping down. This is not an American buggy," but before he had finished the warning, Katherine had jumped lightly on the gravel, and stood waiting for him to drive on. When he came back he found the iron gates open.

"I shall not get in again," she said. "You may leave the pony with this man, George, he will take care of it. We can walk up the avenue to the house."

After a short walk under the spreading old oaks they came in sight of the house, which was of red brick and of the Elizabethan style of architecture.

"I am rather disappointed with that," said George, "I always thought old English homesteads were of stone."

"Well, this one at least is of brick, and I imagine you will find a great many of them are of the same material."

They met with further opposition from the housekeeper who came to the door which the servant had opened after the bell was rung.

She would allow nobody in the house, she said. As for Giles, if he allowed people on the grounds that was his own look-out, but she had been forbidden by the lawyers to allow anybody in the house, and she had let nobody in, and she wasn't going to let anybody in.

"Shall I offer her a tip?" asked George, in a whisper.

"No, don't do that."

"You can't wheedle her like you did the old man, you know. A woman may do a great deal with a man, but when she meets another woman she meets her match. You women know each other, you know."

Meanwhile the housekeeper, who had been about to shut the door, seemed to pause and regard the young lady with a good deal of curiosity. Her attention had before that time been taken up with the gentleman.

"Well, I shall walk to the end of the terrace, and give you a chance to try your wiles. But I am ready to bet ten dollars that you don't succeed."

"I'll take you," answered the young lady.

"Yes, you said you would that night on the steamer."

"Oh, that's a very good way of getting out of a hopeless bet."

"I am ready to make the bet all right enough, but I know you haven't a ten-dollar bill about you."

"Well, that is very true, for I have changed all my money to English currency; but I am willing to bet its equivalent."

Morris walked to the end of the terrace. When he got back he found that the door of the house was as wide open as the gates of the park had been.

"There is something uncanny about all this," he said. "I am just beginning to see that you have a most dangerous power of fascination. I could understand it with old Giles, but I must admit that I thought the stern housekeeper would—"

"My dear George," interrupted Katherine, "almost anything can be accomplished with people, if you only go about it the right way."

"Now, what is there to be seen in this house?"

"All that there is to be seen about any old English house. I thought, perhaps, you might be interested in it."

"Oh, I am. But I mean, isn't there any notable things? For instance, I was in Haddon Hall once, and they showed me the back stairway where a fair lady had eloped with her lover. Have they anything of that kind to show here?"

Miss Earle was silent for a few moments. "Yes," she said, "I am afraid they have."

"Afraid? Why, that is perfectly delightful. Did the young lady of the house elope with her lover?"

"Oh, don't talk in that way, George," she said. "Please don't."

"Well, I won't, if you say so. I admit those little episodes generally turn out badly. Still you must acknowledge that they add a great interest to an old house of the Elizabethan age like this?"

Miss Earle was silent. They had, by this time, gone up the polished stairway, which was dimly lighted by a large window of stained glass.

"Here we are in the portrait hall," said Miss Earle. "There is a picture here that I have never seen, although I have heard of it, and I want to see it. Where is it?" she asked, turning to the housekeeper, who had been following them up the stairs.

"This way, my lady," answered the housekeeper, as she brought them before a painting completely concealed by a dark covering of cloth.

"Why is it covered in that way? To keep the dust from it?"

The housekeeper hesitated for a moment; then she said—

"The old Squire, my lady, put that on when she left, and it has never been taken off since."

"Then take it off at once," demanded Katherine Earle, in a tone that astonished Morris.

The housekeeper, who was too dignified to take down the covering herself, went to find the servant, but Miss Earle, with a gesture of impatience, grasped the cloth and tore it from its place, revealing the full-length portrait of a young lady.

Morris looked at the portrait in astonishment, and then at the girl by his side.

"Why, Katherine," he cried, "it is your picture!"

The young lady was standing with her hands tightly clenched and her lips quivering with nervous excitement. There were tears in her eyes, and she did not answer her lover for a moment; then she said—

"No, it is not my picture. This is a portrait of my mother."

Mrs. Tremain

"And Woman, wit a flaming torch

Sings heedless, in a powder—

Her careless smiles they warp and scorch

Man's heart, as fire the pine

Cuts keener than the thrust of lance

Her glance"

The trouble about this story is that it really has no ending. Taking an ocean voyage is something like picking up an interesting novel, and reading a chapter in the middle of it. The passenger on a big steamer gets glimpses of other people's lives, but he doesn't know what the beginning was, nor what the ending will be.

The last time I saw Mrs. Tremain she was looking over her shoulder and smiling at Glendenning as she walked up the gangway plank at Liverpool, hanging affectionately on the arm of her husband. I said to myself at the time, "You silly little handsome idiot, Lord only knows what trouble you will cause before flirting has lost its charm for you." Personally I would like to have shoved Glendenning off the gangway plank into the dark Mersey; but that would have been against the laws of the country on which we were then landing.

Mrs. Tremain was a woman whom other women did not like, and whom men did. Glendenning was a man that the average man detested, but he was a great favourite with the ladies.

I shall never forget the sensation Mrs. Tremain caused when she first entered the saloon of our steamer. I wish I were able to describe accurately just how she was dressed; for her dress, of course, had a great deal to do with her appearance, notwithstanding the fact that she was one of the loveliest women

I ever saw in my life. But it would require a woman to describe her dress with accuracy, and I am afraid any woman who was on board the steamer that trip would decline to help me. Women were in the habit of sniffing when Mrs. Tremain's name was mentioned. Much can be expressed by a woman's sniff. All that I can say about Mrs. Tremain's dress is that it was of some dark material, brightly shot with threads of gold, and that she had looped in some way over her shoulders and around her waist a very startlingly coloured silken scarf, while over her hair was thrown a black lace arrangement that reached down nearly to her feet, giving her a half-Spanish appearance. A military-looking gentleman, at least twice her age, was walking beside her. He was as grave and sober as she appeared light and frivolous, and she walked by his side with a peculiar elastic step, that seemed hardly to touch the carpet, laughing and talking to him just as if fifty pair of eyes were not riveted upon her as the pair entered. Everybody thought her a Spanish woman; but, as it turned out afterward, she was of Spanish-Mexican-American origin, and whatever beauty there is in those three nationalities seemed to be blended in some subtle, perfectly indescribable way in the face and figure of Mrs. Tremain.

The grave military-looking gentleman at her side was Captain Tremain, her husband, although in reality he was old enough to be her father. He was a captain in the United States army, and had been stationed at some fort near the Mexican border where he met the young girl whom he made his wife. She had seen absolutely nothing of the world, and they were now on their wedding trip to Europe, the first holiday he had taken for many a year.

In an incredibly short space of time Mrs. Tremain was the acknowledged belle of the ship. She could not have been more than nineteen or twenty years of age, yet she was as perfectly at her ease, and as thoroughly a lady as if she had been accustomed to palaces and castles for years. It was astonishing to see how naturally she took to it. She had lived all her life in a rough village in the wilds of the South-West, yet she had the bearing of a duchess or a queen.

The second day out she walked the deck with the captain, which, as everybody knows, is a very great honour. She always had a crowd of men around her, and apparently did not care the snap of her pretty fingers whether a woman on board spoke to her or not. Her husband was one of those slow-going, sterling men whom you meet now and again, with no nonsense about him, and with a perfect trust in his young wife. He was delighted to see her enjoying her voyage so well, and proud of the universal court that was paid to her. It was quite evident to everybody on board but himself that Mrs. Tremain was a born coquette, and the way she could use those dark, languishing, Spanish-Mexican eyes of hers was a lesson to flirts all the world over. It didn't, apparently, so much matter as long as her smiles were distributed pretty evenly over the whole masculine portion of the ship. But by-and-by things began to simmer down until the smiles were concentrated on the most utterly objectionable man on board—Glendenning. She walked the deck with him, she sat in cozy corners of the saloon with him, when there were not many people there, and at night they placed their chairs in a little corner of the deck where the electric light did not shine. One by one the other admirers dropped off, and left her almost entirely to Glendenning.

Of all those of us who were deserted by Mrs. Tremain none took it so hard as young Howard of Brooklyn. I liked Howard, for he was so palpably and irretrievably young, through no fault of his own, and so thoroughly ashamed of it. He wished to be considered a man of the world, and he had grave opinions on great questions, and his opinions were ever so much more settled and firm than those of us older people.

Young Howard confided a good deal in me, and even went so far one time as to ask if I thought he appeared very young, and if I would believe he was really as old as he stated.

I told him frankly I had taken him to be a very much older man than that, and the only thing about him I didn't like was a certain cynicism and knowledge of the world which didn't look well in a man who ought to be thinking about the serious things of life. After this young Howard confided in me even more than before. He said that he didn't care for Mrs. Tremain in that sort of way at all. She was simply an innocent child, with no knowledge of the world whatever, such as he and I possessed. Her husband—and in this I quite agreed with him—had two bad qualities: in the first place he was too easy going at the present, and in the second place he was one of those quiet men who would do something terrible if once he were aroused.

101

One day, as young Howard and I walked the deck together, he burst out with this extraordinary sentiment—

"All women," he said, "are canting hypocrites."

"When a man says that," I answered, "he means some particular woman. What woman have you in your eye, Howard?"

"No, I mean all women. All the women on board this boat, for instance."

"Except one, of course," I said.

"Yes," he answered, "except one. Look at the generality of women," he cried bitterly; "especially those who are what they call philanthropic and good. They will fuss and mourn over some drunken wretch who cannot be reclaimed, and would be no use if he could, and they will spend their time and sympathy over some creature bedraggled in the slums, whose only hope can be death, and that as soon as possible, yet not one of them will lift a finger to save a fellow creature from going over the brink of ruin. They will turn their noses in the air when a word from them would do some good, and then they will spend their time fussing and weeping over somebody that nothing on earth can help."

"Now, Howard," I said, "that's your cynicism which I've so often deplored. Come down to plain language, and tell me what you mean?"

"Look at the women on board this steamer," he cried indignantly. "There's pretty little Mrs. Tremain, who seems to have become fascinated by that scoundrel Glendenning. Any person can see what kind of a man he is—any one but an innocent child, such as Mrs. Tremain is. Now, no man can help. What she needs is some good kindly woman to take her by the hand and give her a word of warning. Is there a woman on board of this steamer who will do it? Not one. They see as plainly as any one else how things are drifting; but it takes a man who has murdered his wife to get sympathy and flowers from the modern so-called lady."

"Didn't you ever hear of the man, Howard, who made a large sum of money, I forget at the moment exactly how much, by minding his own business?"

"Oh yes, it's all very well to talk like that; but I would like to pitch Glendenning overboard."

"I admit that it would be a desirable thing to do, but if anybody is to do it, it is Captain Tremain and not you. Are you a married man, Howard?"

"No," answered Howard, evidently very much flattered by the question.

"Well, you see, a person never can tell on board ship; but, if you happen to be, it seems to me that you wouldn't care for any outsider to interfere in a matter such as we are discussing. At any rate Mrs. Tremain is a married woman, and I can't see what interest you should have in her. Take my advice and leave her alone, and if you want to start a reforming crusade among women, try to convert the rest of the ladies of the ship to be more charitable and speak the proper word in time."

"You may sneer as much as you like," answered young Howard, "but I will tell you what I am going to do. Two is company, and three is none; I'm going to make the third, as far as Mrs. Tremain and Glendenning are concerned."

"Supposing she objects to that?"

"Very likely she will; I don't care. The voyage lasts only a few days longer, and I am going to make the third party at any tête-à-tête."

"Dangerous business, Howard; first thing, you know, Glendenning will be wanting to throw you overboard."

"I would like to see him try it," said the young fellow, clenching his fist.

And young Howard was as good as his word. It was very interesting to an onlooker to see the way the different parties took it. Mrs. Tremain seemed to be partly amused with the boy, and think it all rather good fun. Glendenning scowled somewhat, and tried to be silent; but, finding that made no particular difference, began to make allusions to the extreme youth of young Howard, and seemed to try to provoke him, which laudable intention, to young Howard's great credit, did not succeed.

One evening I came down the forward narrow staircase, that leads to the long corridor running from the saloon, and met, under the electric light at the foot, Mrs. Tremain, young Howard, and Glendenning. They were evidently about to ascend the stairway; but, seeing me come down, they paused, and I stopped for a moment to have a chat with them, and see how things were going on.

Glendenning said, addressing me, "Don't you think it's time for children to be in bed?"

"If you mean me," I answered, "I am just on my way there."

Mrs. Tremain and young Howard laughed, and Glendenning after that ignored both Howard and myself.

He said to Mrs. Tremain, "I never noticed you wearing that ring before. It is a very strange ornament."

"Yes," answered Mrs. Tremain, turning it round and round. "This is a Mexican charmed ring. There is a secret about it, see if you can find it out." And with that she pulled off the ring, and handed it to Glendenning.

"You ought to give it to him as a keepsake," said young Howard, aggressively. "The ring, I notice, is a couple of snakes twisted together."

"Little boys," said Mrs. Tremain, laughing, "shouldn't make remarks like that. They lead to trouble."

Young Howard flushed angrily as Mrs. Tremain said this. He did not seem to mind it when Glendenning accused him of his youth, but he didn't like it coming from her.

Meanwhile Glendenning was examining the ring, and suddenly it came apart in his hand. The coils of the snake were still linked together, but instead of composing one solid ring they could now be spread several inches apart like the links of a golden chain. Mrs. Tremain turned pale, and gave a little shriek, as she saw this.

"Put it together again," she cried; "put it together quickly."

"What is the matter?" said Glendenning, looking up at her. She was standing two or three steps above him; Glendenning was at the bottom of the stair; young Howard stood on the same step as Mrs. Tremain, and I was a step or two above them.

"Put it together," cried Mrs. Tremain again. "I am trying to," said Glendenning, "is there a spring somewhere?"

"Oh, I cannot tell you," she answered, nervously clasping and unclasping her hands; "but if you do not put it together without help, that means very great ill-luck for both you and me."

"Does it?" said Glendenning, looking up at her with a peculiar glance, quite ignoring our presence.

"Yes, it does," she said; "try your best to put that ring together as you found it." It was quite evident that Mrs. Tremain had all the superstition of Mexico.

Glendenning fumbled with the ring one way and another, and finally said, "I cannot put it together."

"Let me try," said young Howard.

"No, no, that will do no good." Saying which Mrs. Tremain snatched the links from Glendenning, slipped them into one ring again, put it on her finger, and dashed quickly up the stairs without saying a word of good night to any of us.

Glendenning was about to proceed up the stair after her, when young Howard very ostentatiously placed himself directly in his path. Glendenning seemed to hesitate for a moment, then thought better of it, turned on his heel and walked down the passage towards the saloon.

"Look here, Howard," I said, "you are going to get yourself into trouble. There's sure to be a fuss on board this steamer before we reach Liverpool."

"I wouldn't be at all surprised," answered young Howard.

"Well, do you think it will be quite fair to Mrs. Tremain?"

"Oh, I shan't bring her name into the matter."

"The trouble will be to keep her name out. It may not be in your power to do that. A person who interferes in other people's affairs must do so with tact and caution."

Young Howard looked up at me with a trace of resentment in his face. "Aren't you interfering now?" he said.

"You are quite right, I am. Good night." And I went up the stairway. Howard shouted after me, but I did not see him again that night.

Next day we were nearing Queenstown, and, as I had letters to write, I saw nothing of young Howard till the evening. I found him unreasonably contrite for what he had said to me the night before; and when I told him he had merely spoken the truth, and was quite justified in doing so, he seemed more miserable than ever.

"Come," he said, "let us have a walk on the deck."

It was between nine and ten o'clock; and when we got out on the deck, I said to him, "Without wishing to interfere any further—"

"Now, don't say that," he cried; "it is cruel."

"Well, I merely wanted to know where your two charges are."

"I don't know," he answered, in a husky whisper; "they are not in the usual corner to-night, and I don't know where they are."

"She is probably with her husband," I suggested.

"No, he is down in the saloon reading."

As young Howard was somewhat prone to get emphatic when he began to talk upon this subject, and as there was always a danger of other people overhearing what he said, I drew him away to a more secluded part of the ship. On this particular boat there was a wheelhouse aft unused, and generally filled up with old steamer chairs. A narrow passage led around this at the

106

curving stern, seldom used by promenaders because of certain obstructions which, in the dark, were apt to trip a person up. Chains or something went from this wheelhouse to the sides of the ship, and, being covered up by boxes of plank, made this part of the deck hard to travel on in the dark. As we went around this narrow passage young Howard was the first to stop. He clutched my arm, but said nothing. There in the dark was the faint outline of two persons, with their backs towards us, leaning over the stern of the ship. The vibration at this part of the boat, from the throbbing of the screw, made it impossible for them to hear our approach. They doubtless thought they were completely in the dark; but they were deluded in that idea, because the turmoil of the water left a brilliant phosphorescent belt far in the rear of the ship, and against this bright, faintly yellow luminous track their forms were distinctly outlined. It needed no second glance to see that the two were Glendenning and Mrs. Tremain. Her head rested on his shoulder, and his arm was around her waist.

"Let us get back," I said in a whisper; and, somewhat to my surprise, young Howard turned back with me. I felt his hand trembling on my arm, but he said nothing. Before we could say a word to each other a sadden and unexpected complication arose. We met Captain Tremain, with a shawl on his arm, coming towards us.

"Good evening, captain," I said; "have a turn on the deck with us?"

"No, thanks," he replied, "I am looking for my wife. I want to give her this shawl to put over her shoulders. She is not accustomed to such chilly weather as we are now running into, and I am afraid she may take cold."

All this time young Howard stood looking at him with a startled expression in his eyes, and his lower jaw dropped. I was afraid Captain Tremain would see him, and wonder what was the matter with the boy. I tried to bring him to himself by stamping my heel—not too gently—on his toes, but he turned his face in the semi-darkness toward me without changing its expression. The one idea that had taken possession of my mind was that Captain Tremain must not be allowed to go further aft than he was, and I tried by looks and nudges to tell young Howard to go back and give her warning, but the boy seemed to be completely dazed with the unexpected horror of the situation. To have this calm, stern, unsuspecting man come suddenly upon what we had seen at the stern of the boat was simply appalling to think of. He certainly would have killed Glendenning where he stood, and very likely Mrs. Tremain as well. As Captain Tremain essayed to pass us I collected my wits as well as I could, and said—

"Oh, by the way, captain, I wanted to speak to you about Mexico. Do you—do you—think that it is a good—er—place for investment?"

"Well," said Captain Tremain, pausing, "I am not so sure about that. You see, their Government is so very unstable. The country itself is rich enough in mineral wealth, if that is what you mean." All the while Howard stood there with his mouth agape, and I felt like shoving my fist into it.

"Here, Howard," I said, "I want to speak to Captain Tremain for a moment. Take this shawl and find Mrs. Tremain, and give it to her." Saying this, I took the shawl from the captain's arm and threw it at young Howard. He appeared then to realise, for the first time, what was expected of him, and, giving me a grateful look, disappeared toward the stern.

"What I wanted more particularly to know about Mexico," I said to the captain, who made no objection to this move, "was whether there would be any more—well, likely to have trouble—whether we would have trouble with them in a military way, you know—that's more in your line."

"Oh, I think not," said the captain. "Of course, on the boundary where we were, there was always more or less trouble with border ruffians, sometimes on one side of the line and sometimes on the other. There is a possibility always that complications may arise from that sort of thing. Our officers might go over into the Mexican territory and seize a desperado there, or they might come over into ours. Still, I don't think anything will happen to bring on a war such as we had once or twice with Mexico."

At this moment I was appalled to hear Glendenning's voice ring out above the noise of the vibration of the vessel.

"What do you mean by that, you scoundrel," he said.

"Hallo," exclaimed the captain, "there seems to be a row back there. I wonder what it is?"

"Oh, nothing serious, I imagine. Probably some steerage passengers have come on the cabin deck. I heard them having a row with some one to-day on that score. Let's walk away from it."

The captain took my arm, and we strolled along the deck while he gave me a great deal of valuable information about Mexico and the state of things along the border line, which I regret to say I cannot remember a word of. The impressions of a man who has been on the spot are always worth hearing, but my ears were strained to catch a repetition of the angry cry I had heard, or the continuation of the quarrel which it certainly seemed to be the beginning of. As we came up the deck again we met young Howard with the shawl still on his arm and Mrs. Tremain walking beside him. She was laughing in a somewhat hysterical manner, and his face was as pale as ashes with a drawn look about the corners of his lips, but the captain's eyes were only on his wife.

"Why don't you put on the shawl, my dear?" he said to her affectionately. "The shawl?" she answered. Then, seeing it on young Howard's arm, she laughed, and said, "He never offered it to me."

Young Howard made haste to place the shawl on her shoulders, which she arranged around herself in a very coquettish and charming way. Then she took her husband's arm.

"Good night," she said to me; "good night, and thanks, Mr. Howard."

"Good night," said the captain; "I will tell you more about that mine to-morrow."

We watched them disappear towards the companion-way. I drew young Howard towards the side of the boat.

"What happened?" I asked eagerly. "Did you have trouble?"

"Very nearly, I made a slip of the tongue. I called her Mrs. Glendenning."

"You called her what?"

"I said, 'Mrs. Glendenning, your husband is looking for you.' I had come right up behind them, and they hadn't heard me, and of course both were very much startled. Glendenning turned round and shouted, 'What do you mean by that, you scoundrel?' and caught me by the throat. She instantly sprang between us, pushing him toward the stern of the boat, and me against the wheelhouse. "'Hush, hush,' she whispered; 'you mean, Mr. Howard, that my husband is there, do you not?'

"'Yes,' I answered, 'and he will be here in a moment unless you come with me.' With that she said 'Good night, Mr. Glendenning,' and took my arm, and he, like a thief, slunk away round the other side of the wheelhouse. I was very much agitated. I suppose I acted like a fool when we met the captain, didn't I?"

"You did," I answered; "go on."

"Well, Mrs. Tremain saw that, and she laughed at me, although I could see she was rather disturbed herself."

Some time that night we touched at Queenstown, and next evening we were in Liverpool. When the inevitable explosion came, I have no means of knowing, and this, as I have said before, is a story without a conclusion.

Mrs. Tremain the next day was as bright and jolly as ever, and the last time I saw her, she was smiling over her shoulder at Glendenning, and not paying the slightest attention to either her husband on whose arm she hung, or to young Howard, who was hovering near.

Share and Share Alike

"The quick must haste to vengeance taste,

For time is on his head;

But he can wait at the door of fate,

Though the stay be long and the hour be late—

The dead."

Melville Hardlock stood in the centre of the room with his feet wide apart and his hands in his trousers pockets, a characteristic attitude of his. He gave a quick glance at the door, and saw with relief that the key was in the lock, and that the bolt prevented anybody coming in unexpectedly. Then he gazed once more at the body of his friend, which lay in such a helpless-looking attitude upon the floor. He looked at the body with a feeling of mild curiosity, and wondered what there was about the lines of the figure on the floor that so certainly betokened death rather than sleep, even though the face was turned away from him. He thought, perhaps, it might be the hand with its back to the floor and its palm towards the ceiling; there was a certain look of hopelessness about that. He resolved to investigate the subject some time when he had leisure. Then his thoughts turned towards the subject of murder. It was so easy to kill, he felt no pride in having been able to accomplish that much. But it was not everybody who could escape the consequences of his crime. It required an acute brain to plan after events so that shrewd detectives would be baffled. There was a complacent conceit about Melville Hardlock, which was as much a part of him as his intense selfishness, and this conceit led him to believe that the future path he had outlined for himself would not be followed by justice.

With a sigh Melville suddenly seemed to realise that while there was no necessity for undue haste, yet it was not wise to be too leisurely in some things, so he took his hands from his pockets and drew to the middle of the floor a large Saratoga trunk. He threw the heavy lid open, and in doing so showed that the trunk was empty. Picking up the body of his friend, which he was surprised to note was so heavy and troublesome to handle, he with some difficulty doubled it up so that it slipped into the trunk. He piled on top of it some old coats, vests, newspapers, and other miscellaneous articles until the space above the body was filled. Then he pressed down the lid and locked it, fastening the catches at each end. Two stout straps were now placed around the trunk and firmly buckled after he had drawn them as tight as possible. Finally he damped the gum side of a paper label, and when he had pasted it on the end of the trunk, it showed the words in red letters, "S.S. Platonic, cabin, wanted." This done, Melville threw open the window to allow the fumes of chloroform to dissipate themselves in the outside air. He placed a closed, packed and labelled portmanteau beside the trunk, and a valise beside that again, which, with a couple of handbags, made up his luggage. Then he unlocked the door, threw back the bolt, and, having turned the key again from the outside, strode down the thickly-carpeted stairs of the hotel into the large pillared and marble-floored vestibule where the clerk's office was. Strolling up to the counter behind which stood the clerk of the hotel, he shoved his key across to that functionary, who placed it in the pigeon-hole marked by the number of his room.

"Did my friend leave for the West last night, do you know?"

"Yes," answered the clerk, "he paid his bill and left. Haven't you seen him since?"

"No," replied Hardlock.

"Well, he'll be disappointed about that, because he told me he expected to see you before he left, and would call up at your room later. I suppose he didn't have time. By the way, he said you were going back to England to-morrow. Is that so?"

"Yes, I sail on the Platonic. I suppose I can have my luggage sent to the steamer from here without further trouble?"

"Oh, certainly," answered the clerk; "how many pieces are there? It will be fifty cents each."

"Very well; just put that down in my bill with the rest of the expenses, and let me have it to-night. I will settle when I come in. Five pieces of luggage altogether."

"Very good. You'll have breakfast to-morrow, I suppose?"

"Yes, the boat does not leave till nine o'clock."

"Very well; better call you about seven, Mr. Hardlock. Will you have a carriage?"

"No, I shall walk down to the boat. You will be sure, of course, to have my things there in time."

"Oh, no fear of that. They will be on the steamer by half-past eight."

"Thank you."

As Mr. Hardlock walked down to the boat next morning he thought he had done rather a clever thing in sending his trunk in the ordinary way to the steamer. "Most people," he said to himself, "would have made the mistake of being too careful about it. It goes along in the ordinary course of business. If anything should go wrong it will seem incredible that a sane man would send such a package in an ordinary express waggon to be dumped about, as they do dump luggage about in New York."

He stood by the gangway on the steamer watching the trunks, valises, and portmanteaus come on board.

"Stop!" he cried to the man, "that is not to go down in the hold; I want it. Don't you see it's marked 'wanted?'"

"It is very large, sir," said the man; "it will fill up a state-room by itself."

"I have the captain's room," was the answer.

So the man flung the trunk down on the deck with a crash that made even the cool Mr. Hardlock shudder.

"Did you say you had the captain's room, sir?" asked the steward standing near.

"Yes."

"Then I am your bedroom steward," was the answer; "I will see that the trunk is put in all right."

The first day out was rainy but not rough; the second day was fair and the sea smooth. The second night Hardlock remained in the smoking-room until the last man had left. Then, when the lights were extinguished, he went out on the upper deck, where his room was, and walked up and down smoking his cigar. There was another man also walking the deck, and the red glow of his cigar, dim and bright alternately, shone in the darkness like a glow-worm.

Hardlock wished that he would turn in, whoever he was. Finally the man flung his cigar overboard and went down the stairway. Hartlock had now the dark deck to himself. He pushed open the door of his room and turned out the electric light. It was only a few steps from his door to the rail of the vessel high above the water. Dimly on the bridge he saw the shadowy figure of an officer walking back and forth. Hardlock looked over the side at the phosphorescent glitter of the water which made the black ocean seem blacker still. The sharp ring of the bell betokening midnight made Melville start as if a hand had touched him, and the quick beating of his heart took some moments to subside. "I've been smoking too much to-day," he said to himself. Then looking quickly up and down the deck, he walked on tip toe to his room, took the trunk by its stout leather handle and pulled it over the ledge in the doorway. There were small wheels at the bottom of the trunk, but although they made the pulling of it easy, they seemed to creak with appalling loudness. He realised the fearful weight of the trunk as he lifted the end of it up on the rail. He balanced it there for a moment, and glanced sharply around him, but there was nothing to alarm him. In spite of his natural coolness, he felt a strange, haunting dread of some undefinable disaster, a dread which had been completely absent from him at the time he committed the murder. He shoved off the trunk before he had quite intended to do so, and the next instant he nearly bit through his tongue to suppress a groan of agony. There passed half a dozen moments of supreme pain and fear before he realised what had happened. His wrist had caught in the strap handle of the trunk, and his shoulder was dislocated. His right arm was stretched taut and helpless, like a rope holding up the frightful and ever-increasing weight that hung between him and the sea. His breast was pressed against the rail and his left hand gripped the iron stanchion to keep himself from going over. He felt that his feet were slipping, and he set his teeth and gripped the iron with a grasp that was itself like iron. He hoped the trunk would slip from his useless wrist, but it rested against the side of the vessel, and the longer it hung the more it pressed the hard strap handle into his nerveless flesh. He had realised from the first that he dare not cry for help, and his breath came hard through his clenched teeth as the weight grew heavier and heavier. Then, with his eyes strained by the fearful pressure, and perhaps dazzled by the glittering phosphorescence running so swiftly by the side of the steamer far below, he seemed to see from out the trunk something in the form and semblance of his dead friend quivering like summer heat below him. Sometimes it was the shimmering phosphorescence, then again it was the wraith hovering over the trunk. Hardlock, in spite of his agony, wondered which it really was; but he wondered no longer when it spoke to him.

"Old Friend," it said, "you remember our compact when we left England. It was to be share and share alike, my boy—share and share alike. I have had my share. Come!"

Then on the still night air came the belated cry for help, but it was after the foot had slipped and the hand had been wrenched from the iron stanchion.

An International Row

"A simple child

That lightly draws its breath,

And feels its life in every limb,

What should it know of—kicking up a row

(*Note.*—Only the last four words of the above poem are claimed as original.)

"Then America declared war on England."—*History of 1812*

Lady, not feeling particularly well, reclining in a steamer chair, covered up with rugs. Little girl beside her, who wants to know. Gentleman in an adjoining steamer chair. The little girl begins to speak.

"And do you have to pay to go in, mamma?"

"Yes, dear."

"How much do you have to pay? As much as at a theatre?"

"Oh, you need not pay anything particular—no set sum, you know. You pay just what you can afford."

"Then it's like a collection at church, mamma?"

"Yes, dear."

"And does the captain get the money, mamma?"

"No, dear; the money goes to the poor orphans, I think."

"Where are the orphans, mamma?"

"I don't know, dear, I think they are in Liverpool."

"Whose orphans are they, mamma?"

"They are the orphans of sailors, dear."

"What kind of sailors, mamma?"

"British sailors, darling."

"Aren't there any sailors in America, mamma?"

"Oh yes, dear, lots of them."

"And do they have any orphans?"

"Yes, dear, I suppose there are orphans there too."

"And don't they get any of the money, mamma?"

"I am sure I do not know, dear. By the way, Mr. Daveling, how is that? Do they give any of the money to American orphans?"

"I believe not, madam. Subscriptions at concerts given on board British steamers are of course donated entirely to the Seamen's Hospital or Orphanage of Liverpool."

"Well, that doesn't seem to be quite fair, does it? A great deal of the money is subscribed by Americans."

"Yes, madam, that is perfectly true."

"I should think that ten Americans cross on these lines for every one Englishman."

"I am sure I do not know, madam, what the proportion is. The Americans are great travellers, so are the English too, for that matter."

"Yes; but I saw in one of the papers that this year alone over a hundred thousand persons had taken their passage from New York to England. It seems to me, that as all of them contribute to the receipts of the concerts, some sort of a division should be made."

"Oh, I have no doubt if the case were presented to the captain, he would be quite willing to have part of the proceeds at least go to some American seamen's charity."

"I think that would be only fair."

Two young ladies, arm in arm, approach, and ask Mrs. Pengo how she is feeling to-day.

Mrs. Pengo replies that she doesn't suppose she will feel any better as long as this rolling of the ship continues.

They claim, standing there, endeavouring to keep as perpendicular as possible, that the rolling is something simply awful.

Then the lady says to them, "Do you know, girls, that all the money subscribed at the concerts goes to England?"

"Why, no; I thought it went to some charity."

"Oh, it does go to a charity. It goes to the Liverpool Seamen's Hospital."

"Well, isn't that all right?"

"Yes, it's all right enough; but, as Sadie was just suggesting now, it doesn't seem quite fair, when there are orphans of sailors belonging to America, and as long as such large sums are subscribed by Americans, that the money should not be divided and part of it at least given to an American charity."

"Why, that seems perfectly fair, doesn't it, Mr. Daveling?"

"Yes, it is perfectly fair. I was just suggesting that perhaps if the state of things was presented to the captain, he would doubtless give a portion at least of the proceeds to an American Seamen's Home—if such an institution exists."

"Then," remarked the other girl, "I propose we form a committee, and interview the captain. I think that if Americans subscribe the bulk of the money, which they certainly do, they should have a voice in the disposal of it."

This was agreed to on all hands, and so began one of the biggest rows that ever occurred on board an Atlantic liner. Possibly, if the captain had had any tact, and if he had not been so thoroughly impressed with his own tremendous importance, what happened later on would not have happened.

The lady in the steamer chair took little part in the matter, in fact it was not at that time assumed to be of any importance whatever; but the two young American girls were enthusiastic, and they spoke to several of the passengers about it, both American and English. The English passengers all recognised the justice of the proposed plan, so a committee of five young ladies, and one young gentleman as spokesman, waited upon the captain. The young ladies at first had asked the doctor of the ship to be the spokesman; but when the doctor heard what the proposal was, he looked somewhat alarmed, and stroked his moustache thoughtfully.

"I don't know about that," he said; "it is a little unusual. The money has always gone to the Liverpool Seamen's Hospital, and—well, you see, we are a conservative people. We do a thing in one way for a number of years, and then keep on doing it because we have always done it in that way."

"Yes," burst out one of the young ladies, "that is no reason why an unjust thing should be perpetuated. Merely because a wrong has been done is no reason why it should be done again."

"True," said the doctor, "true," for he did not wish to fall out with the young lady, who was very pretty; "but, you see, in England we think a great deal of precedent."

And so the result of it all was that the doctor demurred at going to see the captain in relation to the matter. He said it wouldn't be the thing, as he was an official, and that it would be better to get one of the passengers.

I was not present at the interview, and of course know only what was told me by those who were there. It seems that the captain was highly offended at being approached on such a subject at all. A captain of an ocean liner, as I have endeavoured to show, is a very great personage indeed. And sometimes I imagine the passengers are not fully aware of this fact, or at least they do not show it as plainly as they ought to. Anyhow, the committee thought the captain had been exceedingly gruff with them, as well as just a trifle impolite. He told them that the money from the concerts had always gone to the Liverpool Seamen's Hospital, and always would while he was commanding a ship. He seemed to infer that the permission given them to hold a concert on board the ship was a very great concession, and that people should be thankful for the privilege of contributing to such a worthy object.

So, beginning with the little girl who wanted to know, and ending with the captain who commanded the ship, the conflagration was started.

Such is British deference to authority that, as soon as the captain's decision was known, those who had hitherto shown an open mind on the subject, and even those who had expressed themselves as favouring the dividing of the money, claimed that the captain's dictum had settled the matter. Then it was that every passenger had to declare himself. "Those who are not with us," said the young women, "are against us." The ship was almost immediately divided into two camps. It was determined to form a committee of Americans to take the money received from the second concert; for it was soon resolved to hold two concerts, one for the American Seamen's Orphans' Home and the other for that at Liverpool.

One comical thing about the row was, that nobody on board knew whether an American Seamen's Orphans' Home existed or not. When this problem was placed before the committee of young people, they pooh-poohed the matter. They said it didn't make any difference at all; if there was no Seamen's Hospital in America, it was quite time there should be one; and so they proposed that the money should be given to the future hospital, if it did not already exist.

When everything was prepared for the second concert there came a bolt from the blue. It was rumoured round the ship that the captain had refused his permission for the second concert to be held. The American men, who had up to date looked with a certain amused indifference on the efforts of the ladies, now rallied and held a meeting in the smoking-room. Every one felt that a crisis had come, and that the time to let loose the dogs of war— sea-dogs in this instance—had arrived. A committee was appointed to wait upon the captain next day. The following morning the excitement was at its highest pitch. It was not safe for an American to be seen conversing with an

Englishman, or vice versâ

Rumour had it at first—in fact all sorts of wild rumours were flying around the whole forenoon—that the captain refused to see the delegation of gentlemen who had requested audience with him. This rumour, however, turned out to be incorrect. He received the delegation in his room with one or two of the officers standing beside him. The spokesman said—

"Captain, we are informed that you have concluded not to grant permission to the Americans to hold a concert in aid of the American Seamen's Orphans' Home. We wish to know if this is true?"

"You have been correctly informed," replied the captain.

"We are sorry to hear that," answered the spokesman. "Perhaps you will not object to tell us on what grounds you have refused your permission?"

"Gentlemen," said the captain, "I have received you in my room because you requested an interview. I may say, however, that I am not in the habit of giving reasons for anything I do, to the passengers who honour this ship with their company."

"Then," said the spokesman, endeavouring to keep calm, but succeeding only indifferently, "it is but right that we should tell you that we regard such a proceeding on your part as a high handed outrage; that we will appeal against your decision to the owners of this steamship, and that, unless an apology is tendered, we will never cross on this line again, and we will advise all our compatriots never to patronise a line where such injustice is allowed."

"Might I ask you," said the captain very suavely, "of what injustice you complain?"

"It seems to us," said the spokesman, "that it is a very unjust thing to allow one class of passengers to hold a concert, and to refuse permission to another class to do the same thing."

"If that is all you complain of," said the captain, "I quite agree with you. I think that would be an exceedingly unjust proceeding."

"Is not that what you are about to do?"

"Not that I am aware of."

"You have prohibited the American concert?"

"Certainly. But I have prohibited the English concert as well."

The American delegates looked rather blankly at each other, and then the spokesman smiled. "Oh, well," he said, "if you have prohibited both of them, I don't see that we have anything to grumble at."

"Neither do I," said the captain.

The delegation then withdrew; and the passengers had the unusual pleasure of making one ocean voyage without having to attend the generally inevitable amateur concert.

A Ladies Man

"Jest w'en we guess we've covered the trail

So's no one can't foller, w'y then we fail

W'en we feel safe hid. Nemesis, the cuss,

Waltzes up with nary a warnin' nor fuss.

Grins quiet like, and says, 'How d'y do,

So glad we've met, I'm a-lookin' fer you'"

I do not wish to particularise any of the steamers on which the incidents given in this book occurred, so the boat of which I now write I shall call The Tub. This does not sound very flattering to the steamer, but I must say The Tub was a comfortable old boat, as everybody will testify who has ever taken a voyage in her. I know a very rich man who can well afford to take the best room in the best steamer if he wants to, but his preference always is for a slow boat like The Tub. He says that if you are not in a hurry, a slow boat is preferable to one of the new fast liners, because you have more individuality there, you get more attention, the officers are flattered by your preference for their ship, and you are not merely one of a great mob of passengers as in a crowded fast liner. The officers on a popular big and swift boat are prone to be a trifle snobbish. This is especially the case on the particular liner which for the moment stands at the top—a steamer that has broken the record, and is considered the best boat in the Atlantic service for the time being. If you get a word from the captain of such a boat you may consider yourself a peculiarly honoured individual, and even the purser is apt to answer you very shortly, and make you feel you are but a worm of the dust, even though you have paid a very large price for your state-room. On The Tub there was nothing of this. The officers were genial good fellows who admitted their boat was not the fastest on the Atlantic, although at one time she had been; but if The Tub never broke the record, on the other hand, she never broke a shaft, and so things were evened up. She wallowed her way across the Atlantic in a leisurely manner, and there was no feverish anxiety among the passengers when they reached Queenstown, to find whether the rival boat had got in ahead of us or not.

Everybody on board The Tub knew that any vessel which started from New York the same day would reach Queenstown before us. In fact, a good smart sailing vessel, with a fair wind, might have made it lively for us in an ocean race. The Tub was a broad slow boat, whose great speciality was freight, and her very broadness, which kept her from being a racer, even if her engines had had the power, made her particularly comfortable in a storm. She rolled but little; and as the state-rooms were large and airy, every passenger on board The Tub was sure of a reasonably pleasant voyage.

It was always amusing to hear the reasons each of the passengers gave for being on board The Tub. A fast and splendid liner of an opposition company left New York the next day, and many of our passengers explained to me they had come to New York with the intention of going by that boat, but they found all the rooms taken, that is, all the desirable rooms. Of course they might have had a room down on the third deck; but they were accustomed in travelling to have the best rooms, and if they couldn't be had, why it didn't much matter what was given them, so that was the reason they took passage on The Tub. Others were on the boat because they remembered the time when she was one of the fastest on the ocean, and they didn't like changing ships. Others again were particular friends of the captain, and he would have been annoyed if they had taken any other steamer. Everybody had some particularly valid reason for choosing The Tub, that is, every reason except economy, for it was well known that The Tub was one of the cheapest boats crossing the ocean. For my own part I crossed on her, because the purser was a particular friend of mine, and knew how to amalgamate fluids and different solid substances in a manner that produced a very palatable refreshment. He has himself deserted The Tub long ago, and is now purser on one of the new boats of the same line.

When the gong rang for the first meal on hoard The Tub after leaving New York, we filed down from the smoking-room to the great saloon to take our places at the table. There were never enough passengers on board

The Tub to cause a great rush for places at the table; but on this particular occasion, when we reached the foot of the stairway, two or three of us stood for a moment both appalled and entranced. Sitting at the captain's right hand was a somewhat sour and unattractive elderly woman, who was talking to that smiling and urbane official. Down the long table from where she sat, in the next fifteen seats were fifteen young and pretty girls, most of them looking smilingly and expectantly toward the stairway down which we were descending. The elderly woman paused for a moment in her conversation with the captain, glanced along the line of beauty, said sharply, 'Girls!' and instantly every face was turned demurely toward the plate that was in front of it, and then we, who had hesitated for a moment on the stairway, at once made a break, not for our seats at the table, but for the purser.

"It's all right, gentlemen," said that charming man, before we could speak; "it's all right. I've arranged your places down the table on the opposite side. You don't need to say a word, and those of you who want to change from the small tables to the large one, will find your names on the long table as well as at the small tables, where you have already chosen your places. So, you see, I knew just how you wished things arranged; but," he continued, lowering his voice, "boys, there's a dragon in charge. I know her. She has crossed with us two or three times. She wanted me to arrange it so that fifteen ladies should sit opposite her fifteen girls; but, of course, we couldn't do that, because there aren't fifteen other ladies on board, and there had to be one or two ladies placed next the girls at the foot of the table, so that no girl should have a young man sitting beside her. I have done the best I could, gentlemen, and, if you want the seats rearranged, I think we can manage it for you. Individual preferences may crop up, you know." And the purser smiled gently, for he had crossed the ocean very, very often.

We all took our places, sternly scrutinised by the lady, whom the purser had flatteringly termed the "dragon." She evidently didn't think very much of us as a crowd, and I am sure in my own heart I cannot blame her. We were principally students going over to German colleges on the cheap, some commercial travellers, and a crowd generally who could not afford to take a better boat, although we had all just missed the fast liner that had left a few days before, or had for some reason not succeeded in securing a berth on the fast boat, which was to leave the day after.

If any of the fifteen young ladies were aware of our presence, they did not show it by glancing toward us. They seemed to confine their conversation to whispers among themselves, and now and then a little suppressed giggle arose from one part of the line or the other, upon which the "dragon" looked along the row, and said severely, "Girls!" whereupon everything was quiet again, although some independent young lady generally broke the silence by another giggle just at the time the stillness was becoming most impressive.

After dinner, in the smoking-room, there was a great deal of discussion about the fifteen pretty girls and about the "dragon." As the officers on board The Tub were gentlemen whom an ordinary person might speak to, a delegation of one was deputed to go to the purser's room and find out all that could be learned in relation to the young and lovely passengers.

The purser said that the dragon's name was Mrs. Scrivener-Yapling, with a hyphen. The hyphen was a very important part of the name, and Mrs. Scrivener-Yapling always insisted upon it. Any one who ignored that hyphen speedily fell from the good graces of Mrs. Scrivener-Yapling. I regret to say, however, in spite of the hyphen, the lady was very generally known as the "dragon" during that voyage. The purser told us further, that Mrs. Scrivener-Yapling was in the habit of coming over once a year with a party of girls whom she trotted around Europe. The idea was that they learnt a great deal of geography, a good deal of French and German, and received in a general way a polish which Europe is supposed to give.

The circular which Mrs. Scrivener-Yapling issued was shown to me once by one of the girls, and it represented that all travelling was first-class, that nothing but the very best accommodations on steamers and in hotels were provided, and on account of Mrs. S. Y.'s intimate knowledge of Europe, and the different languages spoken there, she managed the excursion in a way which any one else would find impossible to emulate, and the advantages accruing from such a trip could not be obtained in any other manner without a very much larger expenditure of money. The girls had the advantage of motherly care during all the time they were abroad, and as the party was strictly limited in number, and the greatest care taken to select members only from the very best families in America, Mrs. Scrivener-Yapling was certain that all her patrons would realise that this was an opportunity of a lifetime, etc., etc.

Even if The Tub were not the finest boat on the Atlantic, she certainly belonged to one of the best lines, and as the circular mentioned the line and not the particular vessel on which the excursion was to go, the whole thing had a very high-class appearance.

The first morning out, shortly after, breakfast, the "dragon" and her girls appeared on deck. The girls walked two and two together, and kept their eyes pretty much on the planks beneath them. The fifteenth girl walked with the "dragon," and thus the eight pairs paced slowly up and down the deck under the "dragon's" eye. When this morning promenade was over the young ladies were marshalled into the ladies' saloon, where no masculine foot was allowed to tread. Shortly before lunch an indignation meeting was held in the smoking-room. Stewart Montague, a commercial traveller from Milwaukee, said that he had crossed the ocean many times, but had never seen such a state of things before. This young ladies' seminary business (he alluded to the two and two walk along the deck) ought not to be permitted on any well regulated ship. Here were a number of young ladies, ranging in age from eighteen upwards, and there lay ahead of us a long and possibly dreary voyage, yet the "dragon" evidently expected that not one of the young ladies was to be allowed to speak to one of the young gentlemen on board, much less walk the deck with him. Now, for his part, said Stewart Montague, he was going to take off his hat the next morning to the young lady who sat opposite him at the dinner-table and boldly ask her to walk the deck with him. If the "dragon" interfered, he proposed that we all mutiny, seize the vessel, put the captain in irons, imprison the "dragon" in the hold, and then take to pirating on the high seas. One of the others pointed out to him an objection to this plan, claiming that The Tub could not overtake anything but a sailing-vessel, while even that was doubtful. Montague explained that the mutiny was only to be resorted to as a last desperate chance. He believed the officers of the boat would give us every assistance possible, and so it was only in case of everything else failing that we should seize the ship.

In a moment of temporary aberration I suggested that the "dragon" might not be, after all, such an objectionable person as she appeared, and that perhaps she could be won over by kindness. Instantly a motion was put, and carried unanimously, appointing me a committee to try the effect of kindness on the "dragon." It was further resolved that the meeting should be adjourned, and I should report progress at the next conclave.

I respectfully declined this mission. I said it was none of my affair. I didn't wish to talk to any of the fifteen girls, or even walk the deck with them. I was perfectly satisfied as I was. I saw no reason why I should sacrifice myself for the good of others. I suggested that the name of Stewart Montague be substituted for mine, and that he should face the "dragon" and report progress.

Mr. Montague said it had been my suggestion, not his, that the "dragon" might be overcome by kindness. He did not believe she could, but he was quite willing to suspend hostilities until my plan had been tried and the result reported to the meeting. It was only when they brought in a motion to expel me from the smoking-room that I succumbed to the pressure. The voyage was just beginning, and what is a voyage to a smoker who dare not set foot in the smoking-room?

I do not care to dwell on the painful interview I had with the "dragon." I put my foot in it at the very first by pretending that I thought she came from New York, whereas she had really come from Boston. To take a New York person for a Bostonian is flattery, but to reverse the order of things, especially with a woman of the uncertain temper of Mrs. Scrivener-Yapling, was really a deadly insult, and I fear this helped to shipwreck my mission, although I presume it would have been shipwrecked in any case. Mrs. Scrivener-Yapling gave me to understand that if there was one thing more than another she excelled in it was the reading of character. She knew at a glance whether a man could be trusted or not; most men were not, I gathered from her conversation. It seems she had taken a great many voyages across the Atlantic, and never in the whole course of her experience had she seen such an objectionable body of young men as on this present occasion. She accused me of being a married man, and I surmised that there were other iniquities of which she strongly suspected me.

The mission was not a success, and I reported at the adjourned meeting accordingly.

Mr. Stewart Montague gave it as his opinion that the mission was hopeless from the first, and in this I quite agreed with him. He said he would try his plan at dinner, but what it was he refused to state. We asked if he would report on the success or failure, and he answered that we would all see whether it was a success or failure for ourselves. So there was a good deal of interest centring around the meal, an interest not altogether called forth by the pangs of hunger.

Dinner had hardly commenced when Mr. Stewart Montague leaned over the table and said, in quite an audible voice, to the young lady opposite him, "I understand you have never been over the ocean before?"

The young lady looked just a trifle frightened, blushed very prettily, and answered in a low voice that she had not.

Then he said, "I envy you the first impressions you will have of Europe. It is a charming country. Where do you go after leaving England?"

"We are going across to Paris first," she replied, still in a low voice.

Most of us, however, were looking at the "dragon." That lady sat bolt upright in her chair as if she could not believe her ears. Then she said, in an acid voice, "Miss Fleming."

"Yes, Mrs. Scrivener-Yapling," answered that young lady.

"Will you oblige me by coming here for a moment?"

Miss Fleming slowly revolved in her circular chair, then rose and walked up to the head of the table.

"Miss Strong," said the "dragon" calmly, to the young lady who sat beside her, "will you oblige me by taking Miss Fleming's place at the centre of the table?"

Miss Strong rose and took Miss Fleming's place.

"Sit down beside me, please?" said the "dragon" to Miss Fleming; and that unfortunate young woman, now as red as a rose, sat down beside the "dragon."

Stewart Montague bit his lip. The rest of us said nothing, and appeared not to notice what had occurred. Conversation went on among ourselves. The incident seemed ended; but, when the fish was brought, and placed before Miss Fleming, she did not touch it. Her eyes were still upon the table. Then, apparently unable to struggle any longer with her emotions, she rose gracefully, and, bowing to the captain, said, "Excuse me, please." She walked down the long saloon with a firm step, and disappeared. The "dragon" tried to resume conversation with the captain as if nothing had happened; but that official answered only in monosyllables, and a gloom seemed to have settled down upon the dinner party.

Very soon the captain rose and excused himself. There was something to attend to on deck, he said, and he left us.

As soon as we had reassembled in the smoking-room, and the steward had brought in our cups of black coffee, Stewart Montague arose and said, "Gentlemen, I know just what you are going to say to me. It was brutal. Of course I didn't think the 'dragon' would do such a thing. My plan was a complete failure. I expected that conversation would take place across the table all along the line, if I broke the ice."

Whatever opinions were held, none found expression, and that evening in the smoking-room was as gloomy as the hour at the dinner-table.

Towards the shank of the evening a gentleman, who had never been in the smoking-room before, entered very quietly. We recognised him as the man who sat to the left of the captain opposite the "dragon." He was a man of middle age and of somewhat severe aspect. He spoke with deliberation when he did speak, and evidently, weighed his words. All we knew of him was that the chair beside his at meal-times had been empty since the voyage began, and it was said that his wife took her meals in her state-room. She had appeared once on deck with him, very closely veiled, and hung upon his arm in a way that showed she was not standing the voyage very well, pleasant as it had been.

"Gentlemen," began the man suavely, "I would like to say a few words to you if I were certain that my remarks would be taken in the spirit in which they are given, and that you would not think me intrusive or impertinent."

"Go ahead," said Montague, gloomily, who evidently felt a premonition of coming trouble.

The serious individual waited until the steward had left the room, then he closed the door. "Gentlemen," he continued, "I will not recur to the painful incident which happened at the dinner-table to-night further than by asking you, as honourable men, to think of Mrs. Scrivener-Yapling's position of great responsibility. She stands in the place of a mother to a number of young ladies who, for the first time in their lives, have left their homes."

"Lord pity them," said somebody, who was sitting in the corner.

The gentleman paid no attention to the remark.

"Now what I wish to ask of you is that you will not make Mrs. Scrivener-Yapling's position any harder by futile endeavours to form the acquaintance of the young ladies."

At this point Stewart Montague broke out. "Who the devil are you, sir, and who gave you the right to interfere?"

"As to who I am," said the gentleman, quietly, "my name is Kensington, and—"

"West or South?" asked the man in the corner.

At this there was a titter of laughter.

"My name is Kensington," repeated the gentleman, "and I have been asked by Mrs. Scrivener-Yapling to interfere, which I do very reluctantly.

As I said at the beginning, I hope you will not think my interference is impertinent. I only do so at the earnest request of the lady I have mentioned, because I am a family man myself, and I understand and sympathise with the lady in the responsibility which she has assumed."

"It seems to me," said the man in the corner, "that if the 'dragon' has assumed responsibilities and they have not been thrust upon her, which I understand they have not, then she must take the responsibility of the responsibilities which she has assumed. Do I make myself clear?"

"Gentlemen," said Mr. Kensington, "it is very painful for me to speak with you upon this subject. I feel that what I have so clumsily expressed may not be correctly understood; but I appeal to your honour as gentlemen, and I am sure I will not appeal in vain when I ask you not to make further effort towards the acquaintance of the young ladies, because all that you can succeed in doing will be to render their voyage unpleasant to themselves, and interrupt, if not seriously endanger, the good feeling which I understand has always existed between Mrs. Scrivener-Yapling and her protégées."

"All right," said the man in the corner. "Have a drink, Mr. Kensington?"

"Thank you, I never drink," answered Mr. Kensington.

"Have a smoke, then?"

"I do not smoke either, thank you all the same for your offer. I hope, gentlemen, you will forgive my intrusion on you this evening. Good night."

"Impudent puppy," said Stewart Montague, as he closed the door behind him.

But in this we did not agree with him, not even the man in the corner.

"He is perfectly right," said that individual, "and I believe that we ought to be ashamed of ourselves. It will only make trouble, and I for one am going to give up the hunt."

So, from that time forward, the smoking-room collectively made no effort towards the acquaintance of the young ladies. The ladies' seminary walk, as it was called, took place every morning punctually, and sometimes Mr. Kensington accompanied the walkers. Nevertheless, individual friendships, in spite of everything that either Mr. Kensington or the "dragon" could do, sprang up between some of the young men and some of the girls, but the "dragon" had an invaluable ally in Mr. Kensington. The moment any of the young ladies began walking with any of the young gentlemen on deck, or the moment they seated themselves in steamer chairs together, the urbane, always polite Mr. Kensington appeared on the scene and said, "Miss So-and-So, Mrs. Scrivener-Yapling would like to speak with you."

Then the young lady would go with Mr. Kensington, while the young gentleman was apt to use strong language and gnash his teeth.

Mr. Kensington seemed lynx-eyed. There was no escaping him. Many in the smoking-room no doubt would have liked to have picked a flaw in his character if they could. One even spoke of the old chestnut about a man who had no small vices being certain to have some very large ones; but even the speakers themselves did not believe this, and any one could see at a glance that Mr. Kensington was a man of sterling character. Some hinted that his wife was the victim of his cruelty, and kept her state-room only because she knew that he was so fond of the "dragon's" company, and possibly that of some of the young ladies as well. But this grotesque sentiment did not pass current even in the smoking-room. Nevertheless, although he was evidently so good a man, he was certainly the most unpopular individual on board The Tub. The hatred that Stewart Montague felt for him ever since that episode in the smoking-room was almost grotesque.

Montague had somehow managed to get a contrite note of apology and distress to Miss Fleming, and several times the alert Mr. Kensington had caught them together, and asked Miss Fleming with the utmost respect to come down and see Mrs. Scrivener-Yapling.

All in all the "dragon" did not have a very easy time of it. She fussed around like any other old hen who had in charge a brood of ducks.

Once I thought there was going to be a row between Montague and Kensington. He met that gentleman in a secluded part of the deck, and, going up to him, said—

"You old wife deserter, why can't you attend to your own affairs?"

Kensington turned deadly pale at this insult, and his fists clinched—

"What do you mean?" he said huskily.

"I mean what I say. Why don't you take your own wife walking on the deck, and leave the young ladies alone. It's none of your business with whom they walk."

Kensington seemed about to reply; but he thought better of it, turned on his heel, and left Montague standing there.

The old Tub worried her way across the ocean, and reached the bar at Liverpool just in time to be too late to cross it that night. Word was passed along that a tender would come out from Liverpool for us, which was not a very cheering prospect, as we would have two hours' sail at least in what was practically an open boat.

Finally the tender came alongside, and the baggage was dumped down upon it. All of us gathered together ready to leave The Tub. Mr. Kensington, with his closely-veiled wife hanging on his arm, was receiving the thanks and congratulations of the "dragon." The fifteen girls were all around her. Before any one started down the sloping gangway plank, however, two policemen, accompanied by a woman, hurried up on board The Tub.

"Now, madam," said the policeman, "is he here?"

We saw that trouble was coming, and everybody looked at everybody else.

"Is he here?" cried the woman excitedly; "there he stands, the villain. Oh, you villain, you scoundrel, you mean rascal, to leave me, as you thought, penniless in New York, and desert your own wife and family for that—that creature!" We all looked at Kensington, and his face was greenish-pale. The heavily veiled woman shrunk behind him and the policeman tried to make the true wife keep quiet.

"Is your name Braughton?"

Kensington did not answer. His eyes were riveted on his wife. "In the name of God," he cried aghast, "how did you come here?"

"How did I come here," she shrieked. "Oh, you thought you slipped away nicely, didn't you? But you forgot that the Clipper left the next day, and I've been here two days waiting for you. You little thought when you deserted me and my children in New York that we would be here to confront you at Liverpool."

"Come, come." said the policeman, "there's no use of this. I am afraid you will have to come with us, sir."

They took him in charge, and the irate wife then turned like a tigress on the heavily veiled woman who was with him.

"No wonder you are ashamed to show your face," she cried.

"Come, come," said the policeman, "come, come." And they managed to induce her to say no more.

"Madam," said young Montague to the speechless 'dragon,' "I want to ask your permission to allow me to carry Miss Fleming's hand- baggage ashore."

"How dare you speak to me, sir?" she answered.

"Because," he said, in a low voice, "I thought perhaps you wouldn't like an account of this affair to go to the Boston newspapers. I'm a newspaper man, you see," he added, with unblushing mendacity. Then, turning to Miss Fleming, he said, "Won't you allow me to carry this for you?"

Miss Fleming surrendered the natty little handbag she had with her, and smiled. The "dragon" made no objection.

A Society For The Reformation Of Poker Players.

"O Unseen Hand that ever makes and deals us,

And plays our game!

That now obscures and then to light reveals us,

Serves blanks of fame

How vain our shuffling, bluff and weak pretending!

Tis Thou alone can name the final ending"

The seductive game of poker is one that I do not understand. I do not care to understand it, because it cannot be played without the putting up of a good deal of the coin of the realm, and although I have nothing to say against betting, my own theory of conduct in the matter is this, that I want no man's money which I do not earn, and I do not want any man to get my money unless he earns it. So it happens, in the matter of cards, I content myself with euchre and other games which do not require the wagering of money.

On board the Atlantic steamers there is always more or less gambling. I have heard it said that men make trips to and fro merely for the purpose of fleecing their fellow-passengers; but, except in one instance, I never had any experience with this sort of thing.

Our little society for the reformation of poker players, or to speak more correctly, for the reformation of one particular poker player, was formed one bright starlight night, latitude such a number, and longitude something else, as four of us sat on a seat at the extreme rear end of the great steamer. We four, with one other, sat at a small table in the saloon. One of the small tables on a Transatlantic steamer is very pleasant if you have a nice crowd with you. A seat at a small table compares with a seat at the large table as living in a village compares with living in a city. You have some individuality at the short table; you are merely one of a crowd at the long table. Our small table was not quite full. I had the honour of sitting at the head of it, and on each side of me were two young fellows, making five altogether. We all rather prided ourselves on the fact that there were no ladies at our little table.

The young Englishman who sat at my right hand at the corner of the table was going out to America to learn farming. I could, myself, have taught him a good deal about it, but I refrained from throwing cold water on his enthusiastic ideas about American agriculture. His notion was that it was an occupation mostly made up of hunting and fishing, and having a good time generally. The profits, he thought, were large and easily acquired. He had guns with him, and beautiful fishing-rods, and things of that sort. He even had a vague idea that he might be able to introduce fox-hunting in the rural district to which he was going. He understood, and regretted the fact, that we in the United States were rather behind-hand in the matter of fox-hunting. He had a good deal of money with him, I understood, and he had already paid a hundred pounds to a firm in England that had agreed to place him on a farm in America. Of course, now that the money had been paid, there was no use in telling the young man he had been a fool. He would find that out soon enough when he got to America. Henry Storm was his name, and a milder mannered man with a more unsuitable name could hardly be found. The first two or three days out he was the life of our party. We all liked him, in fact, nobody could help liking him; but, as the voyage progressed, he grew more and more melancholy, and, what was really serious, took little food, which is not natural in an Englishman. I thought somebody had been telling him what a fool he had been to pay away his hundred pounds before leaving England, but young Smith of Rochester, who sat at my left, told me what the trouble was one day as we walked the deck. "Do you know," he began, "that Henry Storm is being robbed?"

"Being robbed?" I answered; "you mean he has been robbed."

"Well, has been, and is being, too. The thing is going on yet. He is playing altogether too much poker in the smoking-room, and has lost a pile of money—more, I imagine, than he can well afford."

"That's what's the trouble with him, is it? Well, he ought to know better than to play for bigger stakes than he can afford to lose."

"Oh, it's easy to say that; but he's in the hands of a swindler, of a professional gambler. You see that man?" He lowered his voice as he spoke, and I looked in the direction of his glance. By this time we knew, in a way, everybody on board the ship. The particular man Smith pointed out was a fellow I had noticed a good deal, who was very quiet and gentlemanly, interfering with nobody, and talking with few. I had spoken to him once, but he had answered rather shortly, and, apparently to his relief, and certainly to my own, our acquaintance ceased where it began. He had jet black beard and hair, both rather closely clipped; and he wore a fore and aft cap, which never improves a man's appearance very much.

"That man," continued Smith, as he passed us, "was practically under arrest for gambling on the steamer in which I came over. It seems that he is a regular professional gambler, who does nothing but go across the ocean and back again, fleecing young fellows like Storm."

"Does he cheat?" I asked.

"He doesn't need to. He plays poker. An old hand, and a cool one, has no occasion to cheat at that game to get a young one's money away from him."

"Then why doesn't some one warn young Storm?"

"Well, that's just what I wanted to speak to you about. I think it ought to be done. I think we should call a meeting of our table, somewhere out here in the quiet, and have a talk over it, and make up our mind what is to be done. It's a delicate matter, you know, and I am afraid we are a little late as it is. I do believe young Storm has lost nearly all his money to that fellow."

"Can't he be made to disgorge?"

"How? The money has been won fairly enough, as that sort of thing goes. Other fellows have played with them. It isn't as if he had been caught cheating—he hasn't, and won't be. He doesn't cheat—he doesn't need to, as I said before. Now that gambler pretends he is a commercial traveller from Buffalo. I know Buffalo down to the ground, so I took him aside yesterday and said plumply to him, 'What firm in Buffalo do you represent?' He answered shortly that his business was his own affair. I said, 'Certainly it is, and you are quite right in keeping it dark. When I was coming over to Europe, I saw a man in your line of business who looked very much like you, practically put under arrest by the purser for gambling. You were travelling for a St. Louis house then.'"

"What did he say to that?"

"Nothing; he just gave me one of those sly, sinister looks of his, turned on his heel, and left me."

The result of this conversation was the inauguration of the Society for the Reforming of a Poker Player. It was agreed between us that if young Storm had lost all his money we would subscribe enough as a loan to take care of him until he got a remittance from home. Of course we knew that any young fellow who goes out to America to begin farming, does not, as a general rule, leave people in England exceedingly well off, and probably this fact, more than any other, accounted for the remorse visible on Storm's countenance. We knew quite well that the offering of money to him would be a very delicate matter, but it was agreed that Smith should take this in hand if we saw the offer was necessary. Then I, as the man who sat at the head of the table, was selected to speak to young Storm, and, if possible, get him to abandon poker. I knew this was a somewhat impudent piece of business on my part, and so I took that evening to determine how best to perform the task set for me. I resolved to walk the deck with him in the morning, and have a frank talk over the matter.

When the morning came, I took young Storm's arm and walked two or three turns up and down the deck, but all the while I could not get up courage enough to speak with him in relation to gambling. When he left me, I again thought over the matter. I concluded to go into the smoking-room myself, sit down beside him, see him lose some money and use that fact as a test for my coming discourse on the evils of gambling. After luncheon I strolled into the smoking-room, and there sat this dark-faced man with his half-closed eyes opposite young Storm, while two others made up the four-handed game of poker.

Storm's face was very pale, and his lips seemed dry, for he moistened them every now and then as the game went on. He was sitting on the sofa, and I sat down beside him, paying no heed to the dark gambler's look of annoyance. However, the alleged Buffalo man said nothing, for he was not a person who did much talking. Storm paid no attention to me as I sat down beside him. The gambler had just dealt. It was very interesting to see the way he looked at his hand. He allowed merely the edges of the cards to show over each other, and then closed up his hand and seemed to know just what he had. When young Storm looked at his hand he gave a sort of gasp, and for the first time cast his eyes upon me. I had seen his hand, but did not know whether it was a good one or not. I imagined it was not very good, because all the cards were of a low denomination. Threes or fours I think, but four of the cards had a like number of spots. There was some money in the centre of the table. Storm pushed a half-crown in front of him, and the next man did the same. The gambler put down a half-sovereign, and the man at his left, after a moment's hesitation, shoved out an equal amount from the pile of gold in front of him.

Young Storm pushed out a sovereign.

"I'm out," said the man whose next bet it was, throwing down his cards.

The gambler raised it a sovereign, and the man at his left dropped out. It now rested between Storm and the gambler. Storm increased the bet a sovereign. The gambler then put on a five-pound note.

Storm said to me huskily, "Have you any money?"

"Yes," I answered him.

"Lend me five pounds if you can."

Now, the object of my being there was to stop gambling, not to encourage it. I was the president pro tem, of the Society for the Reformation of Poker Players, yet I dived into my pocket, pulled out my purse under the table and slipped a five-pound note into his hand. He put that on the table as if he had just taken it from his own pocket.

"I call you," he said.

"What have you got?" asked the gambler.

"Four fours," said Storm, putting down his hand.

The gambler closed up his and threw the cards over to the man who was to deal. Storm paused a moment and then pulled towards him the money in the centre of the table and handed me my five-pound note.

When the cards were next dealt, Storm seemed to have rather an ordinary hand, so apparently had all the rest, and there was not much money in the pile. But, poor as Storm's hand was, the rest appeared to be poorer, and he raked in the cash. This went on for two or three deals, and finding that, as Storm was winning all the time, although not heavily, I was not getting an object lesson against gambling, I made a move to go.

"Stay where you are," whispered Storm to me, pinching my knee with his hand so hard that I almost cried out.

Then it came to the gambler's turn to deal again. All the time he deftly shuffled the cards he watched the players with that furtive glance of his from out his half-shut eyes.

Storm's hand was a remarkable one, after he had drawn two cards, but I did not know whether it had any special value or not. The other players drew three cards each, and the gambler took one.

"How much money have you got?" whispered Storm to me.

"I don't know," I said, "perhaps a hundred pounds."

"Be prepared to lend me every penny of it," he whispered.

I said nothing; but I never knew the president of a society for the suppression of gambling to be in such a predicament.

Storm bet a sovereign. The player to his left threw down his hand. The gambler pushed out two sovereigns. The other player went out.

Storm said, "I see your bet, and raise you another sovereign." The gambler, without saying a word, shoved forward some more gold.

"Get your money ready," whispered Storm to I did not quite like his tone, but I made allowance for the excitement under which he was evidently labouring.

He threw on a five-pound note. The gambler put down another five-pound note, and then, as if it were the slightest thing possible, put a ten-pound note on top of that, which made the side players gasp. Storm had won sufficient to cover the bet and raise it. After that I had to feed in to him five-pound notes, keeping count of their number on my fingers as I did so. The first to begin to hesitate about putting money forward was the gambler. He shot a glance now and again from under his eyebrows at the young man opposite. Finally, when my last five-pound note had been thrown on the pile, the gambler spoke for the first time.

"I call you," he said.

"Put down another five-pound note," cried the young man.

"I have called you," said the gambler.

Henry Storm half rose from his seat in his excitement. "Put down another five-pound note, if you dare."

"That isn't poker," said the gambler. "I have called you. What have you got?"

"Put down another five-pound note, and I'll put a ten-pound note on top of it."

"I say that isn't poker. You have been called. What have you got?"

"I'll bet you twenty pounds against your five-pound note, if you dare put it down."

By this time Storm was standing up, quivering with excitement, his cards tightly clenched in his hand. The gambler sat opposite him calm and imperturbable.

"What have you got?" said Storm.

"I called you," said the gambler, "show your hand."

"Yes; but when I called you, you asked me what I had, and I told you. What have you got?"

"I am not afraid to show my hand," said the gambler, and he put down on the table four aces.

"There's the king of hearts," said Storm, putting it down on the table. "There's the queen of hearts, there's the knave of hearts, there's the ten of hearts. Now," he cried, waving his other card in the air, "can you tell me what this card is?"

"I am sure I don't know," answered the gambler, quietly, "probably the nine of hearts."

"It is the nine of hearts," shouted Storm, placing it down beside the others.

The gambler quietly picked up the cards, and handed them to the man who was to deal. Storm's hands were trembling with excitement as he pulled the pile of bank notes and gold towards him. He counted out what I had given him, and passed it to me under the table. The rest he thrust into his pocket.

"Come," I said, "it is time to go. Don't strain your luck."

"Another five pounds," he whispered; "sit where you are."

"Nonsense," I said, "another five pounds will certainly mean that you lose, everything you have won. Come away, I want to talk with you."

"Another five pounds, I have sworn it."

"Very well, I shall not stay here any longer."

"No, no," he cried eagerly; "sit where you are, sit where you are."

There was a grim thin smile on the lips of the gambler as this whispered conversation took place.

When the next hand was dealt around and Storm looked at his cards, he gave another gasp of delight. I thought that a poker player should not be so

143

free with his emotions; but of course I said nothing. When it came his time to bet, he planked down a five-pound note on the table. The other two, as was usual, put down their cards. They were evidently very timorous players. The gambler hesitated for a second, then he put a ten-pound note on Storm's five-pounds. Storm at once saw him, and raised him ten. The gambler hesitated longer this time, but at last he said, "I shall not bet. What have you got?"

"Do you call me?" asked Storm. "Put up your money if you do."

"No, I do not call you."

Storm laughed and threw his cards face up on the table. "I have nothing," he said, "I have bluffed you for once."

"It is very often done," answered the gambler, quietly, as Storm drew in his pile of money, stuffing it again in his coat pocket. "Your deal, Storm."

"No, sir," said the young man, rising up; "I'll never touch a poker hand again. I have got my own money back and five or ten pounds over. I know when I've had enough."

Although it was Storm's deal, the gambler had the pack of cards in his hand idly shuffling them to and fro.

"I have often heard," he said slowly without raising his eyes, "that when one fool sits down beside another fool at poker, the player has the luck of two fools—but I never believed it before."

The Man Who was Not on the Passenger List.

"The well-sworn Lie, franked to the world with all

The circumstance of proof,

Cringes abashed, and sneaks along the wall

At the first sight of Truth."

The Gibrontus of the Hot Cross Bun Line was at one time the best ship of that justly celebrated fleet. All steamships have, of course, their turn at the head of the fleet until a better boat is built, but the Gibrontus is even now a reasonably fast and popular boat. An accident happened on board the Gibrontus some years ago which was of small importance to the general public, but of some moment to Richard Keeling—for it killed him. The poor man got only a line or two in the papers when the steamer arrived at New York, and then they spelled his name wrong. It had happened something like this: Keeling was wandering around very late at night, when he should have been in his bunk, and he stepped on a dark place that he thought was solid. As it happened, there was nothing between him and the bottom of the hold but space. They buried Keeling at sea, and the officers knew absolutely nothing about the matter when inquisitive passengers, hearing rumours, questioned them. This state of things very often exists both on sea and land, as far as officials are concerned. Mrs. Keeling, who had been left in England while her husband went to America to make his fortune, and tumbled down a hole instead, felt aggrieved at the company. The company said that Keeling had no business to be nosing around dark places on the deck at that time of night, and doubtless their contention was just. Mrs. Keeling, on the other hand, held that a steamer had no right to have such mantraps open at any time, night or day, without having them properly guarded, and in that she was also probably correct. The company was very sorry, of course, that the thing had occurred; but they refused to pay for Keeling unless compelled to do so by the law of the land, and there matters stood. No one can tell what the law of the land will do when it is put in motion, although many people thought that if Mrs. Keeling had brought a suit against the Hot Cross Bun Company she would have won it. But Mrs. Keeling was a poor woman, and you have to put a penny in the slot when you want the figures of justice to work, so the unfortunate creature signed something which the lawyer of the company had written out, and accepted the few pounds which Keeling had paid for Room 18 on the Gibrontus. It would seem that this ought to have settled the matter, for the lawyer told Mrs. Keeling he thought the company acted very generously in refunding the passage money; but it didn't settle the matter. Within a year from that time, the company voluntarily paid Mrs. Keeling £2100 for her husband. Now that the occurrence is called to your mind, you will perhaps remember the editorial one of the leading London dailies had on the extraordinary circumstance, in which it was very ably shown that the old saying about corporations having no souls to be condemned or bodies to be kicked did not apply in these days of commercial honour and integrity. It was a very touching editorial, and it caused tears to be shed on the Stock Exchange, the members having had no idea, before reading it, that they were so noble and generous.

How, then, was it that the Hot Cross Bun Company did this commendable act when their lawyer took such pains to clear them of all legal liability? The purser of the Gibrontus, who is now old and superannuated, could probably tell you if he liked.

When the negotiations with Mrs. Keeling had been brought to a satisfactory conclusion by the lawyer of the company, and when that gentleman was rubbing his hands over his easy victory, the good ship Gibrontus was steaming out of the Mersey on her way to New York. The stewards in the grand saloon were busy getting things in order for dinner, when a wan and gaunt passenger spoke to one of them.

"Where have you placed me at table?" he asked.

"What name, sir?" asked the steward.

"Keeling."

The steward looked along the main tables, up one side and down the other, reading the cards, but nowhere did he find the name he was in search of. Then he looked at the small tables, but also without success.

"How do you spell it, sir?" he asked the patient passenger.

"K-double-e-l-i-n-g."

"Thank you, sir."

Then he looked up and down the four rows of names on the passenger list he held in his hand, but finally shook his head.

"I can't find your name on the passenger list," he said. "I'll speak to the purser, sir."

"I wish you would," replied the passenger in a listless way, as if he had not much interest in the matter. The passenger, whose name was not on the list, waited until the steward returned. "Would you mind stepping into the purser's room for a moment, sir? I'll show you the way, sir."

When the passenger was shown into the purser's room that official said to him, in the urbane manner of pursers—

"Might I look at your ticket, sir?"

The passenger pulled a long pocket-book from the inside of his coat, opened it, and handed the purser the document it contained. The purser scrutinized it sharply, and then referred to a list he had on the desk before him.

"This is very strange," he said at last. "I never knew such a thing to occur before, although, of course, it is always possible. The people on shore have in some unaccountable manner left your name out of my list. I am sorry you have been put to any inconvenience, sir."

"There has been no inconvenience so far," said the passenger, "and I trust there will be none. You find the ticket regular, I presume?"

"Quite so—quite so," replied the purser. Then, to the waiting steward, "Give Mr. Keeling any place he prefers at the table which is not already taken.

You have Room 18."

"That was what I bought at Liverpool."

"Well, I see you have the room to yourself, and I hope you will find it comfortable. Have you ever crossed with us before, sir? I seem to recollect your face."

"I have never been in America."

"Ah! I see so many faces, of course, that I sometimes fancy I know a man when I don't. Well, I hope you will have a pleasant voyage, sir."

"Thank you."

No. 18 was not a popular passenger. People seemed instinctively to shrink from him, although it must be admitted that he made no advances. All went well until the Gibrontus was about half-way over. One forenoon the chief officer entered the captain's room with a pale face, and, shutting the door after him, said—

"I am very sorry to have to report, sir, that one of the passengers has fallen into the hold."

"Good heavens!" cried the captain. "Is he hurt?"

"He is killed, sir."

The captain stared aghast at his subordinate.

"How did it happen? I gave the strictest orders those places were on no account to be left unguarded."

Although the company had held to Mrs. Keeling that the captain was not to blame, their talk with that gentleman was of an entirely different tone.

"That is the strange part of it, sir. The hatch has not been opened this voyage, sir, and was securely bolted down."

"Nonsense! Nobody will believe such a story! Some one has been careless! Ask the purser to come here, please."

When the purser saw the body, he recollected, and came as near fainting as a purser can.

They dropped Keeling overboard in the night, and the whole affair was managed so quietly that nobody suspected anything, and, what is the most incredible thing in this story, the New York papers did not have a word about it. What the Liverpool office said about the matter nobody knows, but it must have stirred up something like a breeze in that strictly business locality. It is likely they pooh-poohed the whole affair, for, strange to say, when the purser tried to corroborate the story with the dead man's ticket the document was nowhere to be found.

The Gibrontus started out on her next voyage from Liverpool with all her colours flying, but some of her officers had a vague feeling of unrest within them which reminded them of the time they first sailed on the heaving seas. The purser was seated in his room, busy, as pursers always are at the beginning of a voyage, when there was a rap at the door.

"Come in!" shouted the important official, and there entered unto him a stranger, who said—"Are you the purser?"

"Yes, sir. What can I do for you?"

"I have room No. 18."

"What!" cried the purser, with a gasp, almost jumping from his chair. Then he looked at the robust man before him, and sank back with a sigh of relief. It was not Keeling.

"I have room No. 18," continued the passenger, "and the arrangement I made with your people in Liverpool was that I was to have the room to myself. I do a great deal of shipping over your—"

"Yes, my dear sir," said the purser, after having looked rapidly over his list, "you have No. 18 to yourself."

"So I told the man who is unpacking his luggage there; but he showed me his ticket, and it was issued before mine. I can't quite understand why your people should—"

"What kind of a looking man is he?"

"A thin, unhealthy, cadaverous man, who doesn't look as if he would last till the voyage ends. I don't want him for a room mate, if I have to have one. I think you ought—"

"I will, sir. I will make it all right. I suppose, if it should happen that a mistake has been made, and he has the prior claim to the room, you would not mind taking No. 24—it is a larger and better room."

"That will suit me exactly."

So the purser locked his door and went down to No. 18.

"Well?" he said to its occupant.

"Well," answered Mr. Keeling, looking up at him with his cold and fishy eyes.

"You're here again, are you?"

"I'm here again, and I will be here again. And again and again, and again and again."

"Now, what the—" Then the purser hesitated a moment, and thought perhaps he had better not swear, with that icy, clammy gaze fixed upon him. "What object have you in all this?"

"Object? The very simple one of making your company live up to its contract. From Liverpool to New York, my ticket reads. I paid for being landed in the United States, not for being dumped overboard in mid-ocean. Do you think you can take me over? You have had two tries at it and have not succeeded. Yours is a big and powerful company too."

"If you know we can't do it, then why do you—?" The purser hesitated.

"Pester you with my presence?" suggested Mr. Keeling. "Because I want you to do justice. Two thousand pounds is the price, and I will raise it one hundred pounds every trip." This time the New York papers got hold of the incident, but not of its peculiar features. They spoke of the extraordinary carelessness of the officers in allowing practically the same accident to occur twice on the same boat. When the Gibrontus reached Liverpool all the officers, from the captain down, sent in their resignations. Most of the sailors did not take the trouble to resign, but cut for it. The managing director was annoyed at the newspaper comments, but laughed at the rest of the story. He was invited to come over and interview Keeling for his own satisfaction, most of the officers promising to remain on the ship if he did so. He took Room 18 himself. What happened I do not know, for the purser refused to sail again on the Gibrontus, and was given another ship.

But this much is certain. When the managing director got back, the company generously paid Mrs. Keeling £2100.

The Terrible Experience of Plodkins

"Which—life or death? Tis a gambler's chance!

Yet, unconcerned, we spin and dance,

On the brittle thread of circumstance."

I understand that Plodkins is in the habit of referring sceptical listeners to me, and telling them that I will substantiate every word of his story. Now this is hardly fair of Plodkins. I can certainly corroborate part of what he says, and I can bear witness to the condition in which I found him after his ordeal was over. So I have thought it best, in order to set myself right with the public, to put down exactly what occurred. If I were asked whether or not I believe Plodkins' story myself, I would have to answer that sometimes I believe it, and sometimes I do not. Of course Plodkins will be offended when he reads this, but there are other things that I have to say about him which will perhaps enrage him still more; still they are the truth. For instance, Plodkins can hardly deny, and yet probably he will deny, that he was one of the most talented drinkers in America. I venture to say that every time he set foot in Liverpool coming East, or in New York going West, he was just on the verge of delirium tremens, because, being necessarily idle during the voyage, he did little else but drink and smoke. I never knew a man who could take so much liquor and show such small results. The fact was, that in the morning Plodkins was never at his best, because he was nearer sober then than at any other part of the day; but, after dinner, a more entertaining, genial, generous, kind-hearted man than Hiram Plodkins could not be found anywhere.

I want to speak of Plodkins' story with the calm, dispassionate manner of a judge, rather than with the partisanship of a favourable witness; and although my allusion to Plodkins' habits of intoxication may seem to him defamatory in character, and unnecessary, yet I mention them only to show that something terrible must have occurred in the bath-room to make him stop short. The extraordinary thing is, from that day to this Plodkins has not touched a drop of intoxicating liquor, which fact in itself strikes me as more wonderful than the story he tells.

Plodkins was a frequent crosser on the Atlantic steamers. He was connected with commercial houses on both sides of the ocean; selling in America for an English house, and buying in England for an American establishment. I presume it was his experiences in selling goods that led to his terrible habits of drinking. I understood from him that out West, if you are selling goods you have to do a great deal of treating, and every time you treat another man to a glass of wine, or a whiskey cocktail, you have, of course, to drink with him. But this has nothing to do with Plodkins' story.

On an Atlantic liner, when there is a large list of passengers, especially of English passengers, it is difficult to get a convenient hour in the morning at which to take a bath. This being the case, the purser usually takes down the names of applicants and assigns each a particular hour. Your hour may be, say seven o'clock in the morning. The next man comes on at half-past seven, and the third man at eight, and so on. The bedroom steward raps at your door when the proper time arrives, and informs you that the bath is ready. You wrap a dressing-gown or a cloak around you, and go along the silent corridors to the bath-room, coming back, generally before your half hour is up, like a giant refreshed.

Plodkins' bath hour was seven o'clock in the morning. Mine was half-past seven. On the particular morning in question the steward did not call me, and I thought he had forgotten, so I passed along the dark corridor and tried the bath-room door. I found it unbolted, and as everything was quiet inside, I entered. I thought nobody was there, so I shoved the bolt in the door, and went over to see if the water had been turned on. The light was a little dim even at that time of the morning, and I must say I was horror-stricken to see, lying in the bottom of the bath-tub, with his eyes fixed on the ceiling, Plodkins. I am quite willing to admit that I was never so startled in my life. I thought at first Plodkins was dead, notwithstanding his open eyes staring at the ceiling; but he murmured, in a sort of husky far-away whisper, "Thank God," and then closed his eyes.

"What's the matter, Plodkins?" I said. "Are you ill? What's the matter with you? Shall I call for help?"

There was a feeble negative motion of the head. Then he said, in a whisper, "Is the door bolted?"

"Yes," I answered.

After another moment's pause, I said—

"Shall I ring, and get you some whiskey or brandy?"

Again he shook his head.

"Help me to get up," he said feebly.

He was very much shaken, and I had some trouble in getting him on his feet, and seating him on the one chair in the room.

"You had better come to my state-room," I said; "it is nearer than yours. What has happened to you?"

He replied, "I will go in a moment. Wait a minute." And I waited.

"Now," he continued, when he had apparently pulled himself together a bit, "just turn on the electric light, will you?"

I reached up to the peg of the electric light and turned it on. A shudder passed over Plodkins' frame, but he said nothing. He seemed puzzled, and once more I asked him to let me take him to my stateroom, but he shook his head.

"Turn on the water." I did so.

"Turn out the electric light." I did that also.

"Now," he added, "put your hand in the water and turn on the electric light."

I was convinced Plodkins had become insane, but I recollected I was there alone with him, shaky as he was, in a room with a bolted door, so I put my fingers in the water and attempted to turn on the electric light. I got a shock that was very much greater than that which I received when I saw

Plodkins lying at the bottom of the bath-tub. I gave a yell and a groan, and staggered backwards. Then Plodkins laughed a feeble laugh.

"Now," he said, "I will go with you to your state-room."

The laugh seemed to have braced up Plodkins like a glass of liquor would have done, and when we got to my state-room he was able to tell me what had happened. As a sort of preface to his remarks, I would like to say a word or two about that bath-tub. It was similar to bath-tubs on board other steamers; a great and very deep receptacle of solid marble. There were different nickel-plated taps for letting in hot or cold water, or fresh water or salt water as was desired; and the escape-pipe instead of being at the end, as it is in most bath-tubs, was in the centre. It was the custom of the bath-room steward to fill it about half full of water at whatever temperature you desired. Then, placing a couple of towels on the rack, he would go and call the man whose hour it was to bathe.

Plodkins said, "When I went in there everything appeared as usual, except that the morning was very dark. I stood in the bath-tub, the water coming nearly to my knees, and reached up to turn on the electric light. The moment I touched the brass key I received a shock that simply paralyzed me. I think liquor has something to do with the awful effect the electricity had upon me, because I had taken too much the night before, and was feeling very shaky indeed; but the result was that I simply fell full length in the bath-tub just as you found me. I was unable to move anything except my fingers and toes. I did not appear to be hurt in the least, and my senses, instead of being dulled by the shock, seemed to be preternaturally sharp, and I realized in a moment that if this inability to move remained with me for five minutes I was a dead man—dead, not from the shock, but by drowning. I gazed up through that clear green water, and I could see the ripples on the surface slowly subsiding after my plunge into the tub. It reminded me of looking into an aquarium. You know how you see up through the water to the surface with the bubbles rising to the top. I knew that nobody would come in for at least half an hour, and even then I couldn't remember whether I had bolted the door or not. Sometimes I bolt it, and sometimes I don't. I didn't this morning, as it happens. All the time I felt that strength was slowly returning to me, for I continually worked my fingers and toes, and now feeling seemed to be coming up to my wrists and arms. Then I remembered that the vent was in the middle of the bath-tub; so, wriggling my fingers around, I got hold of the ring, and pulled up the plug. In the dense silence that was around me, I could not tell whether the water was running out or not; but gazing up towards the ceiling I thought I saw the surface gradually sinking down and down and down. Of course it couldn't have been more than a few seconds, but it seemed to be years and years and years. I knew that if once I let my breath go I would be drowned, merely by the spasmodic action of my lungs trying to recover air. I felt as if I should burst. It was a match against time, with life or death as the stake. At first, as I said, my senses were abnormally sharp, but, by and by, I began to notice that they were wavering. I thought the glassy surface of the water, which I could see above me, was in reality a great sheet of crystal that somebody was pressing down upon me, and I began to think that the moment it reached my face I would smother. I tried to struggle, but was held with a grip of steel. Finally, this slab of crystal came down to my nose, and seemed to split apart. I could hold on no longer, and with a mighty expiration blew the water up towards the ceiling, and drew in a frightful smothering breath of salt water, that I blew in turn upwards, and the next breath I took in had some air with the water. I felt the water tickling the corners of my mouth, and receding slower and slower down my face and neck. Then I think I must have become insensible until just before you entered the room. Of course there is something wrong with the electric fittings, and there is a leak of electricity; but I think liquor is at the bottom of all this. I don't believe it would have affected me like this if I had not been soaked in whiskey."

"If I were you," I said, "I would leave whiskey alone."

"I intend to," he answered solemnly, "and baths too."

A Case Of Fever

"O, underneath the blood red sun,

No bloodier deed was ever done!

Nor fiercer retribution sought

The hand that first red ruin wrought."

This is the doctor's story—

The doctors on board the Atlantic liners are usually young men. They are good-looking and entertaining as well, and generally they can play the violin or some other instrument that is of great use at the inevitable concert which takes place about the middle of the Atlantic. They are urbane, polite young men, and they chat pleasantly and nicely to the ladies on board. I believe that the doctor on the Transatlantic steamer has to be there on account of the steerage passengers. Of course the doctor goes to the steerage; but I imagine, as a general thing, he does not spend any more time there than the rules of the service compel him to. The ladies, at least, would be unanimous in saying that the doctor is one of the most charming officials on board the ship.

This doctor, who tells the story I am about to relate, was not like the usual Atlantic physician. He was older than the average, and, to judge by his somewhat haggard, rugged face, had seen hard times and rough usage in different parts of the world. Why he came to settle down on an Atlantic steamer—a berth which is a starting-point rather than a terminus—I have no means of knowing. He never told us; but there he was, and one night, as he smoked his pipe with us in the smoking-room, we closed the door, and compelled him to tell us a story.

As a preliminary, he took out of his inside pocket a book, from which he selected a slip of creased paper, which had been there so long that it was rather the worse for wear, and had to be tenderly handled.

"As a beginning," said the doctor, "I will read you what this slip of paper says. It is an extract from one of the United States Government Reports in the Indian department, and it relates to a case of fever, which caused the death of the celebrated Indian chief Wolf Tusk.

"I am not sure that I am doing quite right in telling this story. There may be some risk for myself in relating it, and I don't know exactly what the United States Government might have in store for me if the truth came to be known. In fact, I am not able to say whether I acted rightly or wrongly in the matter I have to tell you about. You shall be the best judges of that. There is no question but Wolf Tusk was an old monster, and there is no question either that the men who dealt with him had been grievously—but, then, there is no use in my giving you too many preliminaries; each one will say for himself whether he would have acted as I did or not. I will make my excuses at the end of the story." Then he read the slip of paper. I have not a copy of it, and have to quote from memory. It was the report of the physician who saw Wolf Tusk die, and it went on to say that about nine o'clock in the morning a heavy and unusual fever set in on that chief. He had been wounded in the battle of the day before, when he was captured, and the fever attacked all parts of his body. Although the doctor had made every effort in his power to relieve the Indian, nothing could stop the ravages of the fever. At four o'clock in the afternoon, having been in great pain, and, during the latter part, delirious, he died, and was buried near the spot where he had taken ill. This was signed by the doctor.

"What I have read you," said the physician, folding up the paper again, and placing it in his pocket-book, "is strictly and accurately true, otherwise, of course, I would not have so reported to the Government. Wolf Tusk was the chief of a band of irreconcilables, who were now in one part of the West and now in another, giving a great deal of trouble to the authorities. Wolf Tusk and his band had splendid horses, and they never attacked a force that outnumbered their own. In fact, they never attacked anything where the chances were not twenty to one in their favour, but that, of course, is Indian warfare; and in this, Wolf Tusk was no different from his fellows.

"On one occasion Wolf Tusk and his band swooped down on a settlement where they knew that all the defenders were away, and no one but women and children were left to meet them. Here one of the most atrocious massacres of the West took place. Every woman and child in the settlement was killed under circumstances of inconceivable brutality. The buildings, such as they were, were burnt down, and, when the men returned, they found nothing but heaps of smouldering ruin.

"Wolf Tusk and his band, knowing there would be trouble about this, had made for the broken ground where they could so well defend themselves. The alarm, however, was speedily given, and a company of cavalry from the nearest fort started in hot pursuit.

"I was the physician who accompanied the troops. The men whose families had been massacred, and who were all mounted on swift horses, begged permission to go with the soldiers, and that permission was granted, because it was known that their leader would take them after Wolf Tusk on his own account, and it was thought better to have every one engaged in the pursuit under the direct command of the chief officer.

"He divided his troop into three parts, one following slowly after Wolf Tusk, and the other two taking roundabout ways to head off the savages from the broken ground and foothills from which no number of United States troops could have dislodged them. These flanking parties were partly successful. They did not succeed in heading off the Indians entirely, but one succeeded in changing their course, and throwing the Indians unexpectedly into the way of the other flanking party, when a sharp battle took place, and, during its progress, we in the rear came up. When the Indians saw our reinforcing party come towards them each man broke away for himself and made for the wilderness. Wolf Tusk, who had been wounded, and had his horse shot under him, did not succeed in escaping. The two flanking parties now having reunited with the main body, it was decided to keep the Indians on the run for a day or two at least, and so a question arose as to the disposal of the wounded chief. He could not be taken with the fighting party; there were no soldiers to spare to take him back, and so the leader of the settlers said that as they had had enough of war, they would convey him to the fort. Why the commander allowed this to be done, I do not know. He must have realized the feelings of the settlers towards the man who massacred their wives and children. However, the request of the settlers was acceded to, and I was ordered back also, as I had been slightly wounded. You can see the mark here on my cheek, nothing serious; but the commander thought I had better get back into the fort, as he was certain there would be no more need of my services. The Indians were on the run, and would make no further stand.

"It was about three days' march from where the engagement had taken place to the fort. Wolf Tusk was given one of the captured Indian horses. I attended to the wound in his leg, and he was strapped on the horse, so that there could be no possibility of his escaping.

"We camped the first night in a little belt of timber that bordered a small stream, now nearly dry. In the morning I was somewhat rudely awakened, and found myself tied hand and foot, with two or three of the settlers standing over me. They helped me to my feet, then half carried and half led me to a tree, where they tied me securely to the trunk.

"'What are you going to do? What is the meaning of this?' I said to them in astonishment.

"'Nothing,' was the answer of the leader; 'that is, nothing, if you will sign a certain medical report which is to go to the Government. You will see, from where you are, everything that is going to happen, and we expect you to report truthfully; but we will take the liberty of writing the report for you.

"Then I noticed that Wolf Tusk was tied to a tree in a manner similar to myself, and around him had been collected a quantity of firewood. This firewood, was not piled up to his feet, but formed a circle at some distance from him, so that the Indian would be slowly roasted.

"There is no use in my describing what took place. When I tell you that they lit the fire at nine o'clock, and that it was not until four in the afternoon that Wolf Tusk died, you will understand the peculiar horror of it.

"'Now,' said the leader to me when everything was over,' here is the report I have written out,' and he read to me the report which I have read to you.

"'This dead villain has murdered our wives and our children. If I could have made his torture last for two weeks I would have done so. You have made every effort to save him by trying to break loose, and you have not succeeded. We are not going to harm you, even though you refuse to sign this report. You cannot bring him to life again, thank God, and all you can do is to put more trouble on the heads of men who have already, through red devils like this, had more trouble than they can well stand and keep sane. Will you sign the report?'

"I said I would, and I did."

How The Captain Got His Steamer Out

"On his own perticular well-wrought row,

That he's straddled for ages—

Learnt its lay and its gages—

His style may seem queer, but permit him to know,

The likeliest, sprightliest, manner to hoe."

"There is nothing more certain than that some day we may have to record a terrible disaster directly traceable to ocean racing.

"The vivid account which one of our reporters gives in another column of how the captain of the Arrowic went blundering across the bar yesterday in one of the densest fogs of the season is very interesting reading. Of course the account does not pretend to be anything more than imaginary, for, until the Arrowic reaches Queenstown, if she ever does under her present captain, no one can tell how much of luck was mixed with the recklessness which took this steamer out into the Atlantic in the midst of the thickest fog we have had this year. All that can be known at present is, that, when the fog lifted, the splendid steamer Dartonia was lying at anchor in the bay, having missed the tide, while the Arrowic was nowhere to be seen. If the fog was too thick for the Dartonia to cross the bar, how, then, did the captain of the Arrowic get his boat out? The captain of the Arrowic should be taught to remember that there are other things to be thought of beside the defeating of a rival steamer. He should be made to understand that he has under his charge a steamer worth a million and a half of dollars, and a cargo probably nearly as valuable. Still, he might have lost his ship and cargo, and we would have had no word to say. That concerns the steamship company and the owners of the cargo; but he had also in his care nearly a thousand human lives, and these he should not be allowed to juggle with in order to beat all the rival steamers in the world."

The above editorial is taken from the columns of the New York Daily

Mentor. The substance of it had been cabled across to London and it made pleasant reading for the captain of the Arrowic at Queenstown. The captain didn't say anything about it; he was not a talkative man. Probably he explained to his chief, if the captain of an ocean liner can possibly have a chief, how he got his vessel out of New York harbour in a fog; but, if he did, the explanation was never made public, and so here's an account of it published for the first time, and it may give a pointer to the captain of the rival liner Dartonia. I may say, however, that the purser was not as silent as the captain. He was very indignant at what he called the outrage of the New York paper, and said a great many unjustifiable things about newspaper men. He knew I was a newspaper man myself, and probably that is the reason he launched his maledictions against the fraternity at my head.

"Just listen to that wretched penny-a-liner," he said, rapping savagely on the paper with the back of his hand.

I intimated mildly that they paid more than a penny a line for newspaper work in New York, but he said that wasn't the point. In fact the purser was too angry to argue calmly. He was angry the whole way from Queenstown to Liverpool.

"Here," he said, "is some young fellow, who probably never saw the inside of a ship in his life, and yet he thinks he can tell the captain of a great ocean liner what should be done and what shouldn't. Just think of the cheek of it."

"I don't see any cheek in it," I said, as soothingly as possible. "You don't mean to pretend to argue, at this time of day that a newspaper man does not know how to conduct every other business as well as his own."

But the purser did make that very contention, although of course he must be excused, for, as I said, he was not in a good temper.

"Newspaper men," he continued, "act as if they did know everything. They pretend in their papers that every man thinks he knows how to run a newspaper or a hotel. But look at their own case. See the advice they give to statesmen. See how they would govern Germany, or England, or any other country under the sun. Does a big bank get into trouble, the newspaper man at once informs the financiers how they should have conducted their business. Is there a great railway smash-up, the newspaper man shows exactly how it could have been avoided if he had had the management of the railway. Is there a big strike, the newspaper man steps in. He tells both sides what they should do. If every man thinks he can run a hotel, or a newspaper—and I am sure most men could run a newspaper as well as the newspapers are conducted now—the conceit of the ordinary man is nothing to the conceit of the newspaper man. He not only thinks he can run a newspaper and a hotel, but every other business under the sun."

"And how do you know he can't," I asked.

But the purser would not listen to reason. He contended that a captain who had crossed the ocean hundreds of times and for years and years had worked his way up, had just as big a sense of responsibility for his passengers and his ship and his cargo as any newspaper man in New York could have, and this palpably absurd contention he maintained all the way to Liverpool.

When a great ocean racer is making ready to put out to sea, there can hardly be imagined a more bustling scene than that which presents itself on the deck and on the wharf. There is the rush of passengers, the banging about of luggage, the hurrying to and fro on the decks, the roar of escaping steam, the working of immense steam cranes hoisting and lowering great bales of merchandise and luggage from the wharf to the hold, and here and there in quiet corners, away from the rush, are tearful people bidding good-bye to one another.

The Arrowic and the Dartonia left on the same day and within the same hour, from wharfs that were almost adjoining each other. We on board the Arrowic could see the same bustle and stir on board the Dartonia that we ourselves were in the midst of.

The Dartonia was timed to leave about half an hour ahead of us, and we heard the frantic ringing of her last bell warning everybody to get on shore who were not going to cross the ocean. Then the great steamer backed slowly out from her wharf.

Of course all of us who were going on the Arrowic were warm champions of that ship as the crack ocean racer; but, as the Dartonia moved backwards with slow stately majesty, all her colours flying, and her decks black with passengers crowding to the rail and gazing towards us, we could not deny that she was a splendid vessel, and "even the ranks of Tuscany could scarce forbear a cheer." Once out in the stream her twin screws enabled her to turn around almost without the help of tugs, and just as our last bell was ringing she moved off down the bay. Then we backed slowly out in the same fashion, and, although we had not the advantage of seeing ourselves, we saw a great sight on the wharf, which was covered with people, ringing with cheers, and white with the flutter of handkerchiefs.

As we headed down stream the day began to get rather thick. It had been gloomy all morning, and by the time we reached the Statue of Liberty it was so foggy that one could hardly see three boats' length ahead or behind. All eyes were strained to catch a glimpse of the Dartonia, but nothing of her was visible. Shortly after, the fog came down in earnest and blotted out everything. There was a strong wind blowing, and the vapour, which was cold and piercing, swept the deck with dripping moisture. Then we came to a standstill. The ship's bell was rung continually forward and somebody was whanging on the gong towards the stern. Everybody knew that, if this sort of thing lasted long, we would not get over the bar that tide, and consequently everybody felt annoyed, for this delay would lengthen the trip, and people, as a general thing, do not take passage on an ocean racer with the idea of getting in a day late. Suddenly the fog lifted clear from shore to shore. Then we saw something that was not calculated to put our minds at ease. A big three-masted vessel, with full sail, dashed past us only a very few yards behind the stern of the mammoth steamer.

"Look at that blundering idiot," said the purser to me, "rushing full speed over crowded New York Bay in a fog as thick as pea-soup. A captain who would do a thing like that ought to be hanged."

Before the fog settled down again we saw the Dartonia with her anchor chain out a few hundred yards to our left, and, farther on, one of the big German steamers, also at anchor.

In the short time that the fog was lifted our own vessel made some progress towards the bar. Then the thickness came down again. A nautical passenger, who had crossed many times, came aft to where I was standing, and said—

"Do you notice what the captain is trying to do?"

"Well," I answered, "I don't see how anybody can do anything in weather like this."

"There is a strong wind blowing," continued the nautical passenger, "and the fog is liable to lift for a few minutes at a time. If it lifts often enough our captain is going to get us over the bar. It will be rather a sharp bit of work if he succeeds. You notice that the Dartonia has thrown out her anchor. She is evidently going to wait where she is until the fog clears away entirely."

So with that we two went forward to see what was being done. The captain stood on the bridge and beside him the pilot, but the fog was now so thick we could hardly see them, although we stood close by, on the piece of deck in front of the wheelhouse. The almost incessant clanging of the bell was kept up, and in the pauses we heard answering bells from different points in the thick fog. Then, for a second time, and with equal suddenness, the fog lifted ahead of us. Behind we could not see either the Dartonia or the German steamer. Our own boat, however, went full speed ahead and kept up the pace till the fog shut down again. The captain now, in pacing the bridge, had his chronometer in his hand, and those of us who were at the front frequently looked at our watches, for of course the nautical passenger knew just how late it was possible for us to cross the bar.

"I am afraid," said the passenger, "he is not going to succeed." But, as he said this, the fog lifted for the third time, and again the mammoth steamer forged ahead.

"If this clearance will only last for ten minutes," said the nautical passenger, "we are all right." But the fog, as if it had heard him, closed down on us again damper and thicker than ever.

"We are just at the bar," said the nautical passenger, "and if this doesn't clear up pretty soon the vessel will have to go back."

The captain kept his eyes fixed on the chronometer in his hand. The pilot tried to peer ahead, but everything was a thick white blank.

"Ten minutes more and it is too late," said the nautical passenger.

There was a sudden rift in the fog that gave a moment's hope, but it closed down again. A minute afterwards, with a suddenness that was strange, the whole blue ocean lay before us. Then full steam ahead. The fog still was thick behind us in New York Bay. We saw it far ahead coming in from the ocean. All at once the captain closed his chronometer with a snap. We were over the bar and into the Atlantic, and that is how the captain got the Arrowic out of New York Bay.

My Stowaway

"Ye can play yer jokes on Nature,

An' play 'em slick,

She'll grin a grin, but, landsakes, friend,

Look out fer the kick!"

One night about eleven o'clock I stood at the stern of that fine Atlantic steamship, the City of Venice, which was ploughing its way through the darkness towards America. I leaned on the rounded bulwark and enjoyed a smoke as I gazed on the luminous trail the wheel was making in the quiet sea. Some one touched me on the shoulder, saying, "Beg pardon, sir;" and, on straightening up, I saw in the dim light a man whom at first I took to be one of the steerage passengers. I thought he wanted to get past me, for the room was rather restricted in the passage between the aft wheelhouse and the stern, and I moved aside. The man looked hurriedly to one side and then the other and, approaching, said in a whisper, "I'm starving, sir!"

"Why don't you go and get something to eat, then? Don't they give you plenty forward?"

"I suppose they do, sir; but I'm a stowaway. I got on at Liverpool. What little I took with me is gone, and for two days I've had nothing."

"Come with me. I'll take you to the steward, he'll fix you all right."

"Oh, no, no, no," he cried, trembling with excitement. "If you speak to any of the officers or crew I'm lost. I assure you, sir, I'm an honest man, I am indeed, sir. It's the old story—nothing but starvation at home, so my only chance seemed to be to get this way to America. If I'm caught I shall get dreadful usage and will be taken back and put in jail."

"Oh, you're mistaken. The officers are all courteous gentlemen."

"Yes, to you cabin passengers they are. But to a stowaway—that's a different matter. If you can't help me, sir, please don't inform on me."

"How can I help you but by speaking to the captain or purser?"

"Get me a morsel to eat."

"Where were you hid?"

"Right here, sir, in this place," and he put his hand on the square deck-edifice beside us. This seemed to be a spare wheel-house, used if anything went wrong with the one in front. It had a door on each side and there were windows all round it. At present it was piled full of cane folding steamer chairs and other odds and ends.

"I crawl in between the chairs and the wall and get under that piece of tarpaulin."

"Well, you're sure of being caught, for the first fine day all these chairs will be taken out and the deck steward can't miss you."

The man sighed as I said this and admitted the chances were much against him. Then, starting up, he cried, "Poverty is the great crime. If I had stolen some one else's money I would have been able to take cabin passage instead of—"

"If you weren't caught."

"Well, if I were caught, what then? I would be well fed and taken care of."

"Oh, they'd take care of you."

"The waste food in this great ship would feed a hundred hungry wretches like me. Does my presence keep the steamer back a moment of time? No. Well, who is harmed by my trying to better myself in a new world? No one. I am begging for a crust from the lavish plenty, all because I am struggling to be honest. It is only when I become a thief that I am out of danger of starvation—caught or free."

"There, there; now, don't speak so loud or you'll have some one here.

You hang round and I'll bring you some provender. What would you like to have? Poached eggs on toast, roast turkey, or—"

The wretch sank down at my feet as I said this, and, recognising the cruelty of it, I hurried down into the saloon and hunted up a steward who had not yet turned in. "Steward," I said, "can you get me a few sandwiches or anything to eat at this late hour?"

"Yessir, certainly, sir; beef or 'am, sir?"

"Both, and a cup of coffee, please."

"Well, sir, I'm afraid there's no coffee, sir; but I could make you a pot of tea in a moment, sir."

"All right, and bring them to my room, please?"

"Yessir."

In a very short time there was that faint steward rap at the state-room door and a most appetising tray-load was respectfully placed at my service.

When the waiter had gone I hurried up the companion-way with much the air of a man who is stealing fowls, and I found my stowaway just in the position I had left him.

"Now, pitch in," I said. "I'll stand guard forward here, and, if you hear me cough, strike for cover. I'll explain the tray matter if it's found."

He simply said, "Thank you, sir," and I went forward. When I came back the tray had been swept clean and the teapot emptied. My stowaway was making for his den when I said, "How about to-morrow?"

He answered, "This'll do me for a couple of days."

"Nonsense. I'll have a square meal for you here in the corner of this wheel-house, so that you can get at it without trouble. I'll leave it about this time to-morrow night."

"You won't tell any one, any one at all, sir?"

"No. At least, I'll think over the matter, and if I see a way out I'll let you know."

"God bless you, sir."

I turned the incident over in my mind a good deal that night, and I almost made a resolution to take Cupples into my confidence. Roger Cupples, a lawyer of San Francisco, sat next me at table, and with the freedom of wild Westerners we were already well acquainted, although only a few days out. Then I thought of putting a supposititious case to the captain—he was a thorough gentleman—and if he spoke generously about the supposititious case I would spring the real one on him. The stowaway had impressed me by his language as being a man worth doing something for.

Nest day I was glad to see that it was rainy. There would be no demand for ship chairs that day. I felt that real sunshiny weather would certainly unearth, or unchair, my stowaway. I met Cupples on deck, and we walked a few rounds together.

At last, Cupples, who had been telling me some stories of court trials in San Francisco, said, "Let's sit down and wrap up. This deck's too wet to walk on."

"All the seats are damp," I said.

"I'll get out my steamer chair. Steward," he cried to the deck steward who was shoving a mop back and forth, "get me my chair. There's a tag on it, 'Berth 96.'"

"No, no," I cried hastily; "let's go into the cabin. It's raining."

"Only a drizzle. Won't hurt you at sea, you know."

By this time the deck steward was hauling down chairs trying to find No. 96, which I felt sure would be near the bottom. I could not control my anxiety as the steward got nearer and nearer the tarpaulin. At last I cried—

"Steward, never mind that chair; take the first two that come handy."

Cupples looked astonished, and, as we sat down, I said—

"I have something to tell you, and I trust you will say nothing about it

171

to any one else. There's a man under those chairs."

The look that came into the lawyer's face showed that he thought me demented; but, when I told him the whole story, the judicial expression came on, and he said, shaking his head—

"That's bad business."

"I know it."

"Yes, but it's worse than you have any idea of. I presume that you don't know what section 4738 of the Revised Statutes says?"

"No; I don't."

"Well, it is to the effect that any person or persons, who wilfully or with malice aforethought or otherwise, shall aid, abet, succor or cherish, either directly or indirectly or by implication, any person who feloniously or secretly conceals himself on any vessel, barge, brig, schooner, bark, clipper, steamship or other craft touching at or coming within the jurisdiction of these United States, the said person's purpose being the defrauding of the revenue of, or the escaping any or all of the just legal dues exacted by such vessel, barge, etc., the person so aiding or abetting, shall in the eye of the law be considered as accomplice before, during and after the illegal act, and shall in such case be subject to the penalties accruing thereunto, to wit—a fine of not more than five thousand dollars, or imprisonment of not more than two years—or both at the option of the judge before whom the party so accused is convicted."

"Great heavens! is that really so?"

"Well, it isn't word for word, but that is the purport. Of course, if I had my books here, I—why, you've doubtless heard of the case of the Pacific Steamship Company versus Cumberland. I was retained on behalf of the company. Now all Cumberland did was to allow the man—he was sent up for two years—to carry his valise on board, but we proved the intent. Like a fool, he boasted of it, but the steamer brought back the man, and Cumberland got off with four thousand dollars and costs. Never got out of that scrape less than ten thousand dollars. Then again, the steamship Peruvian versus McNish;

that is even more to the—"

"See here, Cupples. Come with me to-night and see the man. If you heard him talk you would see the inhumanity—"

"Tush. I'm not fool enough to mix up in such a matter, and look here, you'll have to work it pretty slick if you get yourself out. The man will be caught as sure as fate; then knowingly or through fright he'll incriminate you."

"What would you do if you were in my place?"

"My dear sir, don't put it that way. It's a reflection on both my judgment and my legal knowledge. I couldn't be in such a scrape. But, as a lawyer—minus the fee—I'll tell you what you should do. You should give the man up before witnesses—before witnesses. I'll be one of them myself. Get as many of the cabin passengers as you like out here, to-day, and let the officers search. If he charges you with what the law terms support, deny it, and call attention to the fact that you have given information. By the way, I would give written information and keep a copy."

"I gave the man my word not to inform on him and so I can't do it to-day, but I'll tell him of it to-night."

"And have him commit suicide or give himself up first and incriminate you? Nonsense. Just release yourself from your promise. That's all. He'll trust you."

"Yes, poor wretch, I'm afraid he will."

About ten o'clock that night I resolved to make another appeal to Roger Cupples to at least stand off and hear the man talk. Cupples' state-room, No. 96, was in the forward part of the steamer, down a long passage and off a short side passage. Mine was aft the cabin. The door of 96 was partly open, and inside an astonishing sight met my gaze.

There stood my stowaway.

He was evidently admiring himself in the glass, and with a brush was touching up his face with dark paint here and there. When he put on a woe-begone look he was the stowaway; when he chuckled to himself he was Roger Cupples, Esq.

The moment the thing dawned on me I quietly withdrew and went up the forward companion way. Soon Cupples came cautiously up and seeing the way clear scudded along in the darkness and hid in the aft wheelhouse. I saw the whole thing now. It was a scheme to get me to make a fool of myself some fine day before the rest of the passengers and have a standing joke on me. I walked forward. The first officer was on duty.

"I have reason to believe," I said, "that there is a stowaway in the aft wheelhouse."

Quicker than it takes me to tell it a detachment of sailors were sent aft under the guidance of the third mate. I went through the saloon and smoking room, and said to the gentlemen who were playing cards and reading—"There's a row upstairs of some kind."

We were all on deck before the crew had surrounded the wheelhouse. There was a rattle of steamer folded chairs, a pounce by the third mate, and out came the unfortunate Cupples, dragged by the collar.

"Hold on; let go. This is a mistake."

"You can't both hold on and let go," said Stalker, of Indiana.

"Come out o' this," cried the mate, jerking him forward.

With a wrench the stowaway tore himself free and made a dash for the companion way. A couple of sailors instantly tripped him up.

"Let go of me; I'm a cabin passenger," cried Cupples.

"Bless me!" I cried in astonishment. "This isn't you, Cupples? Why, I acted on your own advice and that of Revised Statutes, No. what ever-they-were."

"Well, act on my advice again," cried the infuriated Cupples, "and go to—the hold."

However, he was better in humour the next day, and stood treat all round. We found, subsequently, that Cupples was a New York actor, and at the entertainment given for the benefit of the sailors' orphans, a few nights after, he recited a piece in costume that just melted the ladies. It was voted a wonderfully touching performance, and he called it "The Stowaway."

The Purser's Story

"O Mother-nature, kind in touch and tone.

Act as we may, thou clearest to thine own"

I don't know that I should tell this story.

When the purser related it to me I know it was his intention to write it out for a magazine. In fact he had written it, and I understand that a noted American magazine had offered to publish it, but I have watched that magazine for over three years and I have not yet seen the purser's story in it. I am sorry that I did not write the story at the time; then perhaps I should have caught the exquisite peculiarities of the purser's way of telling it. I find myself gradually forgetting the story and I write it now in case I shall forget it, and then be harassed all through after life by the remembrance of the forgetting.

There is no position more painful and tormenting than the consciousness of having had something worth the telling, which, in spite of all mental effort, just eludes the memory. It hovers nebulously beyond the outstretched finger-ends of recollection, and, like the fish that gets off the hook, becomes more and more important as the years fade.

Perhaps, when you read this story, you will say there is nothing in it after all. Well, that will be my fault, then, and I can only regret I did not write down the story when it was told to me, for as I sat in the purser's room that day it seemed to me I had never heard anything more graphic.

The purser's room was well forward on the Atlantic steamship. From one of the little red-curtained windows you could look down to where the steerage passengers were gathered on the deck. When the bow of the great vessel plunged down into the big Atlantic waves, the smother of foam that shot upwards would be borne along with the wind, and spatter like rain against the purser's window. Something about this intermittent patter on the pane reminded the purser of the story, and so he told it to me.

There were a great many steerage passengers coming on at Queenstown, he said, and there was quite a hurry getting them aboard. Two officers stood at each side of the gangway and took the tickets as the people crowded forward. They generally had their tickets in their hands and there was usually no trouble. I stood there and watched them coming aboard. Suddenly there was a fuss and a jam. "What is it?" I asked the officer.

"Two girls, sir, say they have lost their tickets."

I took the girls aside and the stream of humanity poured in. One was about fourteen and the other, perhaps, eight years old. The little one had a firm grip of the elder's hand and she was crying. The larger girl looked me straight in the eye as I questioned her.

"Where's your tickets?"

"We lost thim, sur."

"Where?"

"I dunno, sur."

"Do you think you have them about you or in your luggage?"

"We've no luggage, sur."

"Is this your sister?"

"She is, sur."

"Are your parents aboard?"

"They are not, sur."

"Are you all alone?"

"We are, sur."

"You can't go without your tickets."

The younger one began to cry the more, and the elder answered, "Mabbe we can foind thim, sur."

They were bright-looking, intelligent children, and the larger girl gave me such quick, straightforward answers, and it seemed so impossible that children so young should attempt to cross the ocean without tickets that I concluded to let them come, and resolved to get at the truth on the way over.

Next day I told the deck steward to bring the children to my room.

They came in just as I saw them the day before, the elder with a tight grip on the hand of the younger, whose eyes I never caught sight of. She kept them resolutely on the floor, while the other looked straight at me with her big, blue eyes.

"Well, have you found your tickets?"

"No, sur."

"What is your name?"

"Bridget, sur."

"Bridget what?"

"Bridget Mulligan, sur."

"Where did you live?"

"In Kildormey, sur."

"Where did you get your tickets?"

"From Mr. O'Grady, sur."

Now, I knew Kildormey as well as I know this ship, and I knew O'Grady was our agent there. I would have given a good deal at that moment for a few words with him. But I knew of no Mulligans in Kildormey, although, of course, there might be. I was born myself only a few miles from the place. Now, thinks I to myself, if these two children can baffle a purser who has been twenty years on the Atlantic when they say they came from his own town almost, by the powers they deserve their passage over the ocean. I had often seen grown people try to cheat their way across, and I may say none of them succeeded on my ships.

"Where's your father and mother?"

"Both dead, sur."

"Who was your father?"

"He was a pinshoner, sur."

"Where did he draw his pension?"

"I donno, sur."

"Where did you get the money to buy your tickets?"

"The neighbors, sur, and Mr. O'Grady helped, sur."

"What neighbours? Name them."

She unhesitatingly named a number, many of whom I knew; and as that had frequently been done before, I saw no reason to doubt the girl's word.

"Now," I said, "I want to speak with your sister. You may go."

The little one held on to her sister's hand and cried bitterly.

When the other was gone, I drew the child towards me and questioned her, but could not get a word in reply.

For the next day or two I was bothered somewhat by a big Irishman named O'Donnell, who was a fire-brand among the steerage passengers. He would harangue them at all hours on the wrongs of Ireland, and the desirability of blowing England out of the water; and as we had many English and German passengers, as well as many peaceable Irishmen, who complained of the constant ructions O'Donnell was kicking up, I was forced to ask him to keep quiet. He became very abusive one day and tried to strike me. I had him locked up until he came to his senses.

While I was in my room, after this little excitement, Mrs. O'Donnell came to me and pleaded for her rascally husband. I had noticed her before. She was a poor, weak, broken-hearted woman whom her husband made a slave of, and I have no doubt beat her when he had the chance. She was evidently mortally afraid of him, and a look from him seemed enough to take the life out of her. He was a worse tyrant, in his own small way, than England had ever been.

"Well, Mrs. O'Donnell," I said, "I'll let your husband go, but he will have to keep a civil tongue in his head and keep his hands off people. I've seen men, for less, put in irons during a voyage and handed over to the authorities when they landed. And now I want you to do me a favour. There are two children on board without tickets. I don't believe they ever had tickets, and I want to find out. You're a kind-hearted woman, Mrs. O'Donnell, and perhaps the children will answer you." I had the two called in, and they came hand in hand as usual. The elder looked at me as if she couldn't take her eyes off my face.

"Look at this woman," I said to her; "she wants to speak to you. Ask her some questions about herself," I whispered to Mrs. O'Donnell.

"Acushla," said Mrs. O'Donnell with infinite tenderness, taking the disengaged hand of the elder girl. "Tell me, darlint, where yees are from."

I suppose I had spoken rather harshly to them before, although I had not intended to do so, but however that may be, at the first words of kindness from the lips of their countrywoman both girls broke down and cried as if their hearts would break. The poor woman drew them towards her, and, stroking the fair hair of the elder girl, tried to comfort her while the tears streamed down her own cheeks. "Hush, acushla; hush, darlints, shure the gentlemin's not goin' to be hard wid two poor childher going to a strange country."

Of course it would never do to admit that the company could carry emigrants free through sympathy, and I must have appeared rather hard-hearted when I told Mrs. O'Donnell that I would have to take them back with me to Cork. I sent the children away, and then arranged with Mrs. O'Donnell to see after them during the voyage, to which she agreed if her husband would let her. I could get nothing from the girl except that she had lost her ticket; and when we sighted New York, I took them through the steerage and asked the passengers if any one would assume charge of the children and pay their passage. No one would do so.

"Then," I said, "these children will go back with me to Cork; and if I find they never bought tickets, they will have to go to jail."

There were groans and hisses at that, and I gave the children in charge of the cabin stewardess, with orders to see that they did not leave the ship. I was at last convinced that they had no friends among the steerage passengers. I intended to take them ashore myself before we sailed; and I knew of good friends in New York who would see to the little waifs, although I did not propose that any of the emigrants should know that an old bachelor purser was fool enough to pay for the passage of a couple of unknown Irish children.

We landed our cabin passengers, and the tender came alongside to take the steerage passengers to Castle Garden. I got the stewardess to bring out the children, and the two stood and watched every one get aboard the tender.

Just as the tender moved away, there was a wild shriek among the crowded passengers, and Mrs. O'Donnell flung her arms above her head and cried in the most heart-rending tone I ever heard—"Oh, my babies, my babies."

"Kape quiet, ye divil," hissed O'Donnell, grasping her by the arm. The terrible ten days' strain had been broken at last, and the poor woman sank in a heap at his feet.

"Bring back that boat," I shouted, and the tender came back.

"Come aboard here, O'Donnell."

"I'll not!" he yelled, shaking his fist at me.

"Bring that man aboard."

They soon brought him back, and I gave his wife over to the care of the stewardess. She speedily rallied, and hugged and kissed her children as if she would never part with them.

"So, O'Donnell, these are your children?"

"Yis, they are; an' I'd have ye know I'm in a frae country, bedad, and I dare ye to lay a finger on me."

"Don't dare too much," I said, "or I'll show you what can be done in a free country. Now, if I let the children go, will you send their passage money to the company when you get it?"

"I will," he answered, although I knew he lied.

"Well," I said, "for Mrs. O'Donnell's sake, I'll let them go; and I must congratulate any free country that gets a citizen like you."

Of course I never heard from O'Donnell again.

Miss McMillan

"Come hop, come skip, fair children all,

Old Father Time is in the hall.

He'll take you on his knee, and stroke

Your golden hair to silver bright,

Your rosy cheeks to wrinkles white"

In the saloon of the fine Transatlantic liner the Climatus, two long tables extend from the piano at one end to the bookcase at the other end of the ample dining-room.

On each side of this main saloon are four small tables intended to accommodate six or seven persons. At one of these tables sat a pleasant party of four ladies and three gentlemen. Three ladies were from Detroit, and one from Kent, in England. At the head of the table sat Mr. Blair, the frosts of many American winters in his hair and beard, while the lines of care in his ragged, cheerful Scottish face told of a life of business crowned with generous success.

Mr. Waters, a younger merchant, had all the alert vivacity of the pushing American. He had the distinguished honour of sitting opposite me at the small table. Blair and Waters occupied the same room, No. 27. The one had crossed the Atlantic more than fifty times, the other nearly thirty. Those figures show the relative proportion of their business experience.

The presence of Mr. Blair gave to our table a sort of patriarchal dignity that we all appreciated. If a louder burst of laughter than usual came from where we sat and the other passengers looked inquiringly our way the sedate and self-possessed face of Mr. Blair kept us in countenance, and we, who had given way to undue levity, felt ourselves enshrouded by an atmosphere of genial seriousness. This prevented our table from getting the reputation of being funny or frivolous.

Some remark that Blair made brought forth the following extraordinary statement from Waters, who told it with the air of a man exposing the pretensions of a whited sepulchre.

"Now, before this voyage goes any further," he began, "I have a serious duty to perform which I can shirk no longer, unpleasant though it be. Mr. Blair and myself occupy the same state-room. Into that state-room has been sent a most lovely basket of flowers. It is not an ordinary basket of flowers, I assure you, ladies. There is a beautiful floral arch over a bed of colour, and I believe there is some tender sentiment connected with the display;—Bon Voyage, Auf Wiedersehen, or some such motto marked out in red buds. Now those flowers are not for me. I think, therefore, that Mr. Blair owes it to this company, which has so unanimously placed him at the head of the table, to explain how it comes that an elderly gentleman gets such a handsome floral tribute sent him from some unknown person in New York."

We all looked at Mr. Blair, who gazed with imperturbability at Waters.

"If you had all crossed with Waters as often as I have you would know that he is subject to attacks like that. He means well, but occasionally he gives way in the deplorable manner you have just witnessed. Now all there is of it consists in this—a basket of flowers has been sent (no doubt by mistake) to our state-room. There is nothing but a card on it which says 'Room 27.' Steward," he cried, "would you go to room 27, bring that basket of flowers, and set it on this table. We may as well all have the benefit of them."

The steward soon returned with a large and lovely basket of flowers, which he set on the table, shoving the caster and other things aside to make room for it.

We all admired it very much, and the handsome young lady on my left asked Mr. Blair's permission to take one of the roses for her own. "Now, mind you," said Blair, "I cannot grant a flower from the basket, for you see it is as much the property of Waters as of myself, for all of his virtuous indignation. It was sent to the room, and he is one of the occupants. The flowers have evidently been misdirected."

The lady referred to took it upon herself to purloin the flower she wanted.

As she did so a card came in view with the words written in a masculine hand—

To Miss McMillan, With the loving regards of Edwin J—

"Miss McMillan!" cried the lady; "I wonder if she is on board? I'd give anything to know."

"We'll have a glance at the passenger list," said Waters.

Down among the M's on the long list of cabin passengers appeared the name "Miss McMillan."

"Now," said I, "it seems to me that the duty devolves on both Blair and Waters to spare no pains in delicately returning those flowers to their proper owner. I think that both have been very remiss in not doing so long ago. They should apologise publicly to the young lady for having deprived her of the offering for a day and a half, and then I think they owe an apology to this table for the mere pretence that any sane person in New York or elsewhere would go to the trouble of sending either of them a single flower."

"There will be no apology from me," said Waters. "If I do not receive the thanks of Miss McMillan, it will be because good deeds are rarely recognised in this world. I think it must be evident, even to the limited intelligence of my journalistic friend across the table, that Mr. Blair intended to keep those flowers in his state-room, and—of course I make no direct charges—the concealment of that card certainly looks bad. It may have been concealed by the sender of the flowers, but to me it looks bad."

"Of course," said Blair dryly, "to you it looks bad. To the pure, etc."

"Now," said the sentimental lady on my left, "while you gentlemen are wasting the time in useless talk the lady is without her roses. There is one thing that you all seem to miss. It is not the mere value of the bouquet. There is a subtle perfume about an offering like this more delicate than that which Nature gave the flowers—"

"Hear, hear," broke in Waters.

"I told you," said Blair aside, "the kind of fellow Waters is. He thinks

185

nothing of interrupting a lady."

"Order, both of you!" I cried, rapping on the table; "the lady from England has the floor."

"What I was going to say—"

"When Waters interrupted you."

"When Mr. Waters interrupted me I was going to say that there seems to me a romantic tinge to this incident that you old married men cannot be expected to appreciate."

I looked with surprise at Waters, while he sank back in his seat with the resigned air of a man in the hands of his enemies. We had both been carefully concealing the fact that we were married men, and the blunt announcement of the lady was a painful shock. Waters gave a side nod at Blair, as much as to say, "He's given it away." I looked reproachfully at my old friend at the head of the table, but he seemed to be absorbed in what our sentimental lady was saying.

"It is this," she continued. "Here is a young lady. Her lover sends her a basket. There may be some hidden meaning that she alone will understand in the very flowers chosen, or in the arrangement of them. The flowers, let us suppose, never reach their destination. The message is unspoken, or, rather, spoken, but unheard. The young lady grieves at the apparent neglect, and then, in her pride, resents it. She does not write, and he knows not why. The mistake may be discovered too late, and all because a basket of flowers has been missent."

"Now, Blair," said Waters, "if anything can make you do the square thing surely that appeal will."

"I shall not so far forget what is due to myself and to the dignity of this table as to reply to our erratic friend. Here is what I propose to do—first catch our hare. Steward, can you find out for me at what table and at what seat Miss McMillan is?"

While the steward was gone on his errand Mr. Blair proceeded.

"I will become acquainted with her. McMillan is a good Scotch name and Blair is another. On that as a basis I think we can speedily form an acquaintance. I shall then in a casual manner ask her if she knows a young man by the name of Edwin J., and I shall tell you what effect the mention of the name has on her."

"Now, as part owner in the flowers up to date, I protest against that. I insist that Miss McMillan be brought to this table, and that we all hear exactly what is said to her," put in Mr. Waters.

Nevertheless we agreed that Mr. Blair's proposal was a good one and the majority sanctioned it.

Meanwhile our sentimental lady had been looking among the crowd for the unconscious Miss McMillan.

"I think I have found her," she whispered to me. "Do you see that handsome girl at the captain's table. Really the handsomest girl on board."

"I thought that distinction rested with our own table."

"Now, please pay attention. Do you see how pensive she is, with her cheek resting on her hand? I am sure she is thinking of Edwin."

"I wouldn't bet on that," I replied. "There is considerable motion just now, and indications of a storm. The pensiveness may have other causes."

Here the steward returned and reported that Miss McMillan had not yet appeared at table, but had her meals taken to her room by the stewardess.

Blair called to the good-natured, portly stewardess of the Climatus, who at that moment was passing through the saloon.

"Is Miss McMillan ill?" he asked.

"No, not ill," replied Mrs. Kay; "but she seems very much depressed at leaving home, and she has not left her room since we started."

"There!" said our sentimental lady, triumphantly.

"I would like very much to see her," said Mr. Blair; "I have some good news for her."

"I will ask her to come out. It will do her good," said the stewardess, as she went away.

In a few moments she appeared, and, following her, came an old woman, with white hair, and her eyes concealed by a pair of spectacles.

"Miss McMillan," said the stewardess, "this is Mr. Blair, who wanted to speak to you."

Although Mr. Blair was, as we all were, astonished to see our mythical young lady changed into a real old woman, he did not lose his equanimity, nor did his kindly face show any surprise, but he evidently forgot the part he had intended to play.

"You will pardon me for troubling you, Miss McMillan," he said, "but this basket of flowers was evidently intended for you, and was sent to my room by mistake."

Miss McMillan did not look at the flowers, but gazed long at the card with the writing on it, and as she did so one tear and then another stole down the wrinkled face from behind the glasses.

"There is no mistake, is there?" asked Mr. Blair. "You know the writer."

"There is no mistake—no mistake," replied Miss McMillan in a low voice, "he is a very dear and kind friend." Then, as if unable to trust herself further, she took the flowers and hurriedly said, "Thank you," and left us.

"There," I said to the lady on my left, "your romance turns out to be nothing after all."

"No, sir," she cried with emphasis; "the romance is there, and very much more of a romance than if Miss McMillan was a young and silly girl of twenty."

Perhaps she was right.

FROM WHOSE BOURNE

CHAPTER I.

"My dear," said William Brenton to his wife, "do you think I shall be missed if I go upstairs for a while? I am not feeling at all well."

"Oh, I'm so sorry, Will," replied Alice, looking concerned; "I will tell them you are indisposed."

"No, don't do that," was the answer; "they are having a very good time, and I suppose the dancing will begin shortly; so I don't think they will miss me. If I feel better I will be down in an hour or two; if not, I shall go to bed. Now, dear, don't worry; but have a good time with the rest of them."

William Brenton went quietly upstairs to his room, and sat down in the darkness in a rocking chair. Remaining there a few minutes, and not feeling any better, he slowly undressed and went to bed. Faint echoes reached him of laughter and song; finally, music began, and he felt, rather than heard, the pulsation of dancing feet. Once, when the music had ceased for a time, Alice tiptoed into the room, and said in a quiet voice—

"How are you feeling, Will? any better?"

"A little," he answered drowsily. "Don't worry about me; I shall drop off to sleep presently, and shall be all right in the morning. Good night."

He still heard in a dreamy sort of way the music, the dancing, the laughter; and gradually there came oblivion, which finally merged into a dream, the most strange and vivid vision he had ever experienced. It seemed to him that he sat again in the rocking chair near the bed. Although he knew the room was dark, he had no difficulty in seeing everything perfectly. He heard, now quite plainly, the music and dancing downstairs, but what gave a ghastly significance to his dream was the sight of his own person on the bed. The eyes were half open, and the face was drawn and rigid. The colour of the face was the white, greyish tint of death.

"This is a nightmare," said Brenton to himself; "I must try and wake myself." But he seemed powerless to do this, and he sat there looking at his own body while the night wore on. Once he rose and went to the side of the bed. He seemed to have reached it merely by wishing himself there, and he passed his hand over the face, but no feeling of touch was communicated to him. He hoped his wife would come and rouse him from this fearful semblance of a dream, and, wishing this, he found himself standing at her side, amidst the throng downstairs, who were now merrily saying good-bye. Brenton tried to speak to his wife, but although he was conscious of speaking, she did not seem to hear him, or know he was there.

The party had been one given on Christmas Eve, and as it was now two o'clock in the morning, the departing guests were wishing Mrs. Brenton a merry Christmas. Finally, the door closed on the last of the revellers, and Mrs. Brenton stood for a moment giving instructions to the sleepy servants; then, with a tired sigh, she turned and went upstairs, Brenton walking by her side until they came to the darkened room, which she entered on tiptoe.

"Now," said Brenton to himself, "she will arouse me from this appalling dream." It was not that there was anything dreadful in the dream itself, but the clearness with which he saw everything, and the fact that his mind was perfectly wide awake, gave him an uneasiness which he found impossible to shake off.

In the dim light from the hall his wife prepared to retire. The horrible thought struck Brenton that she imagined he was sleeping soundly, and was anxious not to awaken him—for of course she could have no realization of the nightmare he was in—so once again he tried to communicate with her. He spoke her name over and over again, but she proceeded quietly with her preparations for the night. At last she crept in at the other side of the bed, and in a few moments was asleep. Once more Brenton struggled to awake, but with no effect. He heard the clock strike three, and then four, and then five, but there was no apparent change in his dream. He feared that he might be in a trance, from which, perhaps, he would not awake until it was too late. Grey daylight began to brighten the window, and he noticed that snow was quietly falling outside, the flakes noiselessly beating against the window pane. Every one slept late that morning, but at last he heard the preparations for breakfast going on downstairs—the light clatter of china on the table, the rattle of the grate; and, as he thought of these things, he found himself in the dining-room, and saw the trim little maid, who still yawned every now and then, laying the plates in their places. He went upstairs again, and stood watching the sleeping face of his wife. Once she raised her hand above her head, and he thought she was going to awake; ultimately her eyes opened, and she gazed for a time at the ceiling, seemingly trying to recollect the events of the day before.

"Will," she said dreamily, "are you still asleep?"

There was no answer from the rigid figure at the front of the bed. After a few moments she placed her hand quietly over the sleeper's face. As she did so, her startled eyes showed that she had received a shock. Instantly she sat upright in bed, and looked for one brief second on the face of the sleeper beside her; then, with a shriek that pierced the stillness of the room, she sprang to the floor.

"Will! Will!" she cried, "speak to me! What is the matter with you? Oh, my God! my God!" she cried, staggering back from the bed. Then, with shriek after shriek, she ran blindly through the hall to the stairway, and there fell fainting on the floor.

CHAPTER II.

William Brenton knelt beside the fallen lady, and tried to soothe and comfort her, but it was evident that she was insensible.

"It is useless," said a voice by his side.

Brenton looked up suddenly, and saw standing beside him a stranger. Wondering for a moment how he got there, and thinking that after all it was a dream, he said—

"What is useless? She is not dead."

"No," answered the stranger, "but you are."

"I am what?" cried Brenton.

"You are what the material world calls dead, although in reality you have just begun to live."

"And who are you?" asked Brenton. "And how did you get in here?"

The other smiled.

"How did you get in here?" he said, repeating Brenton's words.

"I? Why, this is my own house."

"Was, you mean."

"I mean that it is. I am in my own house. This lady is my wife."

"Was," said the other.

"I do not understand you," cried Brenton, very much annoyed. "But, in any case, your presence and your remarks are out of place here."

"My dear sir," said the other, "I merely wish to aid you and to explain to you anything that you may desire to know about your new condition. You are now free from the incumbrance of your body. You have already had some experience of the additional powers which that riddance has given you. You have also, I am afraid, had an inkling of the fact that the spiritual condition has its limitations. If you desire to communicate with those whom you have left, I would strongly advise you to postpone the attempt, and to leave this place, where you will experience only pain and anxiety. Come with me, and learn something of your changed circumstances."

"I am in a dream," said Brenton, "and you are part of it. I went to sleep last night, and am still dreaming. This is a nightmare and it will soon be over."

"You are saying that," said the other, "merely to convince yourself. It is now becoming apparent to you that this is not a dream. If dreams exist, it was a dream which you left, but you have now become awake. If you really think it is a dream, then do as I tell you—come with me and leave it, because you must admit that this part of the dream is at least very unpleasant."

"It is not very pleasant," assented Brenton. As he spoke the bewildered servants came rushing up the stairs, picked up their fallen mistress, and laid her on a sofa. They rubbed her hands and dashed water in her face. She opened her eyes, and then closed them again with a shudder.

"Sarah," she cried, "have I been dreaming, or is your master dead?"

The two girls turned pale at this, and the elder of them went boldly into the room which her mistress had just left. She was evidently a young woman who had herself under good control, but she came out sobbing, with her apron to her eyes.

"Come, come," said the man who stood beside Brenton, "haven't you had enough of this? Come with me; you can return to this house if you wish;" and together they passed out of the room into the crisp air of Christmas morning. But, although Brenton knew it must be cold, he had no feeling of either cold or warmth.

"There are a number of us," said the stranger to Brenton, "who take turns at watching the sick-bed when a man is about to die, and when his spirit leaves his body, we are there to explain, or comfort, or console. Your death was so sudden that we had no warning of it. You did not feel ill before last night, did you?"

"No," replied Brenton. "I felt perfectly well, until after dinner last night."

"Did you leave your affairs in reasonably good order?"

"Yes," said Brenton, trying to recollect. "I think they will find everything perfectly straight."

"Tell me a little of your history, if you do not mind," inquired the other; "it will help me in trying to initiate you into our new order of things here."

"Well," replied Brenton, and he wondered at himself for falling so easily into the other's assumption that he was a dead man, "I was what they call on the earth in reasonably good circumstances. My estate should be worth $100,000. I had $75,000 insurance on my life, and if all that is paid, it should net my widow not far from a couple of hundred thousand."

"How long have you been married?" said the other.

"Only about six months. I was married last July, and we went for a trip abroad. We were married quietly, and left almost immediately afterwards, so we thought, on our return, it would not be a bad plan to give a Christmas Eve dinner, and invite some of our friends. That," he said, hesitating a moment, "was last night. Shortly after dinner, I began to feel rather ill, and went upstairs to rest for a while; and if what you say is true, the first thing I knew I found myself dead."

"Alive," corrected the other.

"Well, alive, though at present I feel I belong more to the world I have left than I do to the world I appear to be in. I must confess, although you are a very plausible gentleman to talk to, that I expect at any moment to wake and find this to have been one of the most horrible nightmares that I ever had the ill luck to encounter."

The other smiled.

"There is very little danger of your waking up, as you call it. Now, I will tell you the great trouble we have with people when they first come to the spirit-land, and that is to induce them to forget entirely the world they have relinquished. Men whose families are in poor circumstances, or men whose affairs are in a disordered state, find it very difficult to keep from trying to set things right again. They have the feeling that they can console or comfort those whom they have left behind them, and it is often a long time before they are convinced that their efforts are entirely futile, as well as very distressing for themselves."

"Is there, then," asked Brenton, "no communication between this world and the one that I have given up?"

The other paused for a moment before he replied.

"I should hardly like to say," he answered, "that there is no communication between one world and the other; but the communication that exists is so slight and unsatisfactory, that if you are sensible you will see things with the eyes of those who have very much more experience in this world than you have. Of course, you can go back there as much as you like; there will be no interference and no hindrance. But when you see things going wrong, when you see a mistake about to be made, it is an appalling thing to stand there helpless, unable to influence those you love, or to point out a palpable error, and convince them that your clearer sight sees it as such. Of course, I understand that it must be very difficult for a man who is newly married, to entirely abandon the one who has loved him, and whom he loves. But I assure you that if you follow the life of one who is as young and handsome as your wife, you will find some one else supplying the consolations you are unable to bestow. Such a mission may lead you to a church where she is married to her second husband. I regret to say that even the most imperturbable spirits are ruffled when such an incident occurs. The wise men are those who appreciate and understand that they are in an entirely new world, with new powers and new limitations, and who govern themselves accordingly from the first, as they will certainly do later on."

"My dear sir," said Brenton, somewhat offended, "if what you say is true, and I am really a dead man——"

"Alive," corrected the other.

"Well, alive, then. I may tell you that my wife's heart is broken. She will never marry again."

"Of course, that is a subject of which you know a great deal more than I do. I all the more strongly advise you never to see her again. It is impossible for you to offer any consolation, and the sight of her grief and misery will only result in unhappiness for yourself. Therefore, take my advice. I have given it very often, and I assure you those who did not take it expressed their regret afterwards. Hold entirely aloof from anything relating to your former life."

Brenton was silent for some moments; finally he said—

"I presume your advice is well meant; but if things are as you state, then I may as well say, first as last, that I do not intend to accept it."

"Very well," said the other; "it is an experience that many prefer to go through for themselves."

"Do you have names in this spirit-land?" asked Brenton, seemingly desirous of changing the subject.

"Yes," was the answer; "we are known by names that we have used in the preparatory school below. My name is Ferris."

"And if I wish to find you here, how do I set about it?"

"The wish is sufficient," answered Ferris. "Merely wish to be with me, and you are with me."

"Good gracious!" cried Brenton, "is locomotion so easy as that?"

"Locomotion is very easy. I do not think anything could be easier than it is, and I do not think there could be any improvement in that matter."

"Are there matters here, then, that you think could be improved?"

"As to that I shall not say. Perhaps you will be able to give your own opinion before you have lived here much longer."

"Taking it all in all," said Brenton, "do you think the spirit-land is to be preferred to the one we have left?"

"I like it better," said Ferris, "although I presume there are some who do not. There are many advantages; and then, again, there are many—well, I would not say disadvantages, but still some people consider them such. We are free from the pangs of hunger or cold, and have therefore no need of money, and there is no necessity for the rush and the worry of the world below."

"And how about heaven and hell?" said Brenton. "Are those localities all a myth? Is there nothing of punishment and nothing of reward in this spirit-land?"

There was no answer to this, and when Brenton looked around he found that his companion had departed.

CHAPTER III.

William Brenton pondered long on the situation. He would have known
better how to act if he could have been perfectly certain that he was not still
the victim of a dream. However, of one thing there was no doubt—namely,
that it was particularly harrowing to see what he had seen in his own house.
If it were true that he was dead, he said to himself, was not the plan outlined
for him by Ferris very much the wiser course to adopt? He stood now in
one of the streets of the city so familiar to him. People passed and repassed
him—men and women whom he had known in life—but nobody appeared
to see him. He resolved, if possible, to solve the problem uppermost in his
mind, and learn whether or not he could communicate with an inhabitant of
the world he had left. He paused for a moment to consider the best method
of doing this. Then he remembered one of his most confidential friends and
advisers, and at once wished himself at his office. He found the office closed,
but went in to wait for his friend. Occupying the time in thinking over his
strange situation, he waited long, and only when the bells began to ring did
he remember it was Christmas forenoon, and that his friend would not be at
the office that day. The next moment he wished himself at his friend's house,
but he was as unsuccessful as at the office; the friend was not at home. The
household, however, was in great commotion, and, listening to what was said,
he found that the subject of conversation was his own death, and he learned
that his friend had gone to the Brenton residence as soon as he heard the
startling news of Christmas morning.

Once more Brenton paused, and did not know what to do. He went
again into the street. Everything seemed to lead him toward his own home.
Although he had told Ferris that he did not intend to take his advice, yet as a
sensible man he saw that the admonition was well worth considering, and if
he could once become convinced that there was no communication possible
between himself and those he had left; if he could give them no comfort and
no cheer; if he could see the things which they did not see, and yet be unable
to give them warning, he realized that he would merely be adding to his own

misery, without alleviating the troubles of others.

He wished he knew where to find Ferris, so that he might have another talk with him. The man impressed him as being exceedingly sensible. No sooner, however, had he wished for the company of Mr. Ferris than he found himself beside that gentleman.

"By George!" he said in astonishment, "you are just the man I wanted to see."

"Exactly," said Ferris; "that is the reason you do see me."

"I have been thinking over what you said," continued the other, "and it strikes me that after all your advice is sensible."

"Thank you," replied Ferris, with something like a smile on his face.

"But there is one thing I want to be perfectly certain about. I want to know whether it is not possible for me to communicate with my friends. Nothing will settle that doubt in my mind except actual experience."

"And have you not had experience enough?" asked Ferris.

"Well," replied the other, hesitating, "I have had some experience, but it seems to me that, if I encounter an old friend, I could somehow make myself felt by him."

"In that case," answered Ferris, "if nothing will convince you but an actual experiment, why don't you go to some of your old friends and try what you can do with them?"

"I have just been to the office and to the residence of one of my old friends. I found at his residence that he had gone to my"—Brenton paused for a moment—"former home. Everything seems to lead me there, and yet, if I take your advice, I must avoid that place of all others."

"I would at present, if I were you," said Ferris. "Still, why not try it with any of the passers-by?"

Brenton looked around him. People were passing and repassing where the two stood talking with each other. "Merry Christmas" was the word on all lips. Finally Brenton said, with a look of uncertainty on his face—

"My dear fellow, I can't talk to any of these people. I don't know them."

Ferris laughed at this, and replied—

"I don't think you will shock them very much; just try it."

"Ah, here's a friend of mine. You wait a moment, and I will accost him." Approaching him, Brenton held out his hand and spoke, but the traveller paid no attention. He passed by as one who had seen or heard nothing.

"I assure you," said Ferris, as he noticed the look of disappointment on the other's face, "you will meet with a similar experience, however much you try. You know the old saying about one not being able to have his cake and eat it too. You can't have the privileges of this world and those of the world you left as well. I think, taking it all in all, you should rest content, although it always hurts those who have left the other world not to be able to communicate with their friends, and at least assure them of their present welfare."

"It does seem to me," replied Brenton, "that would be a great consolation, both for those who are here and those who are left."

"Well, I don't know about that," answered the other. "After all, what does life in the other world amount to? It is merely a preparation for this. It is of so short a space, as compared with the life we live here, that it is hardly worth while to interfere with it one way or another. By the time you are as long here as I have been, you will realize the truth of this."

"Perhaps I shall," said Brenton, with a sigh; "but, meanwhile, what am I to do with myself? I feel like the man who has been all his life in active business, and who suddenly resolves to enjoy himself doing nothing. That sort of thing seems to kill a great number of men, especially if they put off taking a rest until too late, as most of us do."

"Well," said Ferris, "there is no necessity of your being idle here, I assure you. But before you lay out any work for yourself, let me ask you if there is not some interesting part of the world that you would like to visit?"

"Certainly; I have seen very little of the world. That is one of my regrets at leaving it."

"Bless me," said the other, "you haven't left it."

"Why, I thought you said I was a dead man?"

"On the contrary," replied his companion, "I have several times insisted that you have just begun to live. Now where shall we spend the day?"

"How would London do?"

"I don't think it would do; London is apt to be a little gloomy at this time of the year. But what do you say to Naples, or Japan, or, if you don't wish to go out of the United States, Yellowstone Park?"

"Can we reach any of those places before the day is over?" asked Brenton, dubiously.

"Well, I will soon show you how we manage all that. Just wish to accompany me, and I will take you the rest of the way."

"How would Venice do?" said Brenton. "I didn't see half as much of that city as I wanted to."

"Very well," replied his companion, "Venice it is;" and the American city in which they stood faded away from them, and before Brenton could make up his mind exactly what was happening, he found himself walking with his comrade in St. Mark's Square.

"Well, for rapid transit," said Brenton, "this beats anything I've ever had any idea of; but it increases the feeling that I am in a dream."

"You'll soon get used to it," answered Ferris; "and, when you do, the cumbersome methods of travel in the world itself will show themselves in their right light. Hello!" he cried, "here's a man whom I should like you to meet. By the way, I either don't know your name or I have forgotten it."

"William Brenton," answered the other.

"Mr. Speed, I want to introduce you to Mr. Brenton."

"Ah," said Speed, cordially, "a new-comer. One of your victims, Ferris?"

"Say one of his pupils, rather," answered Brenton.

"Well, it is pretty much the same thing," said Speed. "How long have you been with us, and how do you like the country?"

"You see, Mr. Brenton," interrupted Ferris, "John Speed was a newspaper man, and he must ask strangers how they like the country. He has inquired so often while interviewing foreigners for his paper that now he cannot abandon his old phrase. Mr. Brenton has been with us but a short time," continued Ferris, "and so you know, Speed, you can hardly expect him to answer your inevitable question."

"What part of the country are you from?" asked Speed.

"Cincinnati," answered Brenton, feeling almost as if he were an American tourist doing the continent of Europe.

"Cincinnati, eh? Well, I congratulate you. I do not know any place in America that I would sooner die in, as they call it, than Cincinnati. You see, I am a Chicago man myself."

Brenton did not like the jocular familiarity of the newspaper man, and found himself rather astonished to learn that in the spirit-world there were likes and dislikes, just as on earth.

"Chicago is a very enterprising city," he said, in a non-committal way.

"Chicago, my dear sir," said Speed, earnestly, "is the city. You will see that Chicago is going to be the great city of the world before you are a hundred years older. By the way, Ferris," said the Chicago man, suddenly recollecting something, "I have got Sommers over here with me."

"Ah!" said Ferris; "doing him any good?"

"Well, precious little, as far as I can see."

"Perhaps it would interest Mr. Brenton to meet him," said Ferris. "I think, Brenton, you asked me a while ago if there was any hell here, or any punishment. Mr. Speed can show you a man in hell."

"Really?" asked Brenton.

"Yes," said Speed; "I think if ever a man was in misery, he is. The trouble with Sommers was this. He—well, he died of delirium tremens, and so, of course, you know what the matter was. Sommers had drunk Chicago whisky for thirty-five years straight along, and never added to it the additional horror of Chicago water. You see what his condition became, both physical and mental. Many people tried to reform Sommers, because he was really a brilliant man; but it was no use. Thirst had become a disease with him, and from the mental part of that disease, although his physical yearning is now gone of course, he suffers. Sommers would give his whole future for one glass of good old Kentucky whisky. He sees it on the counters, he sees men drink it, and he stands beside them in agony. That's why I brought him over here. I thought that he wouldn't see the colour of whisky as it sparkles in the glass; but now he is in the Café Quadra watching men drink. You may see him sitting there with all the agony of unsatisfied desire gleaming from his face."

"And what do you do with a man like that?" asked Brenton.

"Do? Well, to tell the truth, there is nothing to do. I took him away from Chicago, hoping to ease his trouble a little; but it has had no effect."

"It will come out all right by-and-by," said Ferris, who noticed the pained look on Brenton's face. "It is the period of probation that he has to pass through. It will wear off. He merely goes through the agonies he would have suffered on earth if he had suddenly been deprived of his favourite intoxicant."

"Well," said Speed, "you won't come with me, then? All right, good-bye. I hope to see you again, Mr. Brenton," and with that they separated.

Brenton spent two or three days in Venice, but all the time the old home hunger was upon him. He yearned for news of Cincinnati. He wanted to be back, and several times the wish brought him there, but he instantly returned. At last he said to Ferris—

"I am tired. I must go home. I have got to see how things are going."

"I wouldn't if I were you," replied Ferris.

"No, I know you wouldn't. Your temperament is indifferent. I would rather be miserable with knowledge than happy in ignorance. Good-bye."

It was evening when he found himself in Cincinnati. The weather was bright and clear, and apparently cold. Men's feet crisped on the frozen pavement, and the streets had that welcome, familiar look which they always have to the returned traveller when he reaches the city he calls his home. The newsboys were rushing through the streets yelling their papers at the top of their voices. He heard them, but paid little attention.

"All about the murder! Latest edition! All about the poison case!"

He felt that he must have a glimpse at a paper, and, entering the office of an hotel where a man was reading one, he glanced over his shoulder at the page before him, and was horror-stricken to see the words in startling headlines—

THE BRENTON MURDER.

The Autopsy shows that Morphine was the Poison used.

Enough found to have killed a Dozen Men.

Mrs. Brenton arrested for Committing the Horrible

Deed.

CHAPTER IV.

For a moment Brenton was so bewildered and amazed at the awful headlines which he read, that he could hardly realize what had taken place. The fact that he had been poisoned, although it gave him a strange sensation, did not claim his attention as much as might have been thought. Curiously enough he was more shocked at finding himself, as it were, the talk of the town, the central figure of a great newspaper sensation. But the thing that horrified him was the fact that his wife had been arrested for his murder. His first impulse was to go to her at once, but he next thought it better to read what the paper said about the matter, so as to become possessed of all the facts. The headlines, he said to himself, often exaggerated things, and there was a possibility that the body of the article would not bear out the naming announcement above it. But as he read on and on, the situation seemed to become more and more appalling. He saw that his friends had been suspicious of his sudden death, and had insisted on a post-mortem examination. That examination had been conducted by three of the most eminent physicians of Cincinnati, and the three doctors had practically agreed that the deceased, in the language of the verdict, had come to his death through morphia poisoning, and the coroner's jury had brought in a verdict that "the said William Brenton had been poisoned by some person unknown." Then the article went on to state how suspicion had gradually fastened itself upon his wife, and at last her arrest had been ordered. The arrest had taken place that day.

After reading this, Brenton was in an agony of mind. He pictured his dainty and beautiful wife in a stone cell in the city prison. He foresaw the horrors of the public trial, and the deep grief and pain which the newspaper comments on the case would cause to a woman educated and refined. Of course, Brenton had not the slightest doubt in his own mind about the result of the trial. His wife would be triumphantly acquitted; but, all the same, the terrible suspense which she must suffer in the meanwhile would not be compensated for by the final verdict of the jury.

Brenton at once went to the jail, and wandered through that gloomy building, searching for his wife. At last he found her, but it was in a very comfortable room in the sheriffs residence. The terror and the trials of the last few days had aged her perceptibly, and it cut Brenton to the heart to think that he stood there before her, and could not by any means say a soothing word that she would understand. That she had wept many bitter tears since the terrible Christmas morning was evident; there were dark circles under her beautiful eyes that told of sleepless nights. She sat in a comfortable armchair, facing the window; and looked steadily out at the dreary winter scene with eyes that apparently saw nothing. Her hands lay idly on her lap, and now and then she caught her breath in a way that was half a sob and half a gasp.

Presently the sheriff himself entered the room.

"Mrs. Brenton," he said, "there is a gentleman here who wishes to see you. Mr. Roland, he tells me his name is, an old friend of yours. Do you care to see any one?"

The lady turned her head slowly round, and looked at the sheriff for a moment, seemingly not understanding what he said. Finally she answered, dreamily—

"Roland? Oh, Stephen! Yes, I shall be very glad to see him. Ask him to come in, please."

The next moment Stephen Roland entered, and somehow the fact that he had come to console Mrs. Brenton did not at all please the invisible man who stood between them.

"My dear Mrs. Brenton," began Roland, "I hope you are feeling better to-day? Keep up your courage, and be brave. It is only for a very short time. I have retained the noted criminal lawyers, Benham and Brown, for the defence. You could not possibly have better men."

At the word "criminal" Mrs. Brenton shuddered.

"Alice," continued Roland, sitting down near her, and drawing his chair closer to her, "tell me that you will not lose your courage. I want you to be brave, for the sake of your friends."

210

He took her listless hand in his own, and she did not withdraw it.

Brenton felt passing over him the pangs of impotent rage, as he saw this act on the part of Roland.

Roland had been an unsuccessful suitor for the hand which he now held in his own, and Brenton thought it the worst possible taste, to say the least, that he should take advantage now of her terrible situation to ingratiate himself into her favour.

The nearest approach to a quarrel that Brenton and his wife had had during their short six months of wedded life was on the subject of the man who now held her hand in his own. It made Brenton impatient to think that a woman with all her boasted insight into character, her instincts as to what was right and what was wrong, had such little real intuition that she did not see into the character of the man whom they were discussing; but a woman never thinks it a crime for a man to have been in love with her, whatever opinion of that man her husband may hold.

"It is awful! awful! awful!" murmured the poor lady, as the tears again rose to her eyes.

"Of course it is," said Roland; "it is particularly awful that they should accuse you, of all persons in the world, of this so-called crime. For my part I do not believe that he was poisoned at all, but we will soon straighten things out. Benham and Brown will give up everything and devote their whole attention to this case until it is finished. Everything will be done that money or friends can do, and all that we ask is that you keep up your courage, and do not be downcast with the seeming awfulness of the situation."

Mrs. Brenton wept silently, but made no reply. It was evident, however, that she was consoled by the words and the presence of her visitor. Strange as it may appear, this fact enraged Brenton, although he had gone there for the very purpose of cheering and comforting his wife. All the bitterness he had felt before against his former rival was revived, and his rage was the more agonizing because it was inarticulate. Then there flashed over him Ferris's sinister advice to leave things alone in the world that he had left. He felt that he could stand this no longer, and the next instant he found himself again in the wintry streets of Cincinnati.

The name of the lawyers, Benham and Brown, kept repeating itself in his mind, and he resolved to go to their office and hear, if he could, what preparations were being made for the defence of a woman whom he knew to be innocent. He found, when he got to the office of these noted lawyers, that the two principals were locked in their private room; and going there, he found them discussing the case with the coolness and impersonal feeling that noted lawyers have even when speaking of issues that involve life or death.

"Yes," Benham was saying, "I think that, unless anything new turns up, that is the best line of defence we can adopt."

"What do you think might turn up?" asked Brown.

"Well, you can never tell in these cases. They may find something else—they may find the poison, for instance, or the package that contained it. Perhaps a druggist will remember having sold it to this woman, and then, of course, we shall have to change our plans. I need not say that it is strictly necessary in this case to give out no opinions whatever to newspaper men. The papers will be full of rumours, and it is just as well if we can keep our line of defence hidden until the time for action comes."

"Still," said Brown, who was the younger partner, "it is as well to keep in with the newspaper fellows; they'll be here as soon as they find we have taken charge of the defence."

"Well, I have no doubt you can deal with them in such a way as to give them something to write up, and yet not disclose anything we do not wish known."

"I think you can trust me to do that," said Brown, with a self-satisfied air.

"I shall leave that part of the matter entirely in your hands," replied Benham. "It is better not to duplicate or mix matters, and if any newspaper man comes to see me I will refer him to you. I will say I know nothing of the case whatever."

"Very well," answered Brown. "Now, between ourselves, what do you think of the case?"

"Oh, it will make a great sensation. I think it will probably be one of the most talked-of cases that we have ever been connected with."

"Yes, but what do you think of her guilt or innocence?"

"As to that," said Benham, calmly, "I haven't the slightest doubt. She murdered him."

As he said this, Brenton, forgetting himself for a moment, sprang forward as if to strangle the lawyer. The statement Benham had made seemed the most appalling piece of treachery. That men should take a woman's money for defending her, and actually engage in a case when they believed their client guilty, appeared to Brenton simply infamous.

"I agree with you," said Brown. "Of course she was the only one to benefit by his death. The simple fool willed everything to her, and she knew it; and his doing so is the more astounding when you remember he was quite well aware that she had a former lover whom she would gladly have married if he had been as rich as Brenton. The supreme idiocy of some men as far as their wives are concerned is something awful."

"Yes," answered Benham, "it is. But I tell you, Brown, she is no ordinary woman. The very conception of that murder had a stroke of originality about it that I very much admire. I do not remember anything like it in the annals of crime. It is the true way in which a murder should be committed. The very publicity of the occasion was a safeguard. Think of poisoning a man at a dinner that he has given himself, in the midst of a score of friends. I tell you that there was a dash of bravery about it that commands my admiration."

"Do you imagine Roland had anything to do with it?"

"Well, I had my doubts about that at first, but I think he is innocent, although from what I know of the man he will not hesitate to share the proceeds of the crime. You mark my words, they will be married within a year from now if she is acquitted. I believe Roland knows her to be guilty."

"I thought as much," said Brown, "by his actions here, and by some remarks he let drop. Anyhow, our credit in the affair will be all the greater if we succeed in getting her off. Yes," he continued, rising and pushing back his chair, "Madam Brenton is a murderess."

CHAPTER V.

Brenton found himself once more in the streets of Cincinnati, in a state of mind that can hardly be described. Rage and grief struggled for the mastery, and added to the tumult of these passions was the uncertainty as to what he should do, or what he could do. He could hardly ask the advice of Ferris again, for his whole trouble arose from his neglect of the counsel that gentleman had already given him. In his new sphere he did not know where to turn. He found himself wondering whether in the spirit-land there was any firm of lawyers who could advise him, and he remembered then how singularly ignorant he was regarding the conditions of existence in the world to which he now belonged. However, he felt that he must consult with somebody, and Ferris was the only one to whom he could turn. A moment later he was face to face with him.

"Mr. Ferris," he said, "I am in the most grievous trouble, and I come to you in the hope that, if you cannot help me, you can at least advise me what to do."

"If your trouble has come," answered Ferris, with a shade of irony in his voice, "through following the advice that I have already given you, I shall endeavour, as well as I am able, to help you out of it."

"You know very well," cried Brenton, hotly, "that my whole trouble has occurred through neglecting your advice, or, at least, through deliberately not following it. I could not follow it."

"Very well, then," said Ferris, "I am not surprised that you are in a difficulty. You must remember that such a crisis is an old story with us here."

"But, my dear sir," said Brenton, "look at the appalling condition of things, the knowledge of which has just come to me. It seems I was poisoned, but of course that doesn't matter. I feel no resentment against the wretch who did it. But the terrible thing is that my wife has been arrested for the crime, and I have just learned that her own lawyers actually believe her guilty."

"That fact," said Ferris, calmly, "will not interfere with their eloquent pleading when the case comes to trial."

Brenton glared at the man who was taking things so coolly, and who proved himself so unsympathetic; but an instant after he realized the futility of quarrelling with the only person who could give him advice, so he continued, with what patience he could command—

"The situation is this: My wife has been arrested for the crime of murdering me. She is now in the custody of the sheriff. Her trouble and anxiety of mind are fearful to contemplate."

"My dear sir," said Ferris, "there is no reason why you or anybody else should contemplate it."

"How can you talk in that cold-blooded way?" cried Brenton, indignantly. "Could you see your wife, or any one you held dear, incarcerated for a dreadful crime, and yet remain calm and collected, as you now appear to be when you hear of another's misfortune?"

"My dear fellow," said Ferris, "of course it is not to be expected that one who has had so little experience with this existence should have any sense of proportion. You appear to be speaking quite seriously. You do not seem at all to comprehend the utter triviality of all this."

"Good gracious!" cried Brenton, "do you call it a trivial thing that a woman is in danger of her life for a crime which she never committed?"

"If she is innocent," said the other, in no way moved by the indignation of his comrade, "surely that state of things will be brought out in the courts, and no great harm will be done, even looking at things from the standpoint of the world you have left. But I want you to get into the habit of looking at things from the standpoint of this world, and not of the other. Suppose that what you would call the worst should happen—suppose she is hanged—what then?"

Brenton stood simply speechless with indignation at this brutal remark.

"If you will just look at things correctly," continued Ferris, imperturbably, "you will see that there is probably a moment of anguish, perhaps not even that moment, and then your wife is here with you in the land of spirits. I am sure that is a consummation devoutly to be wished. Even a man in your state of mind must see the reasonableness of this. Now, looking at the question in what you would call its most serious aspect, see how little it amounts to. It isn't worth a moment's thought, whichever way it goes."

"You think nothing, then, of the disgrace of such a death—of the bitter injustice of it?"

"When you were in the world did you ever see a child cry over a broken toy? Did the sight pain you to any extent? Did you not know that a new toy could be purchased that would quite obliterate all thoughts of the other? Did the simple griefs of childhood carry any deep and lasting consternation to the mind of a grown-up man? Of course it did not. You are sensible enough to know that. Well, we here in this world look on the pain and struggles and trials of people in the world you have left, just as an aged man looks on the tribulations of children over a broken doll. That is all it really amounts to. That is what I mean when I say that you have not yet got your sense of proportion. Any grief and misery there is in the world you have left is of such an ephemeral, transient nature, that when we think for a moment of the free, untrammelled, and painless life there is beyond, those petty troubles sink into insignificance. My dear fellow, be sensible, take my advice. I have really a strong interest in you, and I advise you, entirely for your own welfare, to forget all about it. Very soon you will have something much more important to do than lingering around the world you have left. If your wife comes amongst us I am sure you will be glad to welcome her, and to teach her the things that you will have already found out of your new life. If she does not appear, then you will know that, even from the old-world standpoint, things have gone what you would call 'all right.' Let these trivial matters go, and attend to the vastly more important concerns that will soon engage your attention here."

Ferris talked earnestly, and it was evident, even to Brenton, that he meant what he said. It was hard to find a pretext for a quarrel with a man at once so calm and so perfectly sure of himself.

"We will not talk any more about it," said Brenton. "I presume people here agree to differ, just as they did in the world we have both left."

"Certainly, certainly," answered Ferris. "Of course, you have just heard my opinion; but you will find myriads of others who do not share it with me. You will meet a great many who are interested in the subject of communication with the world they have left. You will, of course, excuse me when I say that I consider such endeavours not worth talking about."

"Do you know any one who is interested in that sort of thing? and can you give me an introduction to him?"

"Oh! for that matter," said Ferris, "you have had an introduction to one of the most enthusiastic investigators of the subject. I refer to Mr. John Speed, late of Chicago."

"Ah!" said Brenton, rather dubiously. "I must confess that I was not very favourably impressed with Mr. Speed. Probably I did him an injustice."

"You certainly did," said Ferris. "You will find Speed a man well worth knowing, even if he does waste himself on such futile projects as a scheme for communicating with a community so evanescent as that of Chicago. You will like Speed better the more you know him. He really is very philanthropic, and has Sommers on his hands just now. From what he said after you left Venice, I imagine he does not entertain the same feeling toward you as you do toward him. I would see Speed if I were you."

"I will think about it," said Brenton, as they separated.

To know that a man thinks well of a person is no detriment to further acquaintance with that man, even if the first impressions have not been favourable; and after Ferris told Brenton that Speed had thought well of him, Brenton found less difficulty in seeking the Chicago enthusiast.

"I have been in a good deal of trouble," Brenton said to Speed, "and have been talking to Ferris about it. I regret to say that he gave me very little encouragement, and did not seem at all to appreciate my feelings in the matter."

"Oh, you mustn't mind Ferris," said Speed. "He is a first-rate fellow, but he is as cold and unsympathetic as—well, suppose we say as an oyster. His great hobby is non-intercourse with the world we have left. Now, in that I don't agree with him, and there are thousands who don't agree with him. I admit that there are cases where a man is more unhappy if he frequents the old world than he would be if he left it alone. But then there are other cases where just the reverse is true. Take my own experience, for example; I take a peculiar pleasure in rambling around Chicago. I admit that it is a grievance to me, as an old newspaper man, to see the number of scoops I could have on my esteemed contemporaries, but—"

"Scoop? What is that?" asked Brenton, mystified.

"Why, a scoop is a beat, you know."

"Yes, but I don't know. What is a beat?"

"A beat or a scoop, my dear fellow, is the getting of a piece of news that your contemporary does not obtain. You never were in the newspaper business? Well, sir, you missed it. Greatest business in the world. You know everything that is going on long before anybody else does, and the way you can reward your friends and jump with both feet on your enemies is one of the delights of existence down there."

"Well, what I wanted to ask you was this," said Brenton. "You have made a speciality of finding out whether there could be any communication between one of us, for instance, and one who is an inhabitant of the other world. Is such communication possible?"

"I have certainly devoted some time to it, but I can't say that my success has been flattering. My efforts have been mostly in the line of news. I have come on some startling information which my facilities here gave me access to, and I confess I have tried my best to put some of the boys on to it. But there is a link loose somewhere. Now, what is your trouble? Do you want to get a message to anybody?"

"My trouble is this," said Brenton, briefly, "I am here because a few days ago I was poisoned."

"George Washington!" cried the other, "you don't say so! Have the newspapers got on to the fact?"

"I regret to say that they have."

"What an item that would have been if one paper had got hold of it and the others hadn't! I suppose they all got on to it at the same time?"

"About that," said Brenton, "I don't know, and I must confess that I do not care very much. But here is the trouble—my wife has been arrested for my murder, and she is as innocent as I am."

"Sure of that?"

"Sure of it?" cried the other indignantly. "Of course I am sure of it."

"Then who is the guilty person?"

"Ah, that," said Brenton, "I do not yet know."

"Then how can you be sure she is not guilty?"

"If you talk like that," exclaimed Brenton, "I have nothing more to say."

"Now, don't get offended, I beg of you. I am merely looking at this from a newspaper standpoint, you know. You must remember it is not you who will decide the matter, but a jury of your very stupid fellow-countrymen. Now, you can never tell what a jury will do, except that it will do something idiotic. Therefore, it seems to me that the very first step to be taken is to find out who the guilty party is. Don't you see the force of that?"

"Yes, I do."

"Very well, then. Now, what were the circumstances of this crime? who was to profit by your death?"

Brenton winced at this.

"I see how it is," said the other, "and I understand why you don't answer. Now—you'll excuse me if I am frank—your wife was the one who benefited most by your death, was she not?"

"No," cried the other indignantly, "she was not the one. That is what the lawyers said. Why in the world should she want to poison me, when she had all my wealth at her command as it was?"

"Yes, that's a strong point," said Speed. "You were a reasonably good husband, I suppose? Rather generous with the cash?"

"Generous?" cried the other. "My wife always had everything she wanted."

"Ah, well, there was no—you'll excuse me, I am sure—no former lover in the case, was there?"

Again Brenton winced, and he thought of Roland sitting beside his wife with her hand in his.

"I see," said Speed; "you needn't answer. Now what were the circumstances, again?"

"They were these: At a dinner which I gave, where some twenty or twenty-five of my friends were assembled, poison, it appears, was put into my cup of coffee. That is all I know of it."

"Who poured out that cup of coffee?"

"My wife did."

"Ah! Now, I don't for a moment say she is guilty, remember; but you must admit that, to a stupid jury, the case might look rather bad against her."

"Well, granted that it does, there is all the more need that I should come to her assistance if possible."

"Certainly, certainly!" said Speed. "Now, I'll tell you what we have to do. We must get, if possible, one of the very brightest Chicago reporters on the track of this thing, and we have to get him on the track of it early. Come with me to Chicago. We will try an experiment, and I am sure you will lend your mind entirely to the effort. We must act in conjunction in this affair, and you are just the man I've been wanting, some one who is earnest and who has something at stake in the matter. We may fail entirely, but I think it's worth the trying. Will you come?"

"Certainly," said Brenton; "and I cannot tell you how much I appreciate your interest and sympathy."

Arriving at a brown stone building on the corner of two of the principal streets in Chicago, Brenton and Speed ascended quickly to one of the top floors. It was nearly midnight, and two upper stories of the huge dark building were brilliantly lighted, as was shown on the outside by the long rows of glittering windows. They entered a room where a man was seated at a table, with coat and vest thrown off, and his hat set well back on his head. Cold as it was outside, it was warm in this man's room, and the room was blue with smoke. A black corn-cob pipe was in his teeth, and the man was writing away as if for dear life, on sheets of coarse white copy paper, stopping now and then to fill up his pipe or to relight it after it had gone out.

"There," said Speed, waving his hand towards the writer with a certain air of proprietory pride, "there sits one of the very cleverest men on the Chicago press. That fellow, sir, is gifted with a nose for news which has no equal in America. He will ferret out a case that he once starts on with an unerringness that would charm you. Yes, sir, I got him his present situation on this paper, and I can tell you it was a good one."

"He must have been a warm friend of yours?" said Brenton, indifferently, as if he did not take much interest in the eulogy.

"Quite the contrary," said Speed. "He was a warm enemy, made it mighty warm for me sometimes. He was on an opposition paper, but I tell you, although I was no chicken in newspaper business, that man would scoop the daylight out of me any time he tried. So, to get rid of opposition, I got the managing editor to appoint him to a place on our paper; and I tell you, he has never regretted it. Yes, sir, there sits George Stratton, a man who knows his business. Now," he said, "let us concentrate our attention on him. First let us see whether, by putting our whole minds to it, we can make any impression on his mind whatever. You see how busily he is engaged. He is thoroughly absorbed in his work. That is George all over. Whatever his assignment is, George throws himself right into it, and thinks of nothing else until it is finished. Now then."

In that dingy, well-lighted room George Stratton sat busily pencilling out the lines that were to appear in next morning's paper. He was evidently very much engrossed in his task, as Speed had said. If he had looked about him, which he did not, he would have said that he was entirely alone. All at once his attention seemed to waver, and he passed his hand over his brow, while perplexity came into his face. Then he noticed that his pipe was out, and, knocking the ashes from it by rapping the bowl on the side of the table, he filled it with an absent-mindedness unusual with him. Again he turned to his writing, and again he passed his hand over his brow. Suddenly, without any apparent cause, he looked first to the right and then to the left of him. Once more he tried to write, but, noticing his pipe was out, he struck another match and nervously puffed away, until clouds of blue smoke rose around him. There was a look of annoyance and perplexity in his face as he bent resolutely to his writing. The door opened, and a man appeared on the threshold.

"Anything more about the convention, George?" he said.

"Yes; I am just finishing this. Sort of pen pictures, you know."

"Perhaps you can let me have what you have done. I'll fix it up."

"All right," said Stratton, bunching up the manuscript in front of him, and handing it to the city editor.

That functionary looked at the number of pages, and then at the writer.

"Much more of this, George?" he said. "We'll be a little short of room in the morning, you know."

"Well," said the other, sitting back in his chair, "it is pretty good stuff that. Folks always like the pen pictures of men engaged in the skirmish better than the reports of what most of them say."

"Yes," said the city editor, "that's so."

"Still," said Stratton, "we could cut it off at the last page. Just let me see the last two pages, will you?"

These were handed to him, and, running his eye through them, he drew

223

his knife across one of the pages, and put at the bottom the cabalistic mark which indicated the end of the copy.

"There! I think I will let it go at that. Old Rickenbeck don't amount to much, anyhow. We'll let him go."

"All right," said the city editor. "I think we won't want anything more to-night."

Stratton put his hands behind his head, with his fingers interlaced, and leaned back in his chair, placing his heels upon the table before him. A thought-reader, looking at his face, could almost have followed the theme that occupied his mind. Suddenly bringing his feet down with a crash to the floor, he rose and went into the city editor's room.

"See here," he said. "Have you looked into that Cincinnati case at all?"

"What Cincinnati case?" asked the local editor, looking up.

"Why, that woman who is up for poisoning her husband."

"Oh yes; we had something of it in the despatches this morning. It's rather out of the local line, you know."

"Yes, I know it is. But it isn't out of the paper's line. I tell you that case is going to make a sensation. She's pretty as a picture. Been married only six months, and it seems to be a dead sure thing that she poisoned her husband. That trial's going to make racy reading, especially if they bring in a verdict of guilty."

The city editor looked interested.

"Want to go down there, George?"

"Well, do you know, I think it'll pay."

"Let me see, this is the last day of the convention, isn't it? And Clark comes back from his vacation to-morrow. Well, if you think it's worth it, take a trip down there, and look the ground over, and give us a special article that we can use on the first day of the trial."

"I'll do it," said George.

Speed looked at Brenton.

"What would old Ferris say now, eh?"

CHAPTER VI.

Next morning George Stratton was on the railway train speeding towards Cincinnati. As he handed to the conductor his mileage book, he did not say to him, lightly transposing the old couplet—

"Here, railroad man, take thrice thy fee,

For spirits twain do ride with me."

George Stratton was a practical man, and knew nothing of spirits, except those which were in a small flask in his natty little valise.

When he reached Cincinnati, he made straight for the residence of the sheriff. He felt that his first duty was to become friends with such an important official. Besides this, he wished to have an interview with the prisoner. He had arranged in his mind, on the way there, just how he would write a preliminary article that would whet the appetite of the readers of the Chicago Argus for any further developments that might occur during and after the trial. He would write the whole thing in the form of a story.

First, there would be a sketch of the life of Mrs. Brenton and her husband. This would be number one, and above it would be the Roman numeral I. Under the heading II. would be a history of the crime. Under III. what had occurred afterwards—the incidents that had led suspicion towards the unfortunate woman, and that sort of thing. Under the numeral IV. would be his interview with the prisoner, if he were fortunate enough to get one. Under V. he would give the general opinion of Cincinnati on the crime, and on the guilt or innocence of Mrs. Brenton. This article he already saw in his mind's eye occupying nearly half a page of the Argus. All would be in leaded type, and written in a style and manner that would attract attention, for he felt that he was first on the ground, and would not have the usual rush in preparing his copy which had been the bane of his life. It would give the Argus practically the lead in this case, which he was convinced would become one of national importance.

The sheriff received him courteously, and, looking at the card he presented, saw the name Chicago Argus in the corner. Then he stood visibly on his guard—an attitude assumed by all wise officials when they find themselves brought face to face with a newspaper man; for they know, however carefully an article may be prepared, it will likely contain some unfortunate overlooked phrase which may have a damaging effect in a future political campaign.

"I wanted to see you," began Stratton, coming straight to the point, "in reference to the Brenton murder."

"I may say at once," replied the sheriff, "that if you wish an interview with the prisoner, it is utterly impossible, because her lawyers, Benham and Brown, have positively forbidden her to see a newspaper man."

"That shows," said Stratton, "they are wise men who understand their business. Nevertheless, I wish to have an interview with Mrs. Brenton. But what I wanted to say to you is this: I believe the case will be very much talked about, and that before many weeks are over. Of course you know the standing the Argus has in newspaper circles. What it says will have an influence, even over the Cincinnati press. I think you will admit that. Now a great many newspaper men consider an official their natural enemy. I do not; at least, I do not until I am forced to. Any reference that I may make to you I am more than willing to submit to you before it goes to Chicago. I will give you my word, if you want it, that nothing will be said referring to your official position, or to yourself personally, that you do not see before it appears in print. Of course you will be up for re-election. I never met a sheriff who wasn't."

The sheriff smiled at this, and did not deny it.

"Very well. Now, I may tell you my belief is that this case is going to have a powerful influence on your re-election. Here is a young and pretty woman who is to be tried for a terrible crime. Whether she is guilty or innocent, public sympathy is going to be with her. If I were in your place, I would prefer to be known as her friend rather than as her enemy."

"My dear sir," said the sheriff, "my official position puts me in the attitude of neither friend nor enemy of the unfortunate woman. I have simply a certain duty to do, and that duty I intend to perform."

"Oh, that's all right!" exclaimed the newspaper man, jauntily. "I, for one, am not going to ask you to take a step outside your duties; but an official may do his duty, and yet, at the same time, do a friendly act for a newspaper man, or even for a prisoner. In the language of the old chestnut, 'If you don't help me, don't help the bear.' That's all I ask."

"You maybe sure, Mr. Stratton, that anything I can do to help you I shall be glad to do; and now let me give you a hint. If you want to see Mrs. Brenton, the best thing is to get permission from her lawyers. If I were you I would not see Benham—he's rather a hard nut, Benham is, although you needn't tell him I said so. You get on the right side of Brown. Brown has some political aspirations himself, and he does not want to offend a man on so powerful a paper as the Argus, even if it is not a Cincinnati paper. Now, if you make him the same offer you have made to me, I think it will be all right. If he sees your copy before it goes into print, and if you keep your word with him that nothing will appear that he does not see, I think you will succeed in getting an interview with Mrs. Brenton. If you bring me a note from Brown, I shall be very glad to allow you to see her."

Stratton thanked the sheriff for his hint. He took down in his note-book the address of the lawyers, and the name especially of Mr. Brown. The two men shook hands, and Stratton felt that they understood each other.

When Mr. Stratton was ushered into the private office of Brown, and handed that gentleman his card, he noticed the lawyer perceptibly freeze over.

"Ahem," said the legal gentleman; "you will excuse me if I say that my time is rather precious. Did you wish to see me professionally?"

"Yes," replied Stratton, "that is, from a newspaper standpoint of the profession."

"Ah," said the other, "in reference to what?"

"To the Brenton case."

"Well, my dear sir, I have had, very reluctantly, to refuse information that I would have been happy to give, if I could, to our own newspaper men; and so I may say to you at once that I scarcely think it will be possible for me to be of any service to an outside paper like the Argus"

"Local newspaper men," said Stratton, "represent local fame. That you already possess. I represent national fame, which, if you will excuse my saying so, you do not yet possess. The fact that I am in Cincinnati to-day, instead of in Chicago, shows what we Chicago people think of the Cincinnati case. I believe, and the Argus believes, that this case is going to be one of national importance. Now, let me ask you one question. Will you state frankly what your objection is to having a newspaper man, for instance, interview Mrs. Brenton, or get any information relating to this case from her or others whom you have the power of controlling?"

"I shall answer that question," said Brown, "as frankly as you put it. You are a man of the world, and know, of course, that we are all selfish, and in business matters look entirely after our own interests. My interest in this case is to defend my client. Your interest in this case is to make a sensational article. You want to get facts if possible, but, in any event, you want to write up a readable column or two for your paper. Now, if I allowed you to see Mrs. Brenton, she might say something to you, and you might publish it, that would not only endanger her chances, but would seriously embarrass us, as her lawyers, in our defence of the case."

"You have stated the objection very plainly and forcibly," said Stratton, with a look of admiration, as if the powerful arguments of the lawyer had had a great effect on him. "Now, if I understand your argument, it simply amounts to this, that you would have no objection to my interviewing Mrs. Brenton if you have the privilege of editing the copy. In other words, if nothing were printed but what you approve of, you would not have the slightest hesitancy about allowing me that interview."

"No, I don't know that I would," admitted the lawyer.

"Very well, then. Here is my proposition to you: I am here to look after the interests of our paper in this particular case. The Argus is probably going to be the first paper outside of Cincinnati that will devote a large amount of space to the Brenton trial, in addition to what is received from the Associated Press dispatches. Now you can give me a great many facilities in this matter if you care to do so, and in return I am perfectly willing to submit to you every line of copy that concerns you or your client before it is sent, and I give you my word of honour that nothing shall appear but what you have seen and approved of. If you want to cut out something that I think is vitally important, then I shall tell you frankly that I intend to print it, but will modify it as much as I possibly can to suit your views."

"I see," said the lawyer. "In other words, as you have just remarked, I am to give you special facilities in this matter, and then, when you find out some fact which I wish kept secret, and which you have obtained because of the facilities I have given to you, you will quite frankly tell me that it must go in, and then, of course, I shall be helpless except to debar you from any further facilities, as you call them. No, sir, I do not care to make any such bargain."

"Well, suppose I strike out that clause of agreement, and say to you that I will send nothing but what you approve of, would you then write me a note to the sheriff and allow me to see the prisoner?"

"I am sorry to say"—the lawyer hesitated for a moment, and glanced at the card, then added—"Mr. Stratton, that I do not see my way clear to granting your request."

"I think," said Stratton, rising, "that you are doing yourself an injustice. You are refusing—I may as well tell you first as last—what is a great privilege. Now, you have had some experience in your business, and I have had some experience in mine, and I beg to inform you that men who are much more prominent in the history of their country than any one I can at present think of in Cincinnati, have tried to balk me in the pursuit of my business, and have failed."

"In that matter, of course," said Brown, "I must take my chances. I don't see the use of prolonging this interview. As you have been so frank as to—I won't say threaten, perhaps warn is the better word—as you have been so good as to warn me, I may, before we part, just give you a word of caution. Of course we, in Cincinnati, are perfectly willing to admit that Chicago people are the smartest on earth, but I may say that if you print a word in your paper which is untrue and which is damaging to our side of the case, or if you use any methods that are unlawful in obtaining the information you so much desire, you will certainly get your paper into trouble, and you will run some little personal risk yourself."

"Well, as you remarked a moment ago, Mr. Brown, I shall have to take the chances of that. I am here to get the news, and if I don't succeed it will be the first time in my life."

"Very well, sir," said the lawyer. "I wish you good evening."

"Just one thing more," said the newspaper man, "before I leave you."

"My dear sir," said the lawyer, impatiently, "I am very busy. I've already given you a liberal share of my time. I must request that this interview end at once."

"I thought," said Mr. Stratton, calmly, "that perhaps you might be interested in the first article that I am going to write. I shall devote one column in the Argus of the day after to-morrow to your defence of the case, and whether your theory of defence is a tenable one or not."

Mr. Brown pushed back his chair and looked earnestly at the young man. That individual was imperturbably pulling on his gloves, and at the moment was buttoning one of them.

"Our defence!" cried the lawyer. "What do you know of our defence?"

"My dear sir," said Stratton, "I know all about it."

"Sir, that is impossible. Nobody knows what our defence is to be except Mr. Benham and myself."

"And Mr. Stratton, of the Chicago Argus," replied the young man, as he buttoned his coat.

"May I ask, then, what the defence is?"

"Certainly," answered the Chicago man. "Your defence is that Mr.

Brenton was insane, and that he committed suicide."

Even Mr. Brown's habitual self-control, acquired by long years of training in keeping his feelings out of sight, for the moment deserted him. He drew his breath sharply, and cast a piercing glance at the young man before him, who was critically watching the lawyer's countenance, although he appeared to be entirely absorbed in buttoning his overcoat. Then Mr. Brown gave a short, dry laugh.

"I have met a bluff before," he said carelessly; "but I should like to know what makes you think that such is our defence?"

"Think!" cried the young man. "I don't think at all; I know it."

"How do you know it?"

"Well, for one thing, I know it by your own actions a moment ago. What first gave me an inkling of your defence was that book which is on your table. It is Forbes Winslow on the mind and the brain; a very interesting book, Mr. Brown, very interesting indeed. It treats of suicide, and the causes and conditions of the brain that will lead up to it. It is a very good book, indeed, to study in such a case. Good evening, Mr. Brown. I am sorry that we cannot co-operate in this matter."

Stratton turned and walked toward the door, while the lawyer gazed after him with a look of helpless astonishment on his face. As Stratton placed his hand on the door knob, the lawyer seemed to wake up as from a dream.

"Stop!" he cried; "I will give you a letter that will admit you to Mrs. Brenton."

CHAPTER VII.

"There!" said Speed to Brenton, triumphantly, "what do you think of that? Didn't I say George Stratton was the brightest newspaper man in Chicago? I tell you, his getting that letter from old Brown was one of the cleverest bits of diplomacy I ever saw. There you had quickness of perception, and nerve. All the time he was talking to old Brown he was just taking that man's measure. See how coolly he acted while he was drawing on his gloves and buttoning his coat as if ready to leave. Flung that at Brown all of a sudden as quiet as if he was saying nothing at all unusual, and all the time watching Brown out of the tail of his eye. Well, sir, I must admit, that although I have known George Stratton for years, I thought he was dished by that Cincinnati lawyer. I thought that George was just gracefully covering up his defeat, and there he upset old Brown's apple-cart in the twinkling of an eye. Now, you see the effect of all this. Brown has practically admitted to him what the line of defence is. Stratton won't publish it, of course; he has promised not to, but you see he can hold that over Brown's head, and get everything he wants unless they change their defence."

"Yes," remarked Brenton, slowly, "he seems to be a very sharp newspaper man indeed; but I don't like the idea of his going to interview my wife."

"Why, what is there wrong about that?"

"Well, there is this wrong about it—that she in her depression may say something that will tell against her."

"Even if she does, what of it? Isn't the lawyer going to see the letter before it is sent to the paper?"

"I am not so sure about that. Do you think Stratton will show the article to Brown if he gets what you call a scoop or a beat?"

"Why, of course he will," answered Speed, indignantly; "hasn't he given him his word that he will?"

"Yes, I know he has," said Brenton, dubiously; "but he is a newspaper man."

"Certainly he is," answered Speed, with strong emphasis; "that is the reason he will keep his word."

"I hope so, I hope so; but I must admit that the more I know you newspaper men, the more I see the great temptation you are under to preserve if possible the sensational features of an article."

"I'll bet you a drink—no, we can't do that," corrected Speed; "but you shall see that, if Brown acts square with Stratton, he will keep his word to the very letter with Brown. There is no use in our talking about the matter here. Let us follow Stratton, and see what comes of the interview."

"I think I prefer to go alone," said Brenton, coldly.

"Oh, as you like, as you like," answered the other, shortly. "I thought you wanted my help in this affair; but if you don't, I am sure I shan't intrude."

"That's all right," said Brenton; "come along. By the way, Speed, what do you think of that line of defence?"

"Well, I don't know enough of the circumstances of the case to know what to think of it. It seems to me rather a good line."

"It can't be a good line when it is not true. It is certain to break down."

"That's so," said Speed; "but I'll bet you four dollars and a half that they'll prove you a raving maniac before they are through with you. They'll show very likely that you tried to poison yourself two or three times; bring on a dozen of your friends to prove that they knew all your life you were insane."

"Do you think they will?" asked Brenton, uneasily.

"Think it? Why, I am sure of it. You'll go down to posterity as one of the most complete lunatics that ever, lived in Cincinnati. Oh, there won't be anything left of you when they get through with you."

Meanwhile, Stratton was making his way to the residence of the sheriff.

"Ah," said that official, when they met, "you got your letter, did you? Well, I thought you would."

"If you had heard the conversation between my estimable friend Mr. Brown and myself, up to the very last moment, you wouldn't have thought it."

"Well, Brown is generally very courteous towards newspaper men, and that's one reason you see his name in the papers a great deal."

"If I were a Cincinnati newspaper man, I can assure you that his name wouldn't appear very much in the columns of my paper."

"I am sorry to hear you say that. I thought Brown was very popular with the newspaper men. You got the letter, though, did you?"

"Yes; I got it. Here it is. Read it."

The sheriff scanned the brief note over, and put it in his pocket.

"Just take a chair for a moment, will you, and I will see if Mrs. Brenton is ready to receive you."

Stratton seated himself, and, pulling a paper from his pocket, was busily reading when the sheriff again entered.

"I am sorry to say," he began, "after you have had all this trouble, that Mrs. Brenton positively refuses to see you. You know I cannot compel a prisoner to meet any one. You understand that, of course."

"Perfectly," said Stratton, thinking for a moment. "See here, sheriff, I have simply got to have a talk with that woman. Now, can't you tell her I knew her husband, or something of that sort? I'll make it all right when I see her."

"The scoundrel!" said Brenton to Speed, as Stratton made this remark.

"My dear sir," said Speed, "don't you see he is just the man we want? This is not the time to be particular."

"Yes, but think of the treachery and meanness of telling a poor unfortunate woman that he was acquainted with her husband, who is only a few days dead."

"Now, see here," said Speed, "if you are going to look on matters in this way you will be a hindrance and not a help in the affair. Don't you appreciate the situation? Why, Mrs. Brenton's own lawyers, as you have said, think her guilty. What, then, can they learn by talking with her, or what good can they do her with their minds already prejudiced against her? Don't you see that?"

Brenton made no answer to this, but it was evident he was very ill at ease.

"Did you know her husband?" asked the sheriff.

"No, to tell you the truth, I never heard of him before. But I must see this lady, both for my good and hers, and I am not going to let a little thing like that stand between us. Won't you tell her that I have come with a letter from her own lawyers? Just show her the letter, and say that I will take up but very little of her time. I am sorry to ask this much of you, but you see how I am placed."

"Oh, that's all right," said the sheriff, good-naturedly; "I shall be very glad to do what you wish," and with that he once more disappeared.

The sheriff stayed away longer this time, and Stratton paced the room impatiently. Finally, the official returned, and said—

"Mrs. Brenton has consented to see you. Come this way, please. You will excuse me, I know," continued the sheriff, as they walked along together, "but it is part of my duty to remain in the room while you are talking with Mrs. Brenton."

"Certainly, certainly," said Stratton; "I understand that."

"Very well; then, if I may make a suggestion, I would say this: you should be prepared to ask just what you want to know, and do it all as speedily as possible, for really Mrs. Brenton is in a condition of nervous exhaustion that renders it almost cruel to put her through any rigid cross-examination."

"I understand that also," said Stratton; "but you must remember that she has a very much harder trial to undergo in the future. I am exceedingly anxious to get at the truth of this thing, and so, if it seems to you that I am asking a lot of very unnecessary questions, I hope you will not interfere with me as long as Mrs. Brenton consents to answer."

"I shall not interfere at all," said the sheriff; "I only wanted to caution you, for the lady may break down at any moment. If you can marshal your questions so that the most important ones come first, I think it will be wise. I presume you have them pretty well arranged in your own mind?"

"Well, I can't say that I have; you see, I am entirely in the dark. I got no help whatever from the lawyers, and from what I know of their defence I am thoroughly convinced that they are on the wrong track."

"What! did Brown say anything about the defence? That is not like his usual caution."

"He didn't intend to," answered Stratton; "but I found out all I wanted to know, nevertheless. You see, I shall have to ask what appears to be a lot of rambling, inconsequential questions because you can never tell in a case like this when you may get the key to the whole mystery."

"Well, here we are," said the sheriff, as he knocked at a door, and then pushed it open.

From the moment George Stratton saw Mrs. Brenton his interest in the case ceased to be purely journalistic.

Mrs. Brenton was standing near the window, and she appeared to be very calm and collected, but her fingers twitched nervously, clasping and unclasping each other. Her modest dress of black was certainly a very becoming one.

George thought he had never seen a woman so beautiful.

As she was standing up, she evidently intended the interview to be a short one.

"Madam," said Stratton, "I am very sorry indeed to trouble you; but

I have taken a great interest in the solution of this mystery, and I have your lawyers' permission to visit you. I assure you, anything you say will be submitted to them, so that there will be no danger of your case being prejudiced by any statements made."

"I am not afraid," said Mrs. Brenton, "that the truth will injure or prejudice my case."

"I am sure of that," answered the newspaper man; and then, knowing that she would not sit down if he asked her to, he continued diplomatically, "Madam, will you permit me to sit down? I wish to write out my notes as carefully as possible. Accuracy is my strong point."

"Certainly," said Mrs. Brenton; and, seeing that it was not probable the interview would be a short one, she seated herself by the window, while the sheriff took a chair in the corner, and drew a newspaper from his pocket.

"Now, madam," said the special, "a great number of the questions I ask you may seem trivial, but as I said to the sheriff a moment ago, some word of yours that appears to you entirely unconnected with the case may give me a clue which will be exceedingly valuable. You will, therefore, I am sure, pardon me if some of the questions I ask you appear irrelevant."

Mrs. Brenton bowed her head, but said nothing.

"Were your husband's business affairs in good condition at the time of his death?"

"As far as I know they were."

"Did you ever see anything in your husband's actions that would lead you to think him a man who might have contemplated suicide?"

Mrs. Brenton looked up with wide-open eyes.

"Certainly not," she said.

"Had he ever spoken to you on the subject of suicide?"

"I do not remember that he ever did."

"Was he ever queer in his actions? In short, did you ever notice anything about him that would lead you to doubt his sanity? I am sorry if questions I ask you seem painful, but I have reasons for wishing to be certain on this point."

"No," said Mrs. Brenton; "he was perfectly sane. No man could have been more so. I am certain that he never thought of committing suicide."

"Why are you so certain on that point?"

"I do not know why. I only know I am positive of it."

"Do you know if he had any enemy who might wish his death?"

"I doubt if he had an enemy in the world. I do not know of any."

"Have you ever heard him speak of anybody in a spirit of enmity?"

"Never. He was not a man who bore enmity against people. Persons whom he did not like he avoided."

"The poison, it is said, was put into his cup of coffee. Do you happen to know," said Stratton, turning to the sheriff, "how they came to that conclusion?"

"No, I do not," answered the sheriff. "In fact, I don't see any reason why they should think so."

"Was morphia found in the coffee cup afterwards?"

"No; at the time of the inquest all the things had been cleared away. I think it was merely presumed that the morphine was put into his coffee."

"Who poured out the coffee he drank that night?"

"I did," answered his wife.

"You were at one end of the table and he at the other, I suppose?"

"Yes."

"How did the coffee cup reach him?"

"I gave it to the servant, and she placed it before him."

"It passed through no other hands, then?"

"No."

"Who was the servant?"

Mrs. Brenton pondered for a moment.

"I really know very little about her. She had been in our house for a couple of weeks only."

"What was her name?"

"Jane Morton, I think."

"Where is she now, do you know?"

"I do not know."

"She appeared at the inquest, of course?" said Stratton, turning to the sheriff.

"I think she did," was the answer. "I am not sure."

He marked her name down in the note-book.

"How many people were there at the dinner?"

"Including my husband and myself, there were twenty-six."

"Could you give me the name of each of them?"

"Yes, I think so."

She repeated the names, which he took down, with certain notes and comments on each.

"Who sat next your husband at the head of the table?"

"Miss Walker was at his right hand, Mr. Roland at his left."

"Now, forgive me if I ask you if you have ever had any trouble with your husband?"

"Never."

"Never had any quarrel?"

Mrs. Brenton hesitated for a moment.

"No, I don't think we ever had what could be called a quarrel."

"You had no disagreement shortly before the dinner?"

Again Mrs. Brenton hesitated.

"I can hardly call it a disagreement," she said. "We had a little discussion about some of the guests who were to be invited."

"Did he object to any that were there?"

"There was a gentleman there whom he did not particularly like, I think, but he made no objection to his coming; in fact, he seemed to feel that I might imagine he had an objection from a little discussion we had about inviting him; and afterwards, as if to make up for that, he placed this guest at his left hand."

Stratton quickly glanced up the page of his notebook, and marked a little cross before the name of Stephen Roland.

"You had another disagreement with him before, if I might term it so, had you not?"

Mrs. Brenton looked at him surprised.

"What makes you think so?" she said.

"Because you hesitated when I spoke of it."

"Well, we had what you might call a disagreement once at Lucerne, Switzerland."

"Will you tell me what it was about?"

"I would rather not."

"Will you tell me this—was it about a gentleman?"

"Yes," said Mrs. Brenton.

"Was your husband of a jealous disposition?"

"Ordinarily I do not think he was. It seemed to me at the time that he was a little unjust—that's all."

"Was the gentleman in Lucerne?"

"Oh no!"

"In Cincinnati?"

"Yes."

"Was his name Stephen Roland?"

Mrs. Brenton again glanced quickly at the newspaper man, and seemed about to say something, but, checking herself, she simply answered—

"Yes."

Then she leaned back in the armchair and sighed.

"I am very tired," she said. "If it is not absolutely necessary, I prefer not to continue this conversation."

Stratton immediately rose.

"Madam," he said, "I am very much obliged to you for the trouble you have taken to answer my questions, which I am afraid must have seemed impertinent to you, but I assure you that I did not intend them to be so. Now, madam, I would like very much to get a promise from you. I wish that you would promise to see me if I call again, and I, on my part, assure you that unless I have something particularly important to tell you, or to ask, I shall not intrude upon you."

"I shall be pleased to see you at any time, sir."

When the sheriff and the newspaper man reached the other room, the former said—

"Well, what do you think?"

"I think it is an interesting case," was the answer.

"Or, to put it in other words, you think Mrs. Brenton a very interesting lady."

"Officially, sir, you have exactly stated my opinion."

"And I suppose, poor woman, she will furnish an interesting article for the paper?"

"Hang the paper!" said Stratton, with more than his usual vim.

The sheriff laughed. Then he said—

"I confess that to me it seems a very perplexing affair all through. Have you got any light on the subject?"

"My dear sir, I will tell you three important things. First, Mrs. Brenton is innocent. Second, her lawyers are taking the wrong line of defence. Third," tapping his breast-pocket, "I have the name of the murderer in my note-book."

CHAPTER VIII.

"Now," said John Speed to William Brenton, "we have got Stratton fairly started on the track, and I believe that he will ferret out the truth in this matter. But, meanwhile, we must not be idle. You must remember that, with all our facilities for discovery, we really know nothing of the murderer ourselves. I propose we set about this thing just as systematically as Stratton will. The chances are that we shall penetrate the mystery of the whole affair very much quicker than he. As I told you before, I am something of a newspaper man myself; and if, with the facilities of getting into any room in any house, in any city and in any country, and being with a suspected criminal night and day when he never imagines any one is near him—if with all those advantages I cannot discover the real author of that crime before George Stratton does, then I'll never admit that I came from Chicago, or belonged to a newspaper."

"Whom do you think Stratton suspects of the crime? He told the sheriff," said Brenton, "that he had the name in his pocket-book."

"I don't know," said Speed, "but I have my suspicions. You see, he has the names of all the guests at your banquet in that pocket-book of his; but the name of Stephen Roland he has marked with two crosses. The name of the servant he has marked with one cross. Now, I suspect that he believes Stephen Roland committed the crime. You know Roland; what do you think of him?"

"I think he is quite capable of it," answered Brenton, with a frown.

"Still, you are prejudiced against the man," put in Speed, "so your evidence is hardly impartial."

"I am not prejudiced against any one," answered Brenton; "I merely know that man. He is a thoroughly despicable, cowardly character. The only thing that makes me think he would not commit a murder, is that he is too craven to stand the consequences if he were caught. He is a cool villain, but he is a coward. I do not believe he has the courage to commit a crime, even if he thought he would benefit by it."

"Well, there is one thing, Brenton, you can't be accused of flattering a man, and if it is any consolation for you to know, you may be pretty certain that George Stratton is on his track."

"I am sure I wish him success," answered Brenton, gloomily; "if he brings Roland to the gallows I shall not mourn over it."

"That's all right," said Speed; "but now we must be up and doing ourselves. Have you anything to propose?"

"No, I have not, except that we might play the detective on Roland."

"Well, the trouble with that is we would merely be duplicating what Stratton is doing himself. Now, I'll tell you my proposal. Supposing that we consult with Lecocq."

"Who is that? The novelist?"

"Novelist? I don't think he has ever written any novels—not that I remember of."

"Ah, I didn't know. It seemed to me that I remembered his name in connection with some novel."

"Oh, very likely you did. He is the hero of more detective stories than any other man I know of. He was the great French detective."

"What, is he dead, then?"

"Dead? Not a bit of it; he's here with us. Oh, I understand what you mean. Yes, from your point of view, he is dead."

"Where can we find him?"

"Well, I presume, in Paris. He's a first-rate fellow to know, anyhow, and he spends most of his time around his old haunts. In fact, if you want to be certain to find Lecocq, you will generally get him during office hours in the room he used to frequent while in Paris."

"Let us go and see him, then."

"Monsieur Lecocq," said Speed, a moment afterwards, "I wish to introduce to you a new-comer, Mr. Brenton, recently of Cincinnati."

"Ah, my dear Speed," said the Frenchman, "I am very pleased indeed to meet any friend of yours. How is the great Chicago, the second Paris, and how is your circulation?—the greatest in the world, I suppose."

"Well, it is in pretty good order," said Speed; "we circulated from Chicago to Paris here in a very much shorter time than the journey usually occupies down below. Now, can you give us a little of your time? Are you busy just now?"

"My dear Speed, I am always busy. I am like the people of the second Paris. I lose no time, but I have always time to speak with my friends."

"All right," said Speed. "I am like the people of the second Chicago, generally more intent on pleasure than business; but, nevertheless, I have a piece of business for you."

"The second Chicago?" asked Lecocq. "And where is that, pray?"

"Why, Paris, of course," said Speed.

Lecocq laughed.

"You are incorrigible, you Chicagoans. And what is the piece of business?"

"It is the old thing, monsieur. A mystery to be unravelled. Mr. Brenton here wishes to retain you in his case."

"And what is his case?" was the answer.

Lecocq was evidently pleased to have a bit of real work given him.

Speed briefly recited the facts, Brenton correcting him now and then on little points where he was wrong. Speed seemed to think these points immaterial, but Lecocq said that attention to trivialities was the whole secret of the detective business.

"Ah," said Lecocq, sorrowfully, "there is no real trouble in elucidating that mystery. I hoped it would be something difficult; but, you see, with my experience of the old world, and with the privileges one enjoys in this world, things which might be difficult to one below are very easy for us. Now, I shall show you how simple it is."

"Good gracious!" cried Speed, "you don't mean to say you are going to read it right off the reel, like that, when we have been bothering ourselves with it so long, and without success?"

"At the moment," replied the French detective, "I am not prepared to say who committed the deed. That is a matter of detail. Now, let us see what we know, and arrive, from that, at what we do not know. The one fact, of which we are assured on the statement of two physicians from Cincinnati, is that Mr. Brenton was poisoned."

"Well," said Speed, "there are several other facts, too. Another fact is that Mrs. Brenton is accused of the crime."

"Ah! my dear sir," said Lecocq, "that is not pertinent."

"No," said Speed, "I agree with you. I call it very impertinent."

Brenton frowned, at this, and his old dislike to the flippant Chicago man rose to the surface again.

The Frenchman continued marking the points on his long forefinger.

"Now, there are two ways by which that result may have been attained. First, Mr. Brenton may have administered to himself the poison; secondly, the poison may have been administered by some one else."

"Yes," said Speed; "and, thirdly, the poison may have been administered accidentally—you do not seem to take that into account."

"I do not take that into account," calmly replied the Frenchman, "because of its improbability. If there were an accident; if, for instance, the poison was in the sugar, or in some of the viands served, then others than Mr. Brenton would have been poisoned. The fact that one man out of twenty-six was poisoned, and the fact that several people are to benefit by his death, point, it seems to me, to murder; but to be sure of that, I will ask Mr. Brenton one question. My dear sir, did you administer this poison to yourself?"

"Certainly not," answered Brenton.

"Then we have two facts. First, Mr. Brenton was poisoned; secondly, he was poisoned by some person who had an interest in his death. Now we will proceed. When Mr. Brenton sat down to that dinner he was perfectly well. When he arose from that dinner he was feeling ill. He goes to bed. He sees no one but his wife after he has left the dinner-table, and he takes nothing between the time he leaves the dinner-table and the moment he becomes unconscious. Now, that poison must have been administered to Mr. Brenton at the dinner-table. Am I not right?"

"Well, you seem to be," answered Speed.

"Seem? Why, it is as plain as day. There cannot be any mistake."

"All right," said Speed; "go ahead. What next?"

"What next? There were twenty-six people around that table, with two servants to wait on them, making twenty-eight in all. There were twenty-six, I think you said, including Mr. Brenton."

"That is correct."

"Very well. One of those twenty-seven persons has poisoned Mr. Brenton. Do you follow me?"

"We do," answered Speed; "we follow you as closely as you have ever followed a criminal! Go on."

"Very well, so much is clear. These are all facts, not theories. Now, what is the thing that I should do if I were in Cincinnati? I would find out whether one or more of those guests had anything to gain by the death of their host. That done, I would follow the suspected persons. I would have my men find out what each of them had done for a month before the time of the crime. Whoever committed it made some preparation. He did something, too, as you say, in America, to cover up his tracks. Very well. By the keen detective these actions are easily traced. I shall at once place twenty-seven of the best men I know on the track of those twenty-seven persons."

"I call that shadowing with a vengeance," remarked the Chicago man.

"It will be very easy. The one who has committed the crime is certain, when he is alone in his own room, to say something, or to do something, that will show my detective that he is the criminal. So, gentlemen, if you can tell me who those twenty-seven persons are, in three days or a week from this time I will tell you who gave the poison to Mr. Brenton."

"You seem very sure of that," said Speed.

"Sure of it? It is simply child's play. It is mere waiting. If, for instance, at the trial Mrs. Brenton is found guilty, and sentenced, the one who is the guilty party is certain to betray himself or herself as soon as he or she is alone. If it be a man who hopes to marry Mrs. Brenton, he will be overcome with grief at what has happened. He will wring his hands and try to think what can be done to prevent the sentence being carried out. He will argue with himself whether it is better to give himself up and tell the truth, and if he is a coward he will conclude not to do that, but will try to get a pardon, or at least have the capital sentence commuted into life imprisonment. He will possibly be cool and calm in public, but when he enters his own room, when his door is locked, when he believes no one can see him, when he thinks he is alone, then will come his trial. Then his passions and his emotions will betray him. It is mere child's play, as I tell you, and long before there is a verdict I will give you the name of the murderer."

"Very well, then," said Speed, "that is agreed; we will look you up in a week from now."

"I should be pained," said Lecocq, "to put you to that trouble. As soon as I get the report from my men I will communicate with you and let you know the result. In a few days I shall give you the name of the assassin."

"Good-bye, then, until I see you again," answered Speed; and with this he and Brenton took their departure.

"He seems to be very sure of himself," said Brenton.

"He will do what he says, you may depend on that."

The week was not yet up when Monsieur Lecocq met John Speed in Chicago.

"By the look of satisfaction on your face," said Mr. Speed, "I imagine you have succeeded in unravelling the mystery."

"Ah," replied the Frenchman; "if I have the appearance of satisfaction, it is indeed misplaced."

"Then you have not made any discovery?"

"On the contrary, it is all as plain as your big buildings here. It is not for that reason, but because it is so simple that I should be foolish to feel satisfaction regarding it."

"Then who is the person?"

"The assassin," replied the Frenchman, "is one whom no one has seemed to think of, and yet one on whom suspicion should have been the first to fall. The person who did Monsieur Brenton the honour to poison him is none other than the servant girl, Jane Morton."

CHAPTER IX.

"Jane Morton!" cried Speed; "who is she?"

"She is, as you may remember, the girl who carried the coffee from Mrs. Brenton to monsieur."

"And are you sure she is the criminal?"

The great detective did not answer; he merely gave an expressive little French gesture, as though the question was not worth commenting upon.

"Why, what was her motive?" asked Speed.

For the first time in their acquaintance a shade of perplexity seemed to come over the enthusiastic face of the volatile Frenchman.

"You are what you call smart, you Chicago people," he said, "and you have in a moment struck the only point on which we are at a loss."

"My dear sir," returned Speed, "that is the point in the case. Motive is the first thing to look for, it seems to me. You said as much yourself. If you haven't succeeded in finding what motive Jane Morton had for poisoning her employer, it appears to me that very little has been accomplished."

"Ah, you say that before you know the particulars. I am certain we shall find the motive. What I know now is that Jane Morton is the one who put the poison in his cup of coffee."

"It would take a good deal of nerve to do that with twenty-six people around the table. You forget, my dear sir, that she had to pass the whole length of the table, after taking the cup, before giving it to Mr. Brenton."

"Half of the people had their backs to her, and the other half, I can assure you, were not looking at her. If the poison was ready, it was a very easy thing to slip it into a cup of coffee. There was ample time to do it, and that is how it was done."

"May I ask how you arrived at that conclusion?"

"Certainly, certainly, my dear sir. My detectives report that each one of the twenty-seven people they had to follow were shadowed night and day. But only two of them acted suspiciously. These two were Jane Morton and Stephen Roland. Stephen Roland's anxiety is accounted for by the fact that he is evidently in love with Mrs. Brenton. But the change in Jane Morton has been something terrible. She is suffering from the severest pangs of ineffectual remorse. She has not gone out again to service, but occupies a room in one of the poorer quarters of the city—a room that she never leaves except at night. Her whole actions show that she is afraid of the police—afraid of being tracked for her crime. She buys a newspaper every night, locks and bars the door on entering her room, and, with tears streaming from her eyes, reads every word of the criminal news. One night, when she went out to buy her paper, and what food she needed for the next day, she came unexpectedly upon a policeman at the corner. The man was not looking at her at all, nor for her, but she fled, running like a deer, doubling and turning through alleys and back streets until by a very roundabout road she reached her own room. There she locked herself in, and remained without food all next day rather than go out again. She flung herself terror-stricken on the bed, after her room door was bolted, and cried, 'Oh, why did I do it? why did I do it? I shall certainly be found out. If Mrs. Brenton is acquitted, they will be after me next day. I did it to make up to John what he had suffered, and yet if John knew it, he would never speak to me again.'"

"Who is John?" asked Speed.

"Ah, that," said the detective, "I do not know. When we find out who John is, then we shall find the motive for the crime."

"In that case, if I were you, I should try to find John as quickly as possible."

"Yes, my dear sir, that is exactly what should be done, and my detective is now endeavouring to discover the identity of John. He will possibly succeed in a few days. But there is another way of finding out who John is, and perhaps in that you can help me."

"What other way?"

"There is one man who undoubtedly knows who John is, and that is Mr. Brenton. Now, I thought that perhaps you, who know Brenton better than I do, would not mind asking him who John is."

"My dear sir," said Speed, "Brenton is no particular friend of mine, and I only know him well enough to feel that if there is any cross-examination to be done, I should prefer somebody else to do it."

"Why, you are not afraid of him, are you?" asked the detective.

"Afraid of him? Certainly not, but I tell you that Brenton is just a little touchy and apt to take offence. I have found him so on several occasions. Now, as you have practically taken charge of this case, why don't you go and see him?"

"I suppose I shall have to do that," said the Frenchman, "if you will not undertake it."

"No, I will not."

"You have no objection, have you, to going with me?"

"It is better for you to see Brenton alone. I do not think he would care to be cross-examined before witnesses, you know."

"Ah, then, good-bye; I shall find out from Mr. Brenton who John is."

"I am sure I wish you luck," replied Speed, as Lecocq took his departure.

Lecocq found Brenton and Ferris together. The cynical spirit seemed to have been rather sceptical about the accounts given him of the influence that Speed and Brenton, combined, had had upon the Chicago newspaper man. Yet he was interested in the case, and although he still maintained that no practical good would result, even if a channel of communication could be opened between the two states of existence, he had listened with his customary respect to what Brenton had to say.

"Ah," said Brenton, when he saw the Frenchman, "have you any news for me?"

"Yes, I have. I have news that I will exchange, but meanwhile I want some news from you."

"I have none to give you," answered Brenton.

"If you have not, will you undertake to answer any questions I shall ask you, and not take offence if the questions seem to be personal ones?"

"Certainly," said Brenton; "I shall be glad to answer anything as long as it has a bearing on the case."

"Very well, then, it has a very distinct bearing on the case. Do you remember the girl Jane Morton?"

"I remember her, of course, as one of the servants in our employ. I know very little about her, though."

"That is just what I wish to find out. Do you know anything about her?"

"No; she had been in our employ but a fortnight, I think, or perhaps it was a month. My wife attended to these details, of course. I knew the girl was there, that is all."

The Frenchman looked very dubious as Brenton said this, while the latter rather bridled up.

"You evidently do not believe me?" he cried.

Once more the detective gave his customary gesture, and said—

"Ah, pardon me, you are entirely mistaken. I have this to acquaint you with. Jane Morton is the one who murdered you. She did it, she says, partly for the sake of John, whoever he is, and partly out of revenge. Now, of course, you are the only man who can give me information as to the motive. That girl certainly had a motive, and I should like to find out what the motive was."

Brenton meditated for a few moments, and then suddenly brightened up.

"I remember, now, an incident which happened a week of two before

Christmas, which may have a bearing on the case. One night I heard—or thought I heard—a movement downstairs, when I supposed everybody had retired. I took a revolver in my hand, and went cautiously down the stairs. Of course I had no light, because, if there was a burglar, I did not wish to make myself too conspicuous a mark. As I went along the hall leading to the kitchen, I saw there was a light inside; but as soon as they heard me coming the light was put out. When I reached the kitchen, I noticed a man trying to escape through the door that led to the coalshed. I fired at him twice, and he sank to the floor with a groan. I thought I had bagged a burglar sure, but it turned out to be nothing of the kind. He was merely a young man who had been rather late visiting one of the girls. I suspect now the girl he came to see was Jane Morton. As it was, the noise brought the two girls there, and I never investigated the matter or tried to find out which one it was that he had been visiting. They were both terror-stricken, and the young man himself was in a state of great fear. He thought for a moment that he had been killed. However, he was only shot in the leg, and I sent him to the house of a physician who keeps such patients as do not wish to go to the hospital. I did not care to have him go to the hospital, because I was afraid the newspapers would get hold of the incident, and make a sensation of it. The whole thing was accidental; the young fellow realized that, and so, I thought, did the girls; at least, I never noticed anything in their behaviour to show the contrary."

"What sort of a looking girl is Jane Morton?" asked Ferris.

"She is a tall brunette, with snapping black eyes."

"Ah, then, I remember her going into the room where you lay," said Ferris, "on Christmas morning. It struck me when she came out that she was very cool and self-possessed, and not at all surprised."

"All I can say," said Brenton, "is that I never noticed anything in her conduct like resentment at what had happened. I intended to give the young fellow a handsome compensation for his injury, but of course what occurred on Christmas Eve prevented that: I had really forgotten all about the circumstance, or I should have told you of it before."

"Then," said Lecocq, "the thing now is perfectly clear. That black-eyed vixen murdered you out of revenge."

CHAPTER X.

It was evident to George Stratton that he would have no time before the trial came off in which to prove Stephen Roland the guilty person. Besides this, he was in a strange state of mind which he himself could not understand. The moment he sat down to think out a plan by which he could run down the man he was confident had committed the crime, a strange wavering of mind came over him. Something seemed to say to him that he was on the wrong track. This became so persistent that George was bewildered, and seriously questioned his own sanity. Whenever he sat alone in his own room, the doubts arose and a feeling that he was on the wrong scent took possession of him. This feeling became so strong at times that he looked up other clues, and at one time tried to find out the whereabouts of the servant girls who had been employed by the Brentons. Curiously enough, the moment he began this search, his mind seemed to become clearer and easier; and when that happened, the old belief in the guilt of Stephen Roland resumed its sway again. But the instant he tried to follow up what clues he had in that direction, he found himself baffled and assailed again by doubts, and so every effort he put forth appeared to be nullified. This state of mind was so unusual with him that he had serious thoughts of abandoning the whole case and going back to Chicago. He said to himself, "I am in love with this woman and I shall go crazy if I stay here any longer." Then he remembered the trust she appeared to have in his powers of ferreting out the mystery of the case, and this in turn encouraged him and urged him on.

All trace of the girls appeared to be lost. He hesitated to employ a Cincinnati detective, fearing that what he discovered would be given away to the Cincinnati press. Then he accused himself of disloyalty to Mrs. Brenton, in putting his newspaper duty before his duty to her. He was so torn by his conflicting ideas and emotions that at last he resolved to abandon the case altogether and return to Chicago. He packed up his valise and resolved to leave that night for big city, trial or no trial. He had described his symptoms to a prominent physician, and that physician told him that the case was driving him mad, and the best thing he could do was to leave at once for other scenes. He could do no good, and would perhaps end by going insane himself.

As George Stratton was packing his valise in his room, alone, as he thought, the following conversation was taking place beside him.

"It is no use," said Speed; "we are merely muddling him, and not doing any good. The only thing is to leave him alone. If he investigates the Roland part of the case he will soon find out for himself that he is on the wrong track; then he will take the right one."

"Yes," said Brenton; "but the case comes on in a few days. If anything is to be done, it must be done now."

"In that I do not agree with you," said Speed. "Perhaps everything will go all right at the trial, but even if it does not, there is still a certain amount of time. You see how we have spoiled things by interfering. Our first success with him has misled us. We thought we could do anything; we have really done worse than nothing, because all this valuable time has been lost. If he had been allowed to proceed in his own way he would have ferreted out the matter as far as Stephen Roland is concerned, and would have found that there was no cause for his suspicion. As it is he has done nothing. He still believes, if left alone, that Stephen Roland is the criminal. All our efforts to lead him to the residence of Jane Morton have been unavailing. Now, you see, he is on the eve of going back to Chicago."

"Well, then, let him go," said Brenton, despondently.

"With all my heart, say I," answered Speed; "but in any case let us leave him alone."

Before the train started that night Stratton said to himself that he was a new man. Richard was himself again. He was thoroughly convinced of the guilt of Stephen Roland, and wondered why he had allowed his mind to wander off the topic and waste time with other suspicions, for which he now saw there was no real excuse. He had not the time, he felt, to investigate the subject personally, but he flattered himself he knew exactly the man to put on Roland's track, and, instead of going himself to Chicago, he sent off the following despatch:—

"Meet me to-morrow morning, without fail, at the Gibson House. Answer."

Before midnight he had his answer, and next morning he met a man in whom he had the most implicit confidence, and who had, as he said, the rare and valuable gift of keeping his mouth shut.

"You see this portrait?" Stratton said, handing to the other a photograph of Stephen Roland. "Now, I do not know how many hundred chemist shops there are in Cincinnati, but I want you to get a list of them, and you must not omit the most obscure shop in town. I want you to visit every drug store there is in the city, show this photograph to the proprietor and the clerks, and find out if that man bought any chemicals during the week or two preceding Christmas. Find out what drugs he bought, and where he bought them, then bring the information to me."

"How much time do you give me on this, Mr. Stratton?" was the question.

"Whatever time you want. I wish the thing done thoroughly and completely, and, as you know, silence is golden in a case like this."

"Enough said," replied the other, and, buttoning the photograph in his inside pocket, he left the room.

There is no necessity of giving an elaborate report of the trial. Any one who has curiosity in the matter can find the full particulars from the files of any paper in the country. Mrs. Brenton was very pale as she sat in the prisoner's dock, but George Stratton thought he never saw any one look so beautiful. It seemed to him that any man in that crowded courtroom could tell in a moment that she was not guilty of the crime with which she was charged, and he looked at the jury of twelve supposedly good men, and wondered what they thought of it.

The defence claimed that it was not their place to show who committed the murder. That rested with the prosecution. The prosecution, Mr. Benham maintained, had signally failed to do this. However, in order to aid the prosecution, he was quite willing to show how Mr. Brenton came to his death. Then witnesses were called, who, to the astonishment of Mrs. Brenton, testified that her husband had all along had a tendency to insanity. It was proved conclusively that some of his ancestors had died in a lunatic asylum, and one was stated to have committed suicide. The defence produced certain books from Mr. Brenton's library, among them Forbes Winslow's volume on "The Mind and the Brain," to show that Brenton had studied the subject of suicide.

The judge's charge was very colourless. It amounted simply to this: If the jury thought the prosecution had shown Mrs. Brenton to have committed the crime, they were to bring in a verdict of guilty, and if they thought otherwise they were to acquit her; and so the jury retired.

As they left the court-room a certain gloom fell upon all those who were friendly to the fair prisoner.

Despite the great reputation of Benham and Brown, it was the thought of every one present that they had made a very poor defence. The prosecution, on the other hand, had been most ably conducted. It had been shown that Mrs. Brenton was chiefly to profit by her husband's death. The insurance fund alone would add seventy-five thousand dollars to the money she would control. A number of little points that Stratton had given no heed to had been magnified, and appeared then to have a great bearing on the case. For the first time, Stratton admitted to himself that the prosecution had made out a very strong case of circumstantial evidence. The defence, too, had been so deplorably weak that it added really to the strength of the prosecution. A great speech had been expected of Benham, but he did not rise to the occasion, and, as one who knew him said, Benham evidently believed his client guilty.

As the jury retired, every one in the court-room felt that there was little hope for the prisoner; and this feeling was intensified when, a few moments after, the announcement was made in court, just as the judge was preparing to leave the bench, that the jury had agreed on the verdict.

Stratton, in the stillness of the court-room, heard one lawyer whisper to another, "She's doomed."

There was intense silence as the jury slowly filed into their places, and the foreman stood up.

"Gentlemen of the jury," was the question, "have you agreed upon a verdict?"

"We have," answered the foreman.

"Do you find the prisoner guilty or not guilty?"

"Not guilty," was the clear answer.

At this there was first a moment of silence, and then a ripple of applause, promptly checked.

Mrs. Brenton was free.

CHAPTER XI.

George Stratton sat in the court-room for a moment dazed, before he thought of the principal figure in the trial; then he rose to go to her side, but he found that Roland was there before him. He heard her say, "Get me a carriage quickly, and take me away from here."

So Stratton went back to his hotel to meet his Chicago detective. The latter had nothing to report. He told him the number of drug stores he had visited, but all without avail. No one had recognized the portrait.

"All right," said Stratton; "then you will just have to go ahead until you find somebody who does. It is, I believe, only a question of time and perseverance."

Next morning he arose late. He looked over the report of the trial in the morning paper, and then, turning to the leader page, read with rising indignation the following editorial:—

"THE BRENTON CASE.

"The decision of yesterday shows the glorious uncertainty that attends the finding of the average American jury. If such verdicts are to be rendered, we may as well blot out from the statute-book all punishment for all crimes in which the evidence is largely circumstantial. If ever a strong case was made out against a human being it was the case of the prosecution in the recent trial. If ever there was a case in which the defence was deplorably weak, although ably conducted, it was the case that was concluded yesterday. Should we, then, be prepared to say that circumstantial evidence will not be taken by an American jury as ground for the conviction of a murderer? The chances are that, if we draw this conclusion, we shall be entirely wrong. If a man stood in the dock, in the place of the handsome young woman who occupied it yesterday, he would to-day have been undoubtedly convicted of murder. The conclusion, then, to be arrived at seems to be that, unless there is the direct proof of murder against a pretty woman, it is absolutely impossible to get the average jury of men to convict her. It would seem that the sooner we get women on juries, especially where a woman is on trial, the better it will be for the cause of justice."

Then in other parts of the paper there were little items similar to this—

"If Mrs. Brenton did not poison her husband, then who did?"

That afternoon George Stratton paid a visit to Mrs. Brenton. He had hoped she had not seen the paper in question, but he hoped in vain. He found Mrs. Brenton far from elated with her acquittal.

"I would give everything I possess," she said, "to bring the culprit to justice."

After a talk on that momentous question, and when George Stratton held her hand and said good-bye, she asked him—

"When do you go to Chicago?"

"Madam," he said, "I leave for Chicago the moment I find out who poisoned William Brenton."

She answered sadly—

"You may remain a long time in Cincinnati."

"In some respects," said Stratton, "I like Cincinnati better than Chicago."

"You are the first Chicago man I ever heard say that," she replied.

"Ah, that was because they did not know Cincinnati as I do."

"I suppose you must have seen a great deal of the town, but I must confess that from now on I should be very glad if I never saw Cincinnati again. I would like to consult with you," she continued, "about the best way of solving this mystery. I have been thinking of engaging some of the best detectives I can get. I suppose New York would be the place."

"No; Chicago," answered the young man.

"Well, then, that is what I wanted to see you about. I would like to get the very best detectives that can be had. Don't you think that, if they were promised ample reward, and paid well during the time they were working on the case, we might discover the key to this mystery?"

"I do not think much of our detective system," answered Stratton, "although I suppose there is something in it, and sometimes they manage in spite of themselves to stumble on the solution of a crime. Still, I shall be very glad indeed to give you what advice I can on the subject. I may say I have constituted myself a special detective in this case, and that I hope to have the honour of solving the problem."

"You are very good, indeed," she answered, "and I must ask you to let me bear the expense."

"Oh, the paper will do that. I won't be out of pocket at all," said Stratton.

"Well, I hardly know how to put it; but, whether you are successful or not, I feel very grateful to you, and I hope you will not be offended at what I am going to say. Now, promise me that you won't!"

"I shall not be offended," he answered. "It is a little difficult to offend a Chicago newspaper man, you know."

"Now, you mustn't say anything against the newspaper men, for, in spite of the hard things that some of them have said about me, I like them."

"Individually or collectively?"

"I am afraid I must say individually. You said you wouldn't be offended, so after your search is over you must let me———. The labourer is worthy of his hire, or I should say, his reward—you know what I mean. I presume that a young man who earns his living on the daily press is not necessarily wealthy."

"Why, Mrs. Brenton, what strange ideas you have of the world! We newspaper men work at the business merely because we like it. It isn't at all for the money that's in it."

"Then you are not offended at what I have said?"

"Oh, not in the least. I may say, however, that I look for a higher reward than money if I am successful in this search."

"Yes, I am sure you do," answered the lady, innocently. "If you succeed in this, you will be very famous."

"Exactly; it's fame I'm after," said Stratton, shaking her hand once more, and taking his leave.

When he reached his hotel, he found the Chicago detective waiting for him.

"Well, old man," he said, "anything new?"

"Yes, sir. Something very new."

"What have you found out?"

"Everything."

"Very well, let me have it."

"I found out that this man bought, on December 10th, thirty grains of morphia. He had this morphia put up in five-grain capsules. He bought this at the drug store on the corner of Blank Street and Nemo Avenue."

"Good gracious!" answered Stratton. "Then to get morphia he must have had a physician's certificate. Did you find who the physician was that signed the certificate?"

"My dear sir," said the Chicago man, "this person is himself a physician, unless I am very much mistaken. I was told that this was the portrait of Stephen Roland. Am I right?"

"That is the name."

"Well, then, he is a doctor himself. Not doing a very large practice, it is true, but he is a physician. Did you not know that?"

"No," said Stratton; "how stupid I am! I never thought of asking the man's occupation."

"Very well, if that is what you wanted to know, here's the detailed report of my investigation."

When the man left, Stratton rubbed his hands.

"Now, Mr. Stephen Roland, I have you," he said.

CHAPTER XII.

After receiving this information Stratton sat alone in his room and thought deeply over his plans. He did not wish to make a false step, yet there was hardly enough in the evidence he had secured to warrant his giving Stephen Roland up to the police. Besides this, it would put the suspected man at once on his guard, and there was no question but that gentleman had taken every precaution to prevent discovery. After deliberating for a long while, he thought that perhaps the best thing he could do was to endeavour to take Roland by surprise. Meanwhile, before the meditating man stood Brenton and Speed, and between them there was a serious disagreement of opinion.

"I tell you what it is," said Speed, "there is no use in our interfering with Stratton. He is on the wrong track, but, nevertheless, all the influence we can use on him in his present frame of mind will merely do what it did before—it will muddle the man up. Now, I propose that we leave him severely alone. Let him find out his mistake. He will find it out in some way or other, and then he will be in a condition of mind to turn to the case of Jane Morton."

"But don't you see," argued Brenton, "that all the time spent on his present investigation is so much time lost? I will agree to leave him alone, as you say, but let us get somebody else on the Morton case."

"I don't want to do that," said Speed; "because George Stratton has taken a great deal of interest in this search. He has done a great deal now, and I think we should be grateful to him for it."

"Grateful!" growled Brenton; "he has done it from the most purely selfish motives that a man can act upon. He has done it entirely for his paper—for newspaper fame. He has done it for money."

"Now," said Speed, hotly, "you must not talk like that of Stratton to me. I won't say what I think of that kind of language coming from you, but you can see how seriously we interfered with his work before, and how it nearly resulted in his departure for Chicago. I propose now that we leave him alone."

"Leave him alone, then, for any sake," replied Brenton; "I am sure I build nothing on what he can do anyway."

"All right, then," returned Speed, recovering his good nature. "Now, although I am not willing to put any one else on the track of Miss Jane Morton, yet I will tell you what I am willing to do. If you like, we will go to her residence, and influence her to confess her crime. I believe that can be done."

"Very well; I want you to understand that I am perfectly reasonable about the matter. All I want is not to lose any more time."

"Time?" cried Speed; "why, we have got all the time there is. Mrs. Brenton is acquitted. There is no more danger."

"That is perfectly true, I admit; but still you can see the grief under which she labours, because her name is not yet cleared from the odium of the crime. You will excuse me, Speed, if I say that you seem to be working more in the interests of Stratton's journalistic success than in the interests of Mrs. Brenton's good name."

"Well, we won't talk about that," said Speed; "Stratton is amply able to take care of himself, as you will doubtless see. Now, what do you say to our trying whether or not we can influence Jane Morton to do what she ought to do, and confess her crime?"

"It is not a very promising task," replied Brenton; "it is hard to get a person to say words that may lead to the gallows."

"I'm not so sure about that," said Speed; "you know the trouble of mind she is in. I think it more than probable that, after the terror of the last few weeks, it will be a relief for her to give herself up."

"Very well; let us go."

The two men shortly afterwards found themselves in the scantily furnished room occupied by Jane Morton. That poor woman was rocking herself to and fro and moaning over her trouble. Then she suddenly stopped rocking, and looked around the room with vague apprehension in her eyes.

She rose and examined the bolts of the door, and, seeing everything was secure, sat down again.

"I shall never have any peace in this world again," she cried to herself.

She rocked back and forth silently for a few moments.

"I wish," she said, "the police would find out all about it, and then this agony of mind would end."

Again she rocked back and forth, with her hands helplessly in her lap.

"Oh, I cannot do it, I cannot do it!" she sobbed, still rocking to and fro. Finally she started to her feet.

"I will do it," she cried; "I will confess to Mrs. Brenton herself. I will tell her everything. She has gone through trouble herself, and may have mercy on me."

"There, you see," said Speed to Brenton, "we have overcome the difficulty, after all."

"It certainly looks like it," replied Brenton. "Don't you think, however, that we had better stay with her until she does confess? May she not change her mind?"

"Don't let us overdo the thing," suggested Speed; "if she doesn't, come to time, we can easily have another interview with her. The woman's mind is made up. She is in torment, and will be until she confesses her crime. Let us go and leave her alone."

George Stratton was not slow to act when he had once made up his mind. He pinned to the breast of his vest a little shield, on which was the word "detective." This he had often found useful, in a way that is not at all sanctioned by the law, in ferreting out crime in Chicago. As soon as it was evening he paced up and down in front of Roland's house, and on the opposite side of the road. There was a light in the doctor's study, and he thought that perhaps the best way to proceed was to go boldly into the house and put his scheme into operation. However, as he meditated on this, the light was turned low, and in a few moments the door opened. The doctor came down the steps, and out on the pavement, walking briskly along the street. The reporter followed him on the other side of the thoroughfare. Whether to do it in the dark or in the light, was the question that troubled Stratton. If he did it in the dark, he would miss the expression on the face of the surprised man. If he did it in the light, the doctor might recognize him as the Chicago reporter, and would know at once that he was no detective. Still, he felt that if there was anything in his scheme at all, it was surprise; and he remembered the quick gasp of the lawyer Brown when he told him he knew what his defence was. He must be able to note the expression of the man who was guilty of the terrible crime.

Having made up his mind to this, he stepped smartly after the doctor, and, when the latter came under a lamp-post, placed his hand suddenly on his shoulder, and exclaimed—

"Doctor Stephen Roland, I arrest you for the murder of William Brenton!"

CHAPTER XIII.

Stephen Roland turned quietly around and shook the hand from his shoulder. It was evident that he recognized Stratton instantly.

"Is this a Chicago joke?" asked the doctor.

"If it is, Mr. Roland, I think you will find it a very serious one."

"Aren't you afraid that you may find it a serious one?"

"I don't see why I should have any fears in the premises," answered the newspaper man.

"My dear sir, do you not realize that I could knock you down or shoot you dead for what you have done, and be perfectly justified in doing so?"

"If you either knock or shoot," replied the other, "you will have to do it very quickly, for, in the language of the wild and woolly West, I've got the drop on you. In my coat pocket is a cocked revolver with my forefinger on the trigger. If you make a hostile move I can let daylight through you so quickly that you won't know what has struck you."

"Electric light, I think you mean," answered the doctor, quietly. "Even a Chicago man might find it difficult to let daylight through a person at this time in the evening. Now, this sort of thing may be Chicago manners, but I assure you it will not go down here in Cincinnati. You have rendered yourself liable to the law if I cared to make a point of it, but I do not. Come back with me to my study. I would like to talk with you."

Stratton began to feel vaguely that he had made a fool of himself. His scheme had utterly failed. The doctor was a great deal cooler and more collected than he was. Nevertheless, he had a deep distrust of the gentleman, and he kept his revolver handy for fear the other would make a dash to escape him. They walked back without saying a word to each other until they came to the doctor's office. Into the house they entered, and the doctor bolted the door behind them. Stratton suspected that very likely he was walking into a trap, but he thought he would be equal to any emergency that might arise. The doctor walked into the study, and again locked the door of that. Pulling down the blinds, he turned up the gas to its full force and sat down by a table, motioning the newspaper man to a seat on the other side.

"Now," he said calmly to Stratton, "the reason I did not resent your unwarrantable insult is this: You are conscientiously trying to get at the root of this mystery. So am I. Your reason is that you wish to score a victory for your paper. My motive is entirely different, but our object is exactly the same. Now, by some strange combination of circumstances you have come to the conclusion that I committed the crime. Am I right?"

"You are perfectly correct, doctor," replied Stratton.

"Very well, then. Now, I assure you that I am entirely innocent. Of course, I appreciate the fact that this assurance will not in the slightest degree affect your opinion, but I am interested in knowing why you came to your conclusion, and perhaps by putting our heads together, even if I dislike you and you hate me, we may see some light on this matter that has hitherto been hidden. I presume you have no objection at all to co-operate with me?"

"None in the least," was the reply.

"Very well, then. Now, don't mind my feelings at all, but tell me exactly why you have suspected me of being a murderer."

"Well," answered Stratton, "in the first place we must look for a motive. It seems to me that you have a motive for the crime."

"And might I ask what that motive is, or was?"

"You will admit that you disliked Brenton?"

"I will admit that, yes."

"Very well. You will admit also that you were—well, how shall I put it?—let us say, interested in his wife before her marriage?"

"I will admit that; yes."

"You, perhaps, will admit that you are interested in her now?"

"I do not see any necessity for admitting that; but still, for the purpose of getting along with the case, I will admit it. Go on."

"Very good. Here is a motive for the crime, and a very strong one. First, we will presume that you are in love with the wife of the man who is murdered. Secondly, supposing that you are mercenary, quite a considerable amount of money will come to you in case you marry Brenton's widow. Next, some one at that table poisoned him. It was not Mrs. Brenton, who poured out the cup of coffee. The cup of coffee was placed before Brenton, and my opinion is that, until it was placed there, there was no poison in that cup. The doomed man was entirely unsuspicious, and therefore it was very easy for a person to slip enough poison in that cup unseen by anybody at that table, so that when he drank his coffee nothing could have saved him. He rose from the table feeling badly, and he went to his room and died. Now, who could have placed that poison in his cup of coffee? It must have been one of the two that sat at his right and left hand. A young lady sat at his right hand. She certainly did not commit the crime. You, Stephen Roland, sat at his left hand. Do you deny any of the facts I have recited?"

"That is a very ingenious chain of circumstantial evidence. Of course, you do not think it strong enough to convict a man of such a serious crime as murder?"

"No; I quite realize the weakness of the case up to this point. But there is more to follow. Fourteen days before that dinner you purchased at the drug store on the corner of Blank Street and Nemo Avenue thirty grains of morphia. You had the poison put up in capsules of five grains each. What do you say to that bit of evidence added to the circumstantial chain which you say is ingenious?"

The doctor knit his brows and leaned back in his chair.

"By the gods!" he said, "you are right. I did buy that morphia. I remember it now. I don't mind telling you that I had a number of experiments on hand, as every doctor has, and I had those capsules put up at the drug store, but this tragedy coming on made me forget all about the matter."

"Did you take the morphia with you, doctor?"

"No, I did not. And the box of capsules, I do not think, has been opened. But that is easily ascertained."

The doctor rose, went to his cabinet, and unlocked it. From a number of packages he selected a small one, and brought it to the desk, placing it before the reporter.

"There is the package. That contains, as you say, thirty grains of morphia in half a dozen five-grain capsules. You see that it is sealed just as it left the drug store. Now, open it and look for yourself. Here are scales; if you want to see whether a single grain is missing or not, find out for yourself.

"Perhaps," said the newspaper man, "we had better leave this investigation for the proper authorities."

"Then you still believe that I am the murderer of William Brenton?"

"Yes, I still believe that."

"Very well; you may do as you please. I think, however, in justice to myself, you should stay right here, and see that this box is not tampered with until the proper authorities, as you say, come."

Then, placing his hand on the bell, he continued—"Whom shall I send for? An ordinary policeman, or some one from the central office? But, now that I think of it, here is a telephone. We can have any one brought here that you wish. I prefer that neither you nor I leave this room until that functionary has appeared. Name the authority you want brought here," said the doctor, going to the telephone, "and I will have him here if he is in town."

The newspaper man was nonplussed. The Doctor's actions did not seem like those of a guilty man. If he were guilty he certainly had more nerve than any person Stratton had ever met. So he hesitated. Then he said—

"Sit down a moment, doctor, and let us talk this thing over."

"Just as you say," remarked Roland, drawing up his chair again.

Stratton took the package, and looked it over carefully. It was certainly just in the condition in which it had left the drug store; but still, that could have been easily done by the doctor himself.

"Suppose we open this package?" he said to Roland.

"With all my heart," said the doctor, "go ahead;" and he shoved over to him a little penknife that was on the table.

The reporter took the package, ran the knife around the edge, and opened it. There lay six capsules, filled, as the doctor had said. Roland picked up one of them, and looked at it critically.

"I assure you," he said, "although I am quite aware you do not believe a word I say, that I have not seen those capsules before."

He drew towards him a piece of paper, opened the capsule, and, let the white powder fall on the paper. He looked critically at the powder, and a shade of astonishment came over his face. He picked up the penknife, took a particle on the tip of it, and touched it with his tongue.

"Don't fool with that thing!" said Stratton.

"Oh, my dear fellow," he said, "morphia is not a poison in small quantities."

The moment he had tasted it, however, he suddenly picked up the paper, put the five grains on his tongue, and swallowed them.

Instantly the reporter sprang to his feet. He saw at once the reason for all the assumed coolness. The doctor was merely gaining time in order to commit suicide.

"What have you done?" cried the reporter.

"Done, my dear fellow? nothing very much. This is not morphia; it is sulphate of quinine."

CHAPTER XIV.

In the morning Jane Morton prepared to meet Mrs. Brenton, and make her confession. She called at the Brenton residence, but found it closed, as it had been ever since the tragedy of Christmas morning. It took her some time to discover the whereabouts of Mrs. Brenton, who, since the murder, had resided with a friend except while under arrest.

For a moment Mrs. Brenton did not recognize the thin and pale woman who stood before her in a state of such extreme nervous agitation, that it seemed as if at any moment she might break down and cry.

"I don't suppose you'll remember me, ma'am," began the girl, "but I worked for you two weeks before—before——"

"Oh yes," said Mrs. Brenton, "I remember you now. Have you been ill? You look quite worn and pale, and very different from what you did the last time I saw you."

"Yes," said the girl, "I believe I have been ill.".

"You believe; aren't you sure?"

"I have been very ill in mind, and troubled, and that is the reason I look so badly,—Oh, Mrs. Brenton, I wanted to tell you of something that has been weighing on my mind ever since that awful day! I know you can never forgive me, but I must tell it to you, or I shall go crazy."

"Sit down, sit down," said the lady, kindly; "you know what trouble I have been in myself. I am sure that I am more able to sympathize now with one who is in trouble than ever I was before."

"Yes, ma'am; but you were innocent, and I am guilty. That makes all the difference in the world."

"Guilty!" cried Mrs. Brenton, a strange fear coming over her as she stared at the girl; "guilty of what?"

"Oh, madam, let me tell you all about it. There is, of course, no excuse; but I'll begin at the beginning. You remember a while before Christmas that John came to see me one night, and we sat up very late in the kitchen, and your husband came down quietly, and when we heard him coming we put out the light and just as John was trying to get away, your husband shot twice at him, and hit him the second time?"

"Oh yes," said Mrs. Brenton, "I remember that very well. I had forgotten about it in my own trouble; but I know that my husband intended to do something for the young man. I hope he was not seriously hurt?"

"No, ma'am; he is able to be about again now as well as ever, and is not even lame, which we expected he would be. But at the time I thought he was going to be lame all the rest of his life, and perhaps that is the reason I did what I did. When everything was in confusion in the house, and it was certain that we would all have to leave, I did a very wicked thing. I went to your room, and I stole some of your rings, and some money that was there, as well as a lot of other things that were in the room. It seemed to me then, although, of course, I know now how wicked it was, that you owed John something for what he had gone through, and I thought that he was to be lame, and that you would never miss the things; but, oh! madam, I have not slept a night since I took them. I have been afraid of the police and afraid of being found out. I have pawned nothing, and they are all just as I took them, and I have brought them back here to you, with every penny of the money. I know you can never forgive me, but I am willing now to be given up to the police, and I feel better in my mind than I have done ever since I took the things."

"My poor child!" said Mrs. Brenton, sympathetically, "was that all?"

"All?" cried the girl. "Yes, I have brought everything back."

"Oh, I don't mean that, but I am sorry you have been worried over anything so trivial. I can see how at such a time, and feeling that you had been wronged, a temptation to take the things came to you. But I hope you will not trouble any more about the matter. I will see that John is compensated for all the injury he received, as far as it is possible for money to compensate him. I hope you will keep the money. The other things, of course, I shall take back, and I am glad you came to tell me of it before telling any one else. I think, perhaps, it is better never to say anything to anybody about this. People might not understand just what temptation you were put to, and they would not know the circumstances of the case, because nobody knows, I think, that John was hurt. Now, my dear girl, do not cry. It is all right. Of course you never will touch anything again that does not belong to you, and the suffering you have gone through has more than made up for all the wrong you have done. I am sure that I forgive you quite freely for it, and I think it was very noble of you to come and tell me about it."

Mrs. Brenton took the package from the hands of the weeping girl, and opened it. She found everything there, as the girl had said. She took the money and offered it to Jane Morton. The girl shook her head.

"No," she cried, "I cannot touch it. I cannot, indeed. It has been enough misery to me already."

"Very well," said Mrs. Brenton. "I would like very much to see John. Will you bring him to me?"

The girl looked at her with startled eyes.

"You will not tell him?" she said.

"No indeed, I shall tell him nothing. But I want to do what I can for him as I said. I suppose you are engaged to be married?"

"Yes," answered the girl; "but if he knew of this he never, never would marry me."

"If he did not," said Mrs. Brenton, "he would not be worthy of you. But he shall know nothing about it. You will promise to come here and see me with him, will you not?"

"Yes, madam," said the girl.

"Then good-bye, until I see you again."

Mrs. Brenton sat for a long time thinking over this confession. It took her some time to recover her usual self-possession, because for a moment she had thought the girl was going to confess that she committed murder. In comparison with that awful crime, the theft seemed so trivial that Mrs. Brenton almost smiled when she thought of the girl's distress.

"Well," said John Speed to Mr. Brenton, "if that doesn't beat the Old Harry. Now I, for one, am very glad of it, if we come to the real truth of the matter."

"I am glad also," said Brenton, "that the girl is not guilty, although I must say things looked decidedly against her."

"I will tell you why I am glad," said Speed. "I am glad because it will take some of the superfluous conceit out of that French detective Lecocq. He was so awfully sure of himself. He couldn't possibly be mistaken. Now, think of the mistakes that man must have made while he was on earth, and had the power which was given into his hands in Paris. After all, Stratton is on the right track, and he will yet land your friend Roland in prison. Let us go and find Lecocq. This is too good to keep."

"My dear sir," said Brenton, "you seem to be more elated because of your friend Stratton than for any other reason. Don't you want the matter ferreted out at all?"

"Why, certainly I do; but I don't want it ferreted out by bringing an innocent person into trouble."

"And may not Stephen Roland be an innocent person?"

"Oh, I suppose so; but I do not think he is."

"Why do you not think so?"

"Well, if you want the real reason, simply because George Stratton thinks he isn't. I pin my faith to Stratton."

"I think you overrate your friend Stratton."

"Overrate him, sir? That is impossible. I love him so well that I hope he will solve this mystery himself, unaided and alone, and that in going back to Chicago he will be smashed to pieces in a railway accident, so that we can have him here to congratulate him."

CHAPTER XV.

"I suppose," said Roland, "you thought for a moment I was trying to commit suicide. I think, Mr. Stratton, you will have a better opinion of me by-and-by. I shouldn't be at all surprised if you imagined I induced you to come in here to get you into a trap."

"You are perfectly correct," said Stratton; "and I may say, although that was my belief, I was not in the least afraid of you, for I had you covered all the time."

"Well," remarked Roland, carelessly, "I don't want to interfere with your business at all, but I wish you wouldn't cover me quite so much; that revolver of yours might go off."

"Do you mean to say," said Stratton, "that there is nothing but quinine in those capsules?"

"I'll tell you in a moment," as he opened them one by one. "No, there is nothing but quinine here. Thirty grains put up in five-grain capsules."

George Stratton's eyes began to open. Then he slowly rose, and looked with horrified face at the doctor.

"My God!" he cried; "who got the thirty grains of morphia?"

"What do you mean?" asked the doctor.

"Mean? Why, don't you see it? It is a chemist's mistake. Thirty grains of quinine have been sent you. Thirty grains of morphia have been sent to somebody else. Was it to William Brenton?"

"By Jove!" said the doctor, "there's something in that. Say, let us go to the drug store."

The two went out together, and walked to the drug store on the corner of Blank Street and Nemo Avenue.

"Do you know this writing?" said Doctor Roland to the druggist, pointing to the label on the box.

"Yes," answered the druggist; "that was written by one of my assistants."

"Can we see him for a few moments?"

"I don't know where he is to be found. He is a worthless fellow, and has gone to the devil this last few weeks with a rapidity that is something startling."

"When did he leave?"

"Well, he got drunk and stayed drunk during the holidays, and I had to discharge him. He was a very valuable man when he was sober; but he began to be so erratic in his habits that I was afraid he would make a ghastly mistake some time, so I discharged him before it was too late."

"Are you sure you discharged him before it was too late?"

The druggist looked at the doctor, whom he knew well, and said, "I never heard of any mistake, if he did make it."

"You keep a book, of course, of all the prescriptions sent out?"

"Certainly."

"May we look at that book?"

"I shall be very glad to show it to you. What month or week?"

"I want to see what time you sent this box of morphia to me."

"You don't know about what time it was, do you?"

"Yes; it must have been about two weeks before Christmas."

The chemist looked over the pages of the book, and finally said, "Here it is."

"Will you let me look at that page?"

"Certainly."

The doctor ran his finger down the column, and came to an entry written in the same hand.

"Look here," he said to Stratton, "thirty grains of quinine sent to William Brenton, and next to it thirty grains of morphia sent to Stephen Roland. I see how it was. Those prescriptions were mixed up. My package went to poor Brenton."

The druggist turned pale.

"I hope," he said, "nothing public will come of this."

"My dear sir," said Roland, "something public will have to come of it. You will oblige me by ringing up the central police station, as this book must be given in charge of the authorities."

"Look here," put in Stratton, his newspaper instinct coming uppermost, "I want to get this thing exclusively for the Argus."

"Oh, I guess there will be no trouble about that. Nothing will be made public until to-morrow, and you can telegraph to-night if we find the box of capsules in Brenton's residence. We must take an officer with us for that purpose, but you can caution or bribe him to keep quiet until to-morrow."

When the three went to William Brenton's residence they began a search of the room in which Brenton had died, but nothing was found. In the closet of the room hung the clothes of Brenton, and going through them Stratton found in the vest pocket of one of the suits a small box containing what was described as five-grain capsules of sulphate of quinine. The doctor tore one of these capsules apart, so as to see what was in it. Without a moment's hesitation he said—

"There you are! That is the morphia. There were six capsules in this box, and one of them is missing. William Brenton poisoned himself! Feeling ill, he doubtless took what he thought was a dose of quinine. Many men indulge in what we call the quinine habit. It is getting to be a mild form of tippling. Brenton committed unconscious suicide!"

CHAPTER XVI.

A group of men; who were really alive, but invisible to the searchers, stood in the room where the discovery was made. Two of the number were evidently angry, one in one way and one in another. The rest of the group appeared to be very merry. One angry man was Brenton himself, who was sullenly enraged. The other was the Frenchman, Lecocq, who was as deeply angered as Brenton, but, instead of being sullen, was exceedingly voluble.

"I tell you," he cried, "it is not a mistake of mine. I went on correct principles from the first. I was misled by one who should have known better. You will remember, gentlemen," he continued, turning first to one and then the other, "that what I said was that we had certain facts to go on. One of those facts I got from Mr. Brenton. I said to him in your presence, 'Did you poison yourself?' He answered me, as I can prove by all of you, 'No, I did not.' I took that for a fact. I thought I was speaking to a reasonable man who knew what he was talking about."

"Haven't I told you time and again," answered Brenton, indignantly, "that it was a mistake? You asked me if I poisoned myself. I answered you that I did not. Your question related to suicide. I did not commit suicide. I was the victim of a druggist's mistake. If you had asked me if I had taken medicine before I went to bed, I should have told you frankly, 'Yes. I took one capsule of quinine.' It has been my habit for years, when I feel badly. I thought nothing of that."

"My dear sir," said Lecocq, "I warned you, and I warned these gentlemen, that the very things that seem trivial to a thoughtless person are the things that sometimes count. You should have told me everything. If you took anything at all, you should have said so. If you had said to me, 'Monsieur Lecocq, before I retired I took five grains of quinine,' I should have at once said; 'Find where that quinine is, and see if it is quinine, and see if there has not been a mistake.' I was entirely misled; I was stupidly misled."

"Well, if there was stupidity," returned Brenton, "it was your own."

"Come, come, gentlemen," laughed Speed, "all's well that ends well.

Everybody has been mistaken, that's all about it. The best detective minds of Europe and America, of the world, and of the spirit-land, have been misled. You are all wrong. Admit it, and let it end."

"My dear sir," said Lecocq, "I shall not admit anything. I was not wrong; I was misled. It was this way——"

"Oh, now, for goodness' sake don't go over it all again. We understand the circumstances well enough."

"I tell you," cried Brenton, in an angry tone, "that——

"Come, come," said Speed, "we have had enough of this discussion. I tell you that you are all wrong, every one of you. Come with me, Brenton, and we will leave this amusing crowd."

"I shall do nothing of the kind," answered Brenton, shortly.

"Oh, very well then, do as you please. I am glad the thing is ended, and I am glad it is ended by my Chicago friend."

"Your Chicago friend!" sneered Brenton, slightingly; "It was discovered by Doctor Stephen Roland."

"My dear fellow," said Speed, "Stephen Roland had all his time to discover the thing, and didn't do it, and never would have done it, if George Stratton hadn't encountered him. Well, good-bye, gentlemen; I am sorry to say that I have had quite enough of this discussion. But one thing looms up above it all, and that is that Chicago is ahead of the world in everything—in detection as well as in fires."

"My dear sir," cried Lecocq, "it is not true. I will show you in a moment—"

"You won't show me," said Speed, and he straightway disappeared.

"Come, Ferris," said Brenton, "after all, you are the only friend I seem to have; come with me."

"Where are you going?" asked Ferris, as they left.

"I want to see how my wife takes the news."

"Don't," said Mr. Ferris—"don't do anything of the kind. Leave matters just where they are. Everything has turned out what you would call all right. You see that your interference, as far as it went, was perfectly futile and useless. I want now to draw your attention to other things."

"Very well, I will listen to you," said Brenton, "if you come with me and see how my wife takes the news. I want to enjoy for even a moment or two her relief and pleasure at finding that her good name is clear."

"Very well," assented Ferris, "I will go with you."

When they arrived they found the Chicago reporter ahead of them. He had evidently told Mrs. Brenton all the news, and her face flushed with eager pleasure as she listened to the recital.

"Now," said the Chicago man, "I am going to leave Cincinnati. Are you sorry I am going?"

"No," said Mrs. Brenton, looking him in the face, "I am not sorry."

Stratton flushed at this, and then said, taking his hat in his hand, "Very well, madam, I shall bid you good day."

"I am not sorry," said Mrs. Brenton, holding out her hand, "because I am going to leave Cincinnati myself, and I hope never to see the city again. So if you stayed here, you see, I should never meet you again, Mr. Stratton."

"Alice," cried Stratton, impulsively grasping her hand in both of his, "don't you think you would like Chicago as a place of residence?"

"George," she answered, "I do not know. I am going to Europe, and shall be there for a year or two."

Then he said eagerly—

"When you return, or if I go over there to see you after a year or two, may I ask you that question again?"

"Yes," was the whispered answer.

"Come," said Brenton to Ferris, "let us go."

About Author

Robert Barr (16 September 1849 – 21 October 1912) was a Scottish-Canadian short story writer and novelist.

Early years in Canada

Robert Barr was born in Barony, Lanark, Scotland to Robert Barr and Jane Watson. In 1854, he emigrated with his parents to Upper Canada at the age of four years old. His family settled on a farm near the village of Muirkirk. Barr assisted his father with his job as a carpenter, and developed a sound work ethic. Robert Barr then worked as a steel smelter for a number of years before he was educated at Toronto Normal School in 1873 to train as a teacher.

After graduating Toronto Normal School, Barr became a teacher, and eventually headmaster/principal of the Central School of Windsor, Ontario in 1874. While Barr worked as head master of the Central School of Windsor, Ontario, he began to contribute short stories—often based on personal experiences, and recorded his work. On August 1876, when he was 27, Robert Barr married Ontario-born Eva Bennett, who was 21. According to the 1891 England Census, the couple appears to have had three children, Laura, William, and Andrew.

In 1876, Barr quit his teaching position to become a staff member of publication, and later on became the news editor for the Detroit Free Press. Barr wrote for this newspaper under the pseudonym, "Luke Sharp." The idea for this pseudonym was inspired during his morning commute to work when Barr saw a sign that read "Luke Sharp, Undertaker." In 1881, Barr left Canada to return to England in order to start a new weekly version of "The Detroit Free Press Magazine."

London years

In 1881 Barr decided to "vamoose the ranch", as he called the process of immigration in search of literary fame outside of Canada, and relocated to London to continue to write/establish the weekly English edition of the Detroit Free Press. During the 1890s, he broadened his literary works, and started writing novels from the popular crime genre. In 1892 he founded the magazine The Idler, choosing Jerome K. Jerome as his collaborator (wanting, as Jerome said, "a popular name"). He retired from its co-editorship in 1895.

In London of the 1890s Barr became a more prolific author—publishing a book a year—and was familiar with many of the best-selling authors of his day, including :Arnold Bennett, Horatio Gilbert Parker, Joseph Conrad, Bret Harte, Rudyard Kipling, H. Rider Haggard, H. G. Wells, and George Robert Gissing. Barr was well-spoken, well-cultured due to travel, and considered a "socializer."

Because most of Barr's literary output was of the crime genre, his works were highly in vogue. As Sherlock Holmes stories were becoming well-known, Barr wrote and published in the Idler the first Holmes parody, "The Adventures of "Sherlaw Kombs" (1892), a spoof that was continued a decade later in another Barr story, "The Adventure of the Second Swag" (1904). Despite those jibes at the growing Holmes phenomenon, Barr remained on very good terms with its creator Arthur Conan Doyle. In Memories and Adventures, a serial memoir published 1923–24, Doyle described him as "a volcanic Anglo—or rather Scot-American, with a violent manner, a wealth of strong adjectives, and one of the kindest natures underneath it all".

In 1904, Robert Barr completed an unfinished novel for Methuen & Co. by the recently deceased American author Stephen Crane entitled The O'Ruddy, a romance.Despite his reservations at taking on the project, Barr reluctantly finished the last eight chapters due to his longstanding friendship with Crane and his common-law wife, Cora, the war correspondent and bordello owner.

Death

The 1911 census places Robert Barr, "a writer of fiction," at Hillhead, Woldingham, Surrey, a small village southeast of London, living with his wife, Eva, their son William, and two female servants. At this home, the author died from heart disease on 21 October 1912.

Writing Style

Barr's volumes of short stories were often written with an ironic twist in the story with a witty, appealing narrator telling the story. Barr's other works also include numerous fiction and non-fiction contributions to periodicals. A few of his mystery stories and stories of the supernatural were put in anthologies, and a few novels have been republished. His writings have also attracted scholarly attention. His narrative personae also featured moral and editorial interpolations within their tales. Barr's achievements were recognized by an honorary degree from the University of Michigan in 1900.

His protagonists were journalists, princes, detectives, deserving commercial and social climbers, financiers, the new woman of bright wit and aggressive accomplishment, and lords. Often, his characters were stereotypical and romanticized.

Barr wrote fiction in an episode-like format. He developed this style when working as an editor for the newspaper Detroit Press. Barr developed his skill with the anecdote and vignette; often only the central character serves to link the nearly self-contained chapters of the novels. (Source: Wikipedia)

NOTABLE WORKS

In a Steamer Chair and Other Stories (Thirteen short stories by one of the most famous writers in his day -1892)

"The Face And The Mask" (1894) consists of twenty-four delightful short stories.

In the Midst of Alarms (1894, 1900, 1912), a story of the attempted Fenian invasion of Canada in 1866.

From Whose Bourne (1896) Novel in which the main character, William Brenton, searches for truth to set his wife free.

One Day's Courtship (1896)

Revenge! (Collection of 20 short stories, Alfred Hitchcock-like style, thriller with a surprise ending)

The Strong Arm

A Woman Intervenes (1896), a story of love, finance, and American journalism.

Tekla: A Romance of Love and War (1898)

Jennie Baxter, Journalist (1899)

The Unchanging East (1900)

The Victors (1901)

A Prince of Good Fellows (1902)

Over The Border: A Romance (1903)

The O'Ruddy, A Romance, with Stephen Crane (1903)

A Chicago Princess (1904)

The Speculations of John Steele (1905)

The Tempestuous Petticoat (1905–12)

A Rock in the Baltic (1906)

The Triumphs of Eugène Valmont (1906)

The Measure of the Rule (1907)

Stranleigh's Millions (1909)

The Sword Maker (Medieval action/adventure novel, genre: Historical Fiction-1910)

The Palace of Logs (1912)

"The Ambassadors Pigeons" (1899)

"And the Rigor of the Game" (1892)

"Converted" (1896)

"Count Conrad's Courtship" (1896)

"The Count's Apology" (1896)

"A Deal on Change " (1896)

"The Exposure of Lord Stanford" (1896)

"Gentlemen: The King!"

"The Hour-Glass" (1899)

"An invitation" (1892)

" A Ladies Man"

"The Long Ladder" (1899)

"Mrs. Tremain" (1892)

" Transformation" (1896)

"The Understudy" (1896)

" The Vengeance of the Dead" (1896)

"The Bromley Gibbert's Story" (1896)

" Out of Thun" (1896)

"The Shadow of Greenback" (1896)

"Flight of the Red Dog" (fiction)

"Lord Stranleigh Abroad" (1913)

"One Day's Courtship and the Herald's of Fame" (1896)

"Cardillac"

"Dr. Barr's Tales"

"The Triumphs of Eugene Valmont"